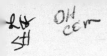

W9-BJS-003

A deep, unfamiliar voice rumbled along Lily's spine.

She curbed her irritation. Time to make nice. She had no choice. If she didn't honor the mayor's request to hire Vaughn Fulton as her deputy, he'd only saddle her with a seventy-year-old retiree. Or he'd veto every candidate she put forth. When Mayor Whitby was coming off a sugar high, that was just the way he rolled.

So suck it up, Lily Anne.

She swiveled toward the counter that separated the office space from the reception area.

A man wearing jeans and a short-sleeved navy T-shirt that barely concealed a hip holster stood in the doorway, shoulder propped against the jamb, posture as cocky as his voice. Midtwenties, six-one or so, trimmed dark hair and troublemaker eyes. One look and she was as clear about who he was as the muscles stretching his shirt. If the man were in motion, he'd be swaggering.

Beside her, Clarissa hummed her approval. Lily could practically hear the drool hitting the floor.

Yeah. Swagger. He planted his palms on the countertop, locked his arms and leaned in.

"Vaughn Fulton reporting for duty, ma'am."

Dear Reader,

It's wonderful to have you back in Castle Creek! You caught a glimpse of the prickly Sheriff Lily Tate in *Staying at Joe's*, and learned of her tragic history in *A Family After All*. In *Tempting the Sheriff*, Lily continues her fight to keep everyone at arm's length—especially city cop Vaughn Fulton, a temporary deputy with a hefty chip on his shoulder. Eventually these two crazy kids fall head over heels, but Vaughn isn't interested in staying in Castle Creek, and Lily herself won't consider moving to the city. So now what?

When I started writing Lily's story, I had already decided which character would risk their entire way of life to make couplehood happen. Imagine my surprise when the *other* character insisted on being the one to make the sacrifice! I hope you find Lily and Vaughn's journey as gratifying as I did.

I always enjoy hearing from readers! You can email me at kathy@kathyaltman.com, or visit me at www.kathyaltman.com, where you can find the recipe for gobs, those Devil Dogs–type treats Vaughn reminisces about. Depending on where you're from, you may know them as whoopie pies, but they'll always be gobs to me, and one of my sweetest memories of Johnstown, PA, where my dad grew up.

All my best,

Kathy Altman

KATHY ALTMAN

Tempting the Sheriff

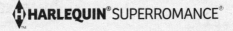
HARLEQUIN® SUPERROMANCE®

If you purchased this book without a cover you should be aware that this book is stolen property. It was reported as "unsold and destroyed" to the publisher, and neither the author nor the publisher has received any payment for this "stripped book."

Recycling programs
for this product may
not exist in your area.

ISBN-13: 978-0-373-61015-0

Tempting the Sheriff

Copyright © 2016 by Kathy Altman

All rights reserved. Except for use in any review, the reproduction or utilization of this work in whole or in part in any form by any electronic, mechanical or other means, now known or hereinafter invented, including xerography, photocopying and recording, or in any information storage or retrieval system, is forbidden without the written permission of the publisher, Harlequin Enterprises Limited, 225 Duncan Mill Road, Don Mills, Ontario M3B 3K9, Canada.

This is a work of fiction. Names, characters, places and incidents are either the product of the author's imagination or are used fictitiously, and any resemblance to actual persons, living or dead, business establishments, events or locales is entirely coincidental.

This edition published by arrangement with Harlequin Books S.A.

For questions and comments about the quality of this book, please contact us at CustomerService@Harlequin.com.

® and TM are trademarks of Harlequin Enterprises Limited or its corporate affiliates. Trademarks indicated with ® are registered in the United States Patent and Trademark Office, the Canadian Intellectual Property Office and in other countries.

Printed in U.S.A.

Kathy Altman writes contemporary romance, romantic suspense and the occasional ode to chocolate. She's also a regular contributor to USATODAY.com's *Happy Ever After* blog. Kathy prefers her chocolate with nuts, her Friday afternoons with wine and her love stories with happy-ever-afters. Find Kathy online at www.kathyaltman.com. She'd enjoy hearing from you!

Books by Kathy Altman

HARLEQUIN SUPERROMANCE

A Family After All
Staying at Joe's
The Other Soldier

To Toni Anderson,
outstanding writer, critique partner and friend.
Here's to the next dozen years of buddy-ship
(and all those bug hugs that keep me going)!

Acknowledgments

I owe a great, big, humongous THANK YOU to editor Claire Caldwell, who is unfailingly gracious, encouraging and all kinds of savvy. Claire, I'm a better writer thanks to you, and I'll miss working with you!

As always, I'm grateful for my entire family, who are even more supportive than they are screwy. (Seriously, folks, that's a lot of support.)

And many, many thanks to the readers who appreciate happy endings as much as I do. I cherish every one of you!

CHAPTER ONE

VAUGHN FULTON TOSSED his shades onto a box marked Kitchen Crap and turned in a slow circle. He'd been played. Suckered, by an eighty-four-year-old man. If Emerson Fulton were still alive, he'd be smirking his ass off because he was about to make good on his promise to see that his nephew stayed in Castle Creek longer than it took to eat a rib eye at the diner and watch a ball game for dessert.

He pushed a breath through his nose. Yeah, he should have visited more often. No doubt about it. He'd let down the old man.

And his uncle had plotted one hell of a payback.

"Bits and pieces, my ass," Vaughn said aloud. The echo he should have heard failed to bounce back at him. No surprise, considering the ceiling-high jumble of boxes and furniture crowding the room. A jumble that hadn't been there two months ago, when he'd stopped in to check on the old man. A week later, Uncle Em was gone.

Vaughn pinched the bridge of his nose.

Near the end, he'd promised to handle the property side of things. Stay at the house as soon as he could manage it. Clear it out and see it sold. Two days max to empty the place, Uncle Em had sworn.

Two days, like hell. It would take two *weeks* to go through everything on the first floor, and that was just the sorting—he'd have to make arrangements for transportation to the landfill and find a charity to take the rest. No way could he take more than one or two items for himself. His apartment in Erie wasn't much bigger than a square of toilet paper.

So much for cranking this out over the weekend.

Vaughn linked his fingers behind his neck and exhaled. He missed his uncle. He missed him bad. His aunt, too. He'd spent a lot of uncomplicated summers in this house. But as grateful as he was that the old man had remembered him in his will, he didn't have time for this. Well, technically he did, since his jackass partner had earned him a thirty-day suspension, but he'd wanted to spend it clearing his name, not clearing a dozen rooms crammed with someone else's crap.

Don't be a dick.

He dropped his arms and carefully wound his way back to the foyer. The afternoon light spilling in through the strip of stained glass in the front door scattered jewel tones across the floor and over the toes of his boots. Along with the faint smell of almond pound cake that was baked into the very walls, it made him nostalgic for a childhood he usually did his damnedest to forget.

Sudden exhaustion tugged at his shoulders. He would have leaned against a wall if it weren't for the piles of junk. Instead he leaned back against the front door and surveyed the hardwood floor, barely visible beneath stacks of old magazines and newspapers, towers of rust-rimmed paint cans and heap after heap of wrinkled clothing.

How had his uncle found the energy to collect all this? What had he done, put up a notice at Cal's Diner? *Help me show my nephew what a jackass he is. Bring your unwanted items, large or small, to 16511 Paisley Place and make him deal with it.*

Vaughn huffed a reluctant chuckle. He'd bet his service weapon that was exactly what Uncle Em had done. He could see the old man now, fixing his invite to the corkboard just inside the diner's door, tongue between his teeth and that tickled-with-himself gleam in his eyes…

Abruptly, Vaughn swung toward the kitchen. He could use a drink. The dust was making his throat scratchy.

The kitchen was the only room in the house that didn't harbor a maze of boxes. Vaughn grabbed a glass and filled it with water from the tap. After downing it he poured another, butted a hip against the sink and took stock. The room—hell, the whole house—was way overdue for a face-lift. Battered white cabinet doors and a scuffed linoleum floor needed to give way to solid maple and Mexican tile, but Uncle Em hadn't wanted to change anything with Aunt Brenda's stamp on it. Vaughn couldn't blame him. Even the thought made Vaughn want to check the wide-eyed ceramic owl cookie jar, see if it held any of the ginger crisps his aunt used to make.

He was stretching toward the jar when his ringtone jolted him upright. Just as well. Considering his aunt had died four years earlier, he doubted he'd enjoy whatever the owl guarded.

He dug his phone out of the front pocket of his jeans. "Fulton here."

"Vaughn? This is Rick Whitby."

"Mayor." Vaughn braced a hand on the edge of the counter. He gazed through the window, studying the generous stretch of brown-tipped grass desperate for a mowing and the intersecting rows of hornbeams that screened the yard from the neighbors. The trees were in serious need of pruning.

For the hundredth time, Vaughn wondered what had drawn his uncle to Whitby, a fifty-year-old player with too much time on his hands, considering he had a county to run. "What can I do for you?" he asked.

"Son, let me say again how sorry I am about your uncle's passing."

"I appreciate that."

"It's been a lot of years since he retired as clerk of the court, but folks at the courthouse still talk about him."

The funeral had been well attended. Vaughn had been touched. "What can I do for you, Mayor?" he asked again.

"In a hurry, are you, son?"

Whitby's chuckle had Vaughn jonesing for a cup of coffee. Hell, even a soda would do. Anything to wash away the taste of ulterior motive. He pushed off the counter and opened the fridge. Nothing but baking soda and a sheet of paper. Vaughn picked up the paper, hip-bumped the door shut and took a closer look.

An estimate, for replacing the roof. It wasn't the fact that his uncle had left it in the fridge that sent Vaughn's oh-shit factor sky-high. It was the total on the dotted line. Five figures.

Vaughn dropped into a chair and double-checked the math.

"Son? You still there?"

"I'm here."

Whitby cleared his throat. "Listen, give me a call when you get into town, will you? I'd like to set up a meeting. Discuss a proposition."

Vaughn fought the urge to admit he'd already arrived. "What's on your mind?"

The mayor hesitated. "What I have to say deserves a face-to-face."

Vaughn's Spidey senses started to tingle. "I'd appreciate a heads-up."

"All righty, then. Our sheriff's department is understaffed. I'm hoping you'll help us out while you're in town."

He had to be kidding. "You want me to be a deputy?"

"I'd make you sheriff if I could."

Vaughn wasn't surprised. He'd never met Sheriff Tate, but he knew she was a hard-ass. From what he'd heard, a man could drop dead in the street and she'd write him a ticket for jaywalking.

Thanks, but no thanks.

"I'll only be around long enough to clean out the house," Vaughn said. "Unless I decide to sell it as is."

"But that's against the terms of your inheritance."

Vaughn shifted his weight, and the chair groaned a threat to break into pieces and dump his ass on the floor. "How do you know that?"

"I helped Emerson draft it. Listen, your uncle wanted the house to stay in the family. More than that, he wanted you to stay in Castle Creek. I promised I'd do my best to talk you into both."

Tension threaded its way through Vaughn's muscles. "He knew better." Besides, the old man had left only half the house to Vaughn—the rest of the estate went to charity. Even if he wanted to, there was no way Vaughn could raise the money to buy the house outright. If Uncle Em had been so gung ho about Vaughn staying, the old man should have left him the whole house.

Not that Vaughn deserved it.

When Whitby spoke again, his voice carried a pout. "That's it? That's all you have to say?"

"I'm sorry you're understaffed, but I don't have time to help, and I have no interest in relocating." Even if he did, it would be to another city, not to a geriatric community that was about as dangerous as a stuffed animal. Yeah, Uncle Em had made noises about Vaughn holding on to the house, but he'd been well aware his nephew could only take so much quiet. By the end of every summer visit, Vaughn had been twitchier than a teenage girl caught speeding in her daddy's brand-new Beemer.

Vaughn liked crowds. Traffic. Noise. *Action*.

"Emerson said you were going to take a leave of absence." The mayor's tone bordered on accusatory.

"I did." Sort of.

"At least let me set up a tour. Show you the facilities, introduce you around."

"Maybe another time."

Vaughn ended the conversation and tossed his phone on the table then zigzagged his way back to the living room. After snagging a box cutter off the tattered seat of a bar stool, he sliced open the Kitchen Crap box. Might as well locate the coffeemaker, because no way was he going to check out the second floor without a hefty dose of caffeine. And maybe a shot of whiskey, if he could find it.

In the dining room behind him, something heavy tumbled to the floor. Vaughn whipped around, automatically slapping a hand to his empty hip. *Easy.* He squinted across the hall and saw that a box had fallen off a stack. Obviously the contents had shifted and gravity had taken over.

Guilt niggled. Had his uncle really counted on his settling here?

He shook his head. *Way to let the mayor work you.*

Ten minutes later, he was rifling through dish towels and pot holders when he heard another thud. Next came a series of scraping sounds, like something being dragged across a sandy floor. *What the hell?*

He grabbed the box cutter and strode into the dining room. "Who's in here?" he demanded.

More thumping, muted this time. He looked to his right. Another box had landed on its side, spilling half-empty bottles of lotion and shampoo. A third carton had fallen behind it. Whatever was in here had to have been inside for a while—the place had been closed up for weeks.

A vision of a rabid raccoon latching onto his jugular while blood sprayed everywhere had him thinking about calling 911. But only for a split second. He couldn't let the overzealous sheriff lock up another Fulton for no good reason.

With a tight grip on the box cutter, Vaughn carefully skirted the mess on the floor, bent down and peered into the upended box.

A black cat stared up at him while kneading the lace tablecloth Aunt Brenda had saved for holidays. Sheepishly, Vaughn retracted the blade on the box cutter and slid the tool into his back pocket.

"Uncle Em might be smirking down on me, but Aunt Brenda's trying to swat you with a broom," he told the cat. The animal yawned and tugged a paw loose from a clinging thread. Vaughn squatted. "How the hell did you get in here?"

The cat hissed and backed farther into the box. Vaughn held up his hands. "Sorry, buddy. Didn't mean to make you nervous."

Jesus. He was talking to a stray cat.

He headed back to the kitchen. As soon as he made this call, the entire county would know he was in town. But someone was missing a pet, and he didn't have time to go knocking on doors.

"Hello, Miss Catlett? This is Vaughn Fulton, next door."

"How are you, Vaughn?"

"Good. Thanks. You?"

"Better if you call me Hazel, sweet cheeks."

While Hazel shared the details of her plantar fasciitis, the cheese ball recipe she'd recently tried and something about a new boyfriend and old lube—*wait, what?*—Vaughn returned to the dining room and checked on his intruder. The cat remained crouched in the corner of the box.

Hazel took a breath and Vaughn took advantage.

"Did my uncle have a cat?"

"No, hon, not that I know of. You have one hanging around outside?"

"Inside, and I have no idea how long he's been in here."

"Oh. Well, if I were you, I'd avoid going barefoot."

"Thanks," Vaughn said dryly. "Any clue where he might have come from?"

"What's he look like?"

"Black, with a white diamond on his chest."

"That could be Franklin. He belongs to the Hockadays, two doors down. But how on earth would he have managed to get in?"

"Probably through one of the big-ass holes in the roof," Vaughn muttered.

"Beg pardon?"

"Just thinking out loud."

"Like my Pete."

"Pete?"

"My sweetie. Pete Lowry. Remember him? Runs Lowry's Garage?"

"Sure do." With a silent huff of relief, Vaughn

perched on the windowsill. That explained the lube comment.

"And yes, we do enjoy wild grease monkey sex."

Or not.

"Hazel. I have an idea." *Please stop talking about your sex life.* "Mind coming over and taking a look at this cat? See if you recognize him?"

She gave a knowing chuckle. "Sure thing, hon. I'll be right over."

Vaughn returned the cat's wary stare. "Franklin. That your name?" When the cat started working his paws into the tablecloth again, Vaughn nodded. "I'll take that as a yes."

He went back across the hall and resumed his quest for the coffeepot.

It took him a few seconds, but he finally recognized that half-buzzing, half-wheezing sound as the doorbell. He set aside the coffee filters he'd discovered in a box marked Cleaning Crap and maneuvered his way back to the front door.

The Catlett sisters stood on the porch, each holding a foil-covered plate, their grins as wide as their makeup was bright. He smiled back, careful not to peer directly into their eye shadow.

The seventysomething Hazel and June, or Hazel and Nut, as some called them, couldn't have been kinder to him when he was a kid. They'd made numerous trips across his uncle's yard during Vaughn's summer visits, toting cakes and cas-

seroles and platters piled high with those round
Devil Dog things they called gobs. It wasn't until
after Aunt Brenda died that Vaughn realized the
sisters had probably used his growing-boy stage
as an excuse to help out his aunt and uncle while
they struggled with his aunt's cancer.

Aunt Brenda's death had hit Vaughn almost as
hard as it had hit Uncle Em. He hadn't handled it
as well as his uncle, though. He'd thrown himself
into his job as a patrol officer with the Erie PD,
with his sights set on becoming a detective. His
visits to Castle Creek had been irregular at best.
He wasn't proud of the distance he'd kept, but it
had helped him manage his grief.

"You just going to stand there, Vaughn Fulton,
or are you going to give us some love?"

Vaughn started. "My apologies, ladies. Please
come in, but watch your step."

They followed him down the hall and into the
kitchen, tut-tutting as they passed the leaning
tower of pizza boxes and five buckets of rags
that were at the top of his list to go to the dump.
The last thing he needed was a fire.

His visitors set their plates on the kitchen table
and exchanged nods of approval.

Hazel beamed at him. "Looks like Emerson
achieved what he set out to do."

"It'll take you weeks to sort this mess." June
lifted her arms. "Hug time."

Vaughn's narrowed gaze traveled from Hazel

to June and back again. Their sweetly familiar, brightly painted faces made him want to smile, but he suppressed the urge. Coconspirators, both of them.

"You were in on it," he said sternly.

Hazel blinked her carrot-colored eyelids and pursed her turquoise lips. Vaughn couldn't help wondering if she'd confused her lipstick for her eye shadow and vice versa. June had avoided that problem by painting both the same color—light purple. Vaughn had to admit it went well with her pink pantsuit.

Hazel patted her short, white hair. "Maybe we were and maybe we weren't," she said cagily.

"Oh, we absolutely were," June said. She wore her silver hair in the same pixie cut as her sister's. "And we loved every minute of it. Emerson let us take a peek at what people were bringing in and I scored two plastic tubs of summer clothes. I'm going to do a reverse Julie Andrews and patch together a set of curtains out of gym shorts." Vaughn let loose his laugh and stepped into her hug. She smelled like peppermint, just as he remembered. Nostalgia backed up in his throat as he bent toward Hazel. She pinched his ass.

"You haven't changed," he said, stepping out of reach.

"You have. You've been working out. That's one fine caboose you have there, Officer."

He gestured at the chaos in the hallway behind

them. "You can help yourself to anything here, except my caboose." He saw her expression and rushed to add, "Or any other body part."

"Fine," Hazel sniffed. "Then I suppose we should go find Franklin."

Vaughn led them to the dining room, where he crouched down to see inside the overturned box. When Hazel and June crowded in behind him, the cat erupted from the box. Front paws scrabbled on dust-covered hardwood as he made for the doorway. The back paws weren't as efficient, and as the cat shuffled past him, Vaughn discovered why. The animal's rear left leg hung at an odd angle, slowing his progress up the stairs.

"I wonder if he hurt himself getting in." He pulled out his cell. "Do you know the Hockadays' number? They'll have better luck getting hold of him."

"I do have their number, but I'm afraid that's not going to do any good." June's hand fluttered to her neck. "Sorry, dear, but that's not Franklin. Your *he* is a *she*. And she's about to have kittens."

Vaughn staggered back a step. "Please tell me you're joking."

Hazel eyed her sister with pride. "Wilmer Fish always said a vet could never ask for a better assistant than June."

While June preened, Hazel started rummaging through one of the boxes toppled by the cat.

Vaughn pushed a hand through his hair. "Neither of you has any idea who that cat might belong to?"

Hazel looked over her shoulder. "I'm thinking it's you."

"The cat seems to be thinking the same thing." June sidled around Vaughn to select her own box to pick through. "Ooh." She held up several pads of paper and a stack of multicolored Post-its. "Would you mind?"

Vaughn shook his head. "Anything else catches your eye, please take it. That includes the cat."

"Nice try, hon. Our Baby Blue would foam at the mouth if we tried to expand our little family. Schnauzers aren't usually superpossessive of their owners, but ours certainly is." Hazel patted him on the cheek. "We need to go. We have a fundraiser to finalize. Good luck with the house. I'm sure you'll get a fine price for it after all the repairs are made."

Vaughn frowned down at her. "I know about the roof. Don't tell me there's more."

"I'm afraid so." June hugged to her chest the office supplies she'd scavenged. "Your uncle had an electrical fire upstairs a few months ago, and there's a problem with the plumbing in the master bath." She squinted up at him. "He didn't tell you?"

Vaughn shook his head. What else had the old man kept from him?

Hazel grimaced. "The way the market is around here, you're not going to find a buyer if they have to invest in major repairs."

Vaughn barely refrained from rubbing his eyes with his knuckles. His halfhearted search for Uncle Em's whiskey stash had now become critical. He didn't have the money to invest in major repairs. His chances for getting a loan weren't good, either. Not when he was already stretched thin. Rent ate up most of his pay.

He thanked the sisters again for the food, apologized for not being able to offer them coffee and walked them out, then shut the front door and glanced at the second floor. That cat could be up there having kittens right this moment. In his *bed*.

Oh, hell, no. Vaughn grabbed his cell and headed for the stairs. Why hadn't he asked June for the vet's number? Before he could do a search on Wilmer Fish, he noticed a text from Whitby.

Forgot to mention it's a paid position. Let's talk salary over dinner. Cal's Diner @ 7? I'm buying.

He hesitated on the top step. As his thumb hovered over Reply, his ringtone blared into the silence. With a sigh, he lifted the phone to his ear.

"Hey, Mom."

"You said you'd call."

"I got caught up in something." He worked his

way toward the room Aunt Brenda had assigned him during his summer visits. So much for hoping the second floor wouldn't also be packed to capacity. It was standing-room-only up here. And it reeked of mothballs.

He stopped in the doorway of the guest room and exhaled. Even his bed was piled high with crap. Though maybe that was a good thing, considering the twin-size mattress looked about five times smaller than he remembered.

His mother gave a disapproving huff. "Do whatever it is you need to do and spend the rest of your break with us. Your father has someone he'd like you to meet."

Vaughn tightened his grip on his phone and swung toward the master bedroom. "I thought I made it clear. Enough with the ambushes."

"Don't be stubborn. So we scheduled a few dinners. You have to eat."

"Mom. I have a job waiting for me in Erie." At least, he hoped he did. "I'm not changing my career."

"Plenty of people your age and even older have made the decision to steer their professional lives in a new direction. It's nothing to be ashamed of."

"I'm not ashamed, I'm resolved. I'm proud of what I do. I plan to continue doing it."

"Vaughn." His mother's voice gentled. "You know your father and I would rather you find a job with actual earning potential. We're trying to look out for you. Don't you want to be able to afford a house someday? A family? Don't you want to have money to travel when you retire?"

He did have a house. His uncle's house. But it was only partly his, and it wasn't in Erie. Not for a moment would he consider staying.

As his mother talked about the trips she and his dad had taken and all of the places they planned to go, Vaughn peered into his uncle's bedroom. *Score.* The bed was empty. No junk, no cat in labor.

He propped a shoulder against the doorjamb and listened to his mother describe the luxury car he could afford if only he earned a decent paycheck.

Most law enforcement parents would worry about their son or daughter getting hurt in the line of duty. Vaughn's folks worried what the neighbors thought of their blue-collar son.

"So when can we expect you?" his mother asked. "I think you should talk to the man from the securities firm first—he has a personal driver *and* a summer house in the Hamptons."

"Not interested, Mom." Did she ever get tired of hearing it? 'Cause he was sure as hell tired of saying it. "Even if I were, I don't have the time."

"You don't have the time to visit your own parents?"

"Not when they won't stop campaigning against my job."

"And anyway, how complicated can it be to put up a For Sale sign?"

Basically what he'd said to Whitby. So why didn't the suggestion sit well?

"It's more involved than that." Just to be difficult, Vaughn added, "Plus they want me to pinch-hit as a deputy while I'm here."

Her reaction didn't disappoint. "That's not going to happen," she said flatly. "As if wasting your potential chasing hardened criminals around the city isn't bad enough."

Vaughn rolled his eyes. "There's a lot more to the job than that. By the way, crime rate's a lot lower here."

"So is the standard of living. What'll I tell the securities broker, that you're busy breaking up a moonshine ring? Please be serious. You'll damage your prospects. You know very well your father and I are not going to let you bury yourself in the country playing cops and robbers with your uncle's cronies."

She wouldn't let her uncle's arrest go. Never mind that Vaughn was still holding his own grudge. His mother didn't blame Sheriff By-The-Book Tate, but Vaughn sure as hell did. "I'm twenty-eight, not twelve," he said. "If I want to play cops and robbers, I'll play cops and robbers and you can't stop me."

He winced at his juvenile tone. After muttering his goodbye, he straightened, drew in a breath and prepared to flush a pregnant cat from her hiding place.

Or maybe he'd just join her there.

WHEN SPEEDY PETE drove past Lily Tate sedately enough that she had time to register his smirk, she realized she'd been had. Squinting after his faded gray Jeep as it disappeared around the bend, she lowered the radar gun and swore. The last time Pete Lowry had driven that slowly, he'd been bringing up the tail end of the Christmas parade, putt-putting down the center of State Street hauling a flatbed crammed with the high school football team, the cheerleading squad, three dozen bales of hay and a celebrity Holstein named Priscilla Mae.

Somehow the smug so-and-so had known Lily was parked at the entrance to the old logging road. But how? The only vehicles she'd seen that afternoon had all been headed in the same direction, away from Castle Creek.

She lifted her hat and blotted the sweat clinging to her bangs. She blinked against the perspiration that stung her eyes and wriggled her shoulders, desperate to free her skin from the short-sleeved uniform shirt plastered to her back. But that wouldn't happen until she was back in the air-conditioned courthouse, and *that* wouldn't happen until she managed to actually write a citation.

Two hours in the August sun and she hadn't issued the first ticket. Today's lack of revenue would not please the mayor. He'd probably auction off her parking space again. Not that she minded the walk, but it always seemed to rain the week she'd been relegated to the back of the lot.

She huffed in exasperation and grabbed at the car door. Time to find out why everyone was driving like the road was coated in ice.

The moment she dropped into her seat, she heard a rattling sound. *What the—oh.* She plucked her cell free of the plastic cup holder. When had she put it on Vibrate? A glance at the screen had her wincing. Burke. Again. She pressed Ignore. The man had to be as tired of hearing *no* as she was of saying it.

She started the car, then lightly bounced her forehead against the wheel. All she wanted was to do her job. Stay busy. Enjoy her privacy.

Forget.

But the mayor was determined to make her job harder, Burke Yancey wouldn't stop asking her out and every time she heard a child laugh—

She pressed her hands against her chest, where sudden pain sliced deep. After a few breathless seconds, she filled her lungs, sat up straight and reached for her seat belt.

Focus. She had a job to do. And doing that

job meant finding out why every driver in Castle Creek had suddenly developed a feather foot.

It didn't take long.

CHAPTER TWO

HALF A MILE past the curve that prevented Lily from seeing oncoming traffic—and prevented oncoming traffic from seeing *her*—she spotted the problem. Jared Ensler.

She should have known.

The skinny preteen stood on the shoulder, his back to Lily. Wincing at his camouflage pants and dark green T-shirt, she pulled off onto the opposite shoulder. At least the kid's blazing orange skullcap made him stand out. Well, that and the poster-sized sheet of cardboard he was toting.

The sound of her engine must have finally registered because he turned. His eyes went wide, his mouth went slack and his arms collapsed. The bottom third of the sign buckled against his shins. Lily eyed the bright red, hand-painted letters and suppressed a grudging smile.

Speed Trap Ahead.

Jared chewed his bottom lip and let the sign drop to his side, but he stood his ground. Ignoring the hat she'd tossed on the passenger seat, Lily pushed herself once more into the thick, sticky heat of the afternoon. A farm stand just down the highway was selling peaches, and she breathed in the heady scent. A mental image of a bowl of vanilla ice cream topped with juicy slices of the ripe fruit was almost enough to forgive the sun for its enthusiasm today.

Almost, but not quite.

The harsh cry of a crow on the power lines overhead had her rolling her eyes at herself. Food fantasies were so not her thing. That's what she got for skipping lunch. And leaving her hat in the car one too many times. With a wistful glance at the distant, dark blue wedge of Lake Erie, she adjusted her sunglasses and crossed the road.

Jared kicked at a dandelion sprouting at the pavement's edge. Bits of white fluff exploded into the air. When the crunch under Lily's boots signaled she'd moved from asphalt to gravel, he lifted his head. His mouth formed an arrogant slash, but his eyes held a hint of panic.

"Am I in trouble?" he asked gruffly.

"Depends. Your mother know what you're up to?"

"I'm used to that kind of trouble. I need to know about the jail kind."

"Why are you out here, if you thought you might be arrested?"

He stacked his hands atop his skullcap. "Am I? Under arrest?"

"Jared." Lily bit back her impatience as sweat

dripped down the back of her neck. "Are you wearing sunscreen?"

He gave her an odd look and shook his head. He wasn't wearing shades, either, but at least he'd been smart enough to bring something to drink. A battered handheld cooler rested on the shoulder behind him.

Lily sighed. "What are you doing out here?"

He glanced around, as if for inspiration. "Something's wrong with our Xbox." When she crossed her arms, he shrugged. "We got bored watching TV. We heard my mom talking on the phone with someone who'd seen you out here—"

"And decided it would be fun to warn everyone I was using radar."

"Yeah." The word carried a lot of *duh*.

"Who's 'we'?"

He hesitated. "Scottie's out here, too, down the road a ways."

His younger brother, on the road by himself. *Fantastic*.

"There hasn't been any traffic from that direction," she said. "How is that less boring than watching TV?"

Jared smirked. "He's doing okay."

"How do you know?" When he pulled a smartphone out of his pocket, Lily nodded, barely resisting the urge to say this *duh* for him. "Let's go get him. I'm taking you two home before you get heatstroke."

"You're not taking us to jail?" His mouth tipped up and then down, as if he didn't know whether to be relieved or disappointed.

"I have a feeling any punishment your mother dishes out will be worse than a stretch in one of my holding cells. What you're doing isn't illegal, but it is dangerous. What if a car came around that corner too fast and swerved onto the shoulder? What if a driver wasn't paying attention and drifted off the road?" She broke off. The possibilities had her lungs floundering.

Jared looked unimpressed.

She breathed in, then out. "How did you even get out here?"

"Our neighbor brought us."

Right. Lily did remember seeing Mrs. Yackley drive by in her lime-green Beetle. "She didn't ask why you and your brother wanted to be dropped off in different locations?" Or wonder if she should leave a twelve-year-old and an eight-year-old out on the highway alone? "What'd you do, tell her you were on some kind of secret mission?"

Jared shook his head. "We told her the truth. She was cool with it, but she said if her taxes went up she wouldn't knit us any more hats."

Lily huffed a laugh. "Okay, then." Apparently Mrs. Yackley had an issue with authority. Or maybe just a soft spot for restless preteens.

Jared picked up his cooler and followed Lily to

her patrol car. She agreed to let him sit up front until they collected his brother. After that, the boys would have to share the backseat—no way was she going to play referee while they argued about who got to sit where.

She drove back to the logging road and eased around the curve beyond it. There stood fair-haired Scottie, wearing a banana-colored T-shirt that hung to his knees and holding a sign identical to his brother's. Except for the message.

Lily snorted. These kids had the perfect setup. After Jared warned drivers of the speed trap, Scottie asked them to show some gratitude.

He held a bucket in his left hand and in his right a sign that read Tip$.

The moment it registered exactly whose car he was signaling, Scottie dropped the sheet of cardboard. The bucket he hugged to his chest.

Once again, Lily steered the car onto the shoulder. This time she parked behind Scottie on the left, so he wouldn't have to cross the road. "Clever scheme," she said.

Jared never glanced up from his perusal of the switches, lights and video screens on her dash. "I know, right?"

Less than five minutes later, Lily had both signs tucked away in her trunk and both Ensler brothers buckled up in her backseat. She nodded in approval at the sound of plastic crackling as they guzzled water. She cranked up the AC and pulled back onto the road, then checked out her passengers in the rearview mirror. "You two trying to earn money for something in particular? A birthday gift for your mom, maybe?"

Jared shot her a disgusted look. "I told you, our Xbox isn't working."

"The red ring of death," Scottie said. His voice was closer than it should be. A glance to her right showed he had his head thrust between the front seats, wide eyes glued to the same panel of switches that had fascinated his brother.

"I need you to sit back, buddy. I know you're curious, but the time to look around isn't when the car's in motion. Jared, make sure your brother's buckled in. So what's the red ring of death?"

"Happens when your console's broke," Scottie said. "The red lights around the power switch come on. When Dad couldn't fix it he said it was about as useful as tits on a boar hog."

Jared hooted, and the sound had her shoulders curving in, her stomach muscles bracing against a surge of acid regret. *Stop that*, she told herself firmly.

She swallowed the misery coating her throat and forced a chuckle. "I doubt your dad would appreciate you repeating that. How much did you make today, anyway?"

Paper shuffled as Scottie counted. After a

whispered consultation in the backseat and a muffled "No, give it *back*" and "It's *not* a secret," he announced, "Forty-five dollars."

Good God. How many tickets should she have written this afternoon?

Jared grunted and crossed his arms. "You gonna confiscate that, too?"

"Not if you promise never to pull something like this again."

"Aw, *man*." Scottie threw his head against the seat back and groaned up at the roof. "But we don't have enough money yet."

"I'm sorry," she said firmly. "You'll have to find a safer way to earn it."

"Shit," Scottie mumbled, and it was so unexpected, Lily was hard put not to laugh. She pressed a palm to her chest again, this time wishing she could trap the unfamiliar lightness there.

"Shh." Jared darted a worried glance at the rearview mirror.

"What? Not like she can arrest us for cussing." A brief pause. "Can she?"

Wait for it...wait for it...

"Sheriff Tate?" Scottie asked meekly.

There it is.

"Yes, Scottie?"

"Can you get arrested for using a bad word?"

"Not unless you're threatening someone. It's never a good idea to be mouthy around the police, though, and it is bad manners. I doubt your parents would approve, so why don't you try and keep it clean, okay?"

He sighed, then grudgingly muttered, "Okay." Neither brother said a word after that.

The sullen silence lasted until she pulled into the Enslers' driveway. "Your mom or dad inside?"

"Dad is," Jared said morosely.

"Before I walk you to the door—" Scottie groaned "—let me set you straight on something."

"He only said that one word and he's sorry," Jared said quickly.

"I'm really sorry," Scottie squeaked.

"Neither of you is in trouble." She retrieved her wallet from the center console, pulled out a twenty and dropped it in Scottie's bucket. "I didn't confiscate your posters," she said. "I bought them." Even though they were about as useful as tits on a boar hog.

Twenty minutes later, Lily had just backed into a new hiding place and pulled out the radar gun when her cell vibrated again. She picked it up and immediately wished she hadn't. The mayor's office. Shouldn't his staff be at Hazel's barbecue?

She swallowed a groan. Chances were that's what they wanted to ask *her*. If the mayor summoned her, she'd have to go. A drop of sweat skated down her temple and she swiped it away with the heel of her hand.

Maybe she'd get lucky and they'd assign her to the dunk tank.

She took the call and moments later dropped her phone back into the cup holder with a scowl. The mayor had summoned her, all right—to his office. On a Saturday?

This did not bode well.

LILY PARKED HER patrol car behind the courthouse, a single-story, faded brick building the sheriff's department shared with the county clerk, the treasurer, the commissioner of revenue and the mayor. With the colossal, pineapple-shaped sugar maple that for decades had served as the front lawn's centerpiece, and the surrounding century-old oaks and lush camellias scattered like guests at a cocktail party, the property was lauded as being especially eye-catching in the autumn. Lily no longer paid attention. Fall had officially become her least favorite season.

The mayor's assistant wasn't at her desk—not surprising, since it was Saturday—so Lily knocked twice on Rick Whitby's open door and strode into his office. Or candy store, as Lily's dispatcher, Clarissa, liked to call it, since the mayor had a credenza lined with clear glass jars he kept well stocked with sweets. Licorice sticks, mini chocolate bars, lollipops, jelly beans—his sweet tooth provided a clever means of staying informed, since the addicts he created couldn't stay out of his office.

As long as he didn't start dealing peanut M&M's, Lily had no problem resisting temptation.

He hadn't heard her knock. He stood with his back to the door, right hand dipping a paper cup into the jelly beans while the left held the lid aloft.

"Mayor Whitby," she said.

The clatter of jelly beans told her she'd startled him. With a muffled *clank*, he replaced the lid on the jar and turned to face her.

The mayor was a lanky, languid man in his fifties with thinning blond hair and a perpetual flush on his face. His title was actually County Executive Officer, but "mayor" was much less of a mouthful. He was popular, a shirtsleeves-and-cold-brew kind of politician, but his hard-at-it look was an act—the man was lazier than an overfed hound sleeping away a hot summer afternoon.

Lily had always suspected he'd run for mayor solely as a means to jump-start his love life. Not long into his term, he'd ended his relationship with his assistant, Paige Southerly, a woman several years his senior. Paige still worked for him and Lily didn't know how she did it, every three or four months taking the newest girlfriend's calls, scheduling dinner dates and sending flowers. Paige insisted their affair had run its course and as long as her boss kept the dish of butterscotch candies stocked, it was all good.

"You're not dressed for the fund-raiser." The mayor gave Lily a once-over as he fished a yellow jelly bean out of his cup.

Yeah, she'd known that was coming. Hazel Catlett and a handful of volunteers were hosting a barbecue to raise money for the citizens' center. As sheriff, Lily should be there, but it was hard to drum up the enthusiasm to mingle with a bunch of happy families.

She needed to get over that. And she would. Just not today.

"JD will be there," she said. "There are only two of us now and you know we can't both go."

When Whitby failed to scold Lily for complaining about her long-ignored deputy vacancy, her stomach did a little side step. Whatever he was about to say would not be pleasant. Not for her, anyway. The gleam in his bright blue eyes indicated *he* was looking forward to it. Either that, or those were damn good jelly beans.

Her fingers curled around her equipment belt and she pulled in a stealthy breath. "What did you want to see me about?"

He held out the cup and rattled it. When she shook her head, he set the cup on the credenza, brushed his hands together and strolled to his desk. "I have something important to discuss with you." He scraped a fingernail over a front tooth to loosen a green gummy wedge. "Here's the thing. I've decided to fill that deputy position like you've been asking."

Lily blinked. "Thank you. JD hasn't had a real vacation in over a year. I'll get busy writing up an ad for the paper—"

"That won't be necessary. I already hired someone."

Damn it. "Without consulting me?"

"I am the mayor." His grin revealed he'd missed a sliver of purple.

"What about the town council?" The mayor did have the right to hire and fire county employees, but he didn't ordinarily do it without the council's okay.

"Bought 'em each a steak dinner and one of Ivy Walker's cheesecakes."

"You *bribed* them?"

"I distracted them." He wilted into his leather club chair, as if her resistance had exhausted him. She wouldn't have been surprised if he'd pressed the back of a hand to his forehead. "Your new deputy is Vaughn Fulton, on temporary loan from the Erie police. He reports on Monday. I asked his captain to email you his qualifications so he can get right to work." He closed his eyes and let his head fall against the back of the padded chair.

Lily tightened her grip on her rig. "May I ask how this Officer Fulton of the Erie PD heard about little ol' Castle Creek and its three-man department?"

"Four again, with Deputy Fulton, and I invited him to apply."

"You mean you offered him the job." She frowned. "Fulton. Any relation to Emerson?" She'd liked that old son of a gun. He'd died a few months back, the weekend she'd been taking her recertification training in Harrisburg. She'd regretted not being able to attend the service.

Slowly, Whitby pushed himself up out of the chair and slid his hands into his pants pockets. "Emerson Fulton was his great-uncle. He was also a good friend of mine. His nephew is on a temporary leave of absence while he handles his uncle's affairs. I gave him a call, asked if he'd be willing to help us out for a while." His voice tightened. "He's a decorated city cop. You should be pleased."

Pleased that he'd casually made her a victim of the old-boy network? That he was forcing her to work with, to entrust JD's life—*her* life—to someone she'd never even met, let alone interviewed?

He had to be kidding.

Too bad he didn't look like he was kidding.

For a while. He'd used the phrase *for a while*.

"So we're only talking a few weeks here," she said carefully.

He shrugged and grabbed his suit coat. "I

imagine he'll be around for a month or two. Maybe even until Thanksgiving."

Oh, come *on*. The first throbs of a headache tapped at her temples and she forced her jaw to unclench. "That's three months away."

He pulled his keys out of his jacket pocket and gave them a jangle before shooing Lily toward the door. "I'm locking up."

For a lazy man, he sure was moving fast.

"I'm the one who's responsible for those in my employ," she reminded him as he herded her into the hallway. "The people of Castle Creek elected me to keep this county safe, and you're making it hard for me to do my job."

"No. You're making it hard for me to do mine." He frowned at the wall, shoved his suit coat at her and straightened a painting. When he turned back around, he caught her off guard with a wink. "And I outrank you."

Hot prickles of resentment chased across Lily's skin and she thrust his jacket back at him. "What if I talk to the council?"

He brushed past her, heading for the front entrance. "How impressed will the people of Castle Creek be when they find out their sheriff refused to work with a fellow officer—an officer who recently lost a well-known and beloved uncle to kidney disease—simply because she couldn't bring herself to trust the word of their mayor?"

"That was a pretty energetic threat," she muttered.

"I know, right? Must have been the jelly beans."

She wasn't going to win this argument. Not when he was in one of his autocratic moods. She chewed the inside of her lip.

If she didn't manage to get reelected, what would she do? Work for her replacement? That would be awkward, to put it mildly. What, then? Move out of Castle Creek?

Her eyes began to sting. She could never do that.

"Fine." Rubbing her temples, she followed the mayor outside and blinked in the sunlight. "Fulton's nephew it is," she said resignedly. "But I'll continue to take applications for when his leave is up."

The mayor gave her the side eye as he aimed his key fob at his Prius.

Lily scowled. "Let me guess. You hope to talk him into staying."

"I'm going to give it a try. You should think about doing the same."

"Staying in Castle Creek?" Her voice was so dry, the words practically scuffed her throat.

"Giving him a try." He rummaged in his suit coat pocket and pulled out two lollipops. He pulled the bright red wrapper from the first, popped it into his mouth and pressed the second into her hand. She waited until he'd left the parking lot before opening her fingers.

Root beer.

Her favorite.

Damn him.

LILY HAD ALREADY switched to decaf by the time her dispatcher came in to start her shift on Monday. Metal clanked as Clarissa deposited her purse in the bottom left drawer of her desk, then came her usual Monday morning sigh, then the click of high heels and the distant clatter of ceramic as she moved into the small break room beside Lily's office and poured herself a cup of coffee.

When the dispatcher appeared in Lily's doorway, she had both hands wrapped around a fading Hello Kitty mug. She looked like a 1950s' starlet with her black-rimmed cat-eye glasses, her *I Love Lucy* hair pulled back in a high ponytail and her plush body showcased in lime capris, a pink-and-lime-striped top and a sheer silk scarf.

While Lily resisted glancing down at her own tan uniform shirt and mud-colored tie, Clarissa checked out the crumpled sub wrappers in the trash can. "Have you been here all weekend again?" she demanded.

"No."

"Are you lying to me?"

Lily shrugged.

Clarissa narrowed her eyes and sipped her coffee. "The only reason I let you off the hook about girls' night out is because you promised you'd do something fun this weekend."

"I remember."

"So what'd you do?"

Lily dropped her pen, tugged off her reading glasses and leaned back in her chair. "Drove up to Erie for the day. Wandered around Presque Isle, treated myself to lunch and did a little antiquing."

"I forget. If someone who's right-handed looks up and to the right when they're talking, does that mean they're lying, or telling the truth?"

Lily shot her dispatcher a wry glance. "If you suspect I'm lying, why would you think I'd answer that question with anything but another lie?"

"Good point." Clarissa tugged at the hem of her top. "Did you find anything? When you were antiquing?"

"I did. I found a vintage set of salt and pepper shakers that'll make a great gift for my mom's birthday. They're cloisonné. She'll go wild."

With a growling sigh, Clarissa plopped down into the chair opposite Lily. "Now I know you're lying. You hate your mom's collections."

"Busted."

"You do realize that being a workaholic is a pathetic cliché?"

"Maybe that fact will sink in the day *you* realize that what I do when I'm off shift is my own business."

"That's the trouble," Clarissa said. "You're never off shift." She caught Lily's look. "And yes, you're right, it's way past time for me to start mine." In the doorway, she pivoted. "I get why you're grumpy. When is the mayor's 'personal favor' supposed to get here?"

Lily tossed her glasses on the desk. "I don't know when he'll be here, but I do know JD's about to earn his vacation all over again. He can take Fulton for the week, get him acclimated to the area before we let him handle calls on his own."

"Sounds like a plan." With a wink Clarissa disappeared into the outer office. Two minutes later, she was back. "You should come listen to this voice mail."

Lily did, and wished she hadn't. "Fudge," she said flatly. Poor JD. Felled by a bad batch of macaroni salad.

She crossed her arms and stared out the windows at the tree-rimmed parking lot behind the sheriff's office. More specifically, she stared at the space where JD's cruiser would *not* be parked for the next few days.

Double fudge.

"Looks like you just lost your rookie wrangler." Clarissa made a sympathetic face and set down her mug. "Tell you what. As soon as this guy shows up, I'll check him out. If I like what I see, I'll gladly play tour guide for you. How's that?"

"If you don't like what you see, I can always use GPS."

The deep, unfamiliar voice rumbled along Lily's spine. She curbed an irritated shudder. *Time to make nice.* She had no choice. If she didn't honor the mayor's request he'd only saddle her with a seventy-year-old retiree once this Fulton guy was gone. Or he'd veto every candidate she put forth. When Rick Whitby was coming off a sugar high, that was just the way he rolled.

So suck it up, Lily Anne.

She swiveled toward the counter that separated the office space from the reception area.

A man wearing jeans and a short-sleeved navy T-shirt that barely concealed a hip holster stood in the doorway, shoulder propped against the jamb, posture as cocky as his voice. Midtwenties, six-one or so, trimmed dark hair and troublemaker eyes. One look and it was as clear-cut as the muscles stretching his shirt. If the man were in motion, he'd be swaggering.

Beside her, Clarissa hummed her approval. Lily could practically hear the drool hitting the floor.

He moved into the office. *Yeah. Swagger.* He planted his palms on the countertop, locked his arms and leaned in. "Vaughn Fulton reporting for duty, ma'am." One eyebrow raised, he made a show of glancing around the area behind the counter then turned a grin on Clarissa. "Looks like I'm first in line for the tour. Guess that means I'll get a good seat."

Clarissa giggled and Lily heaved an inward groan.

Thanks a whole hell of a lot, Whitby. The seventy-year-old retiree would have been a better bet. She'd wanted someone with intelligence, but this guy seemed to carry all his smarts in his ass.

CHAPTER THREE

"THIS IS ONE good deed I'll gladly take the punishment for," Clarissa murmured.

Lily kept an eye roll to herself, but her mind was made up. Whoever ran against Whitby next term—even if ninety-year-old Larry Katz threw his fedora in the ring—Lily's vote was a sure thing.

Kind of like Clarissa, when it came to their new deputy.

Lily snapped out of her inertia and strode over to the counter. After lifting up the section that allowed access to the back, she waved Fulton through. "I expected you an hour ago, Deputy Fulton."

He hesitated. No doubt he was used to hearing *Officer* Fulton. Too bad. He was hers now. So to speak.

"My apologies for being late, Sheriff," he said. "And it's Vaughn."

"Deputy Fulton will do." She gestured at Clarissa, who stepped forward with a wide smile. "Clarissa Dodd, our dispatcher."

He reached for Clarissa's hand. "I'm not a

rookie and I don't need a wrangler. I do know what I'm doing."

After reclaiming her hand, Clarissa smoothed both palms over curvy hips. "I'm sure you do."

"All right, that's enough." Lily clapped once and shooed Clarissa back to her desk. "We're a government office, not a singles' bar." She did wish she could let Clarissa have her fun, since the dispatcher was still reeling from a nasty divorce. But though Clarissa had sworn off romance, she remained a big fan of sex, and Lily didn't need any casual hookups complicating the dynamics of her department.

She turned to Fulton. He didn't look fresh out of the academy, but it was close.

He also looked exceedingly fine in his jeans. *Something you have no business noticing, Lily Anne.* Especially when she suspected he was much younger than she was.

"How long have you been on the force?" she asked, speaking more harshly than she'd intended.

"Six years."

Six years to her eighteen. Damn, she felt old.

He studied her, and one corner of his mouth slanted up. "You plotting revenge against me, or the mayor?"

Both, she wanted to blurt. Instead she said, "What's done is done," and waved him over to the office that had remained empty since Sam

Weems had retired the year Lily won the election. "This is yours," she said, and backed away, eyeing his T-shirt. "You'll need a uniform shirt. JD's office is the next one over. You can borrow his spare until you get one of your own."

"JD. He's out on a call?"

"Out sick." She exhaled. "Guess that means you'll be riding with me."

OUCH. VAUGHN PUSHED a breath through his nose. The sheriff couldn't have made it any clearer that she was less than thrilled to have him around. Not that he'd expected any different, but damn, she'd smacked his ego hard enough to make it sting.

Fine with him. Not like he was thrilled to be working with a woman who would arrest a dying man.

With a curt nod, Vaughn maneuvered around the sheriff and let himself into the office belonging to the absent JD. He glanced around the cramped space—battered metal desk, overcrowded bookshelf, spare chair with a faded cloth seat—but didn't see a coatrack or anything resembling a closet door.

Door. He peered behind the office door. Bingo. A uniform shirt hung on a self-stick hook. Vaughn plucked the shirt free and gave it a sniff. It would do.

He had second thoughts after he'd peeled off his T-shirt and shoved his arms through the sleeves of the borrowed shirt. To say it was a tight fit would be like saying Clarissa Dodd was a little friendly.

Or Sheriff Lily Tate a little hostile.

Outside the door, Clarissa belted out a laugh, and Vaughn's lips twitched at the sound. An odd pair, those two, but the affection between them was obvious. Had they worked together long? Did Clarissa know the reason her boss was such a hard-ass?

Vaughn fumbled a button and swore. *Why do you care?* Damn it, he didn't want to be here in the first place. But after tallying the cost of repairs to the house, and to a cat whose owner was nowhere to be found, he'd realized any kind of income would come in handy. The clincher had been his mother ordering him not to take the job.

A paycheck *and* payback. Childish, yeah, but he hadn't been able to resist.

And he was already regretting it.

He finally managed to button up the shirt, but only just. Shit. If he wore this for long, he'd lose all feeling in his arms. He considered putting his T-shirt back on and letting the uniform shirt hang loose, but he'd never fit the second set of sleeves over top of the first.

"Having difficulties, Deputy Fulton?" The sheriff's long-suffering tone seemed to convey that a mere six years on the force wasn't enough to qualify Vaughn to get into a uniform, let alone wear it.

To hell with it.

He yanked open the door and stepped out. The dispatcher's eyes went wide and she bounced in her high heels when she saw him. Vaughn was proud of himself for not letting his gaze linger on her...bouncy parts.

A throat cleared.

His eyes met those of the sheriff, who was regarding him in a decidedly non-Clarissa kind of way. Then again, pretty much everything about her was non-Clarissa. Her dark hair was short and tousled, her mouth an unfriendly line, and the energy her slim figure radiated was more impatience than cheerfulness.

But the promise of softness was there, in her big hazel eyes and her pale pink lips. With her pointed chin and wide eyes, she looked like a too-tall elf.

An elf with a tendency to bite, he'd do well to remember.

His eyes dropped to the weapon at her hip. Too bad he never had been able to resist a woman in uniform.

Now was probably a good time to start.

Sheriff Tate shook her head at the fabric stretched over his biceps and muttered something about a waste of a good uniform. "It'll do for now," she said.

"I'll say."

The sheriff tossed Clarissa a scowl and the dispatcher stopped bouncing. As soon as the sheriff turned her back, Clarissa sent Vaughn a good-natured wink, then dropped into her chair. She scooted in close to her desk and put on her headset.

Vaughn let his shoulders go lax, which improved the fit of the shirt. A little friendly flirting he could deal with. More, he didn't have time for.

Sheriff Tate was still giving him the evil eye. "Clarissa will give you the grand tour of our offices here," she said.

"Castle Creek Sheriff's Department, how may I help you?" the dispatcher lilted into her microphone. When she started tapping at her keyboard, the sheriff shot Vaughn a disgruntled look.

"Fine," she said. "*I'll* give you the grand tour of our offices." She pointed to the left. "My office." She pointed behind it. "Break room." She pointed straight ahead, at Clarissa. "Dispatch station." She pointed to the two offices across from hers. "Deputies' offices." She pointed to the short hallway to their right, and the door at the end with the electronic keypad beside it. "Bathrooms and holding cells. Any questions?"

He scratched his jaw. "I feel like I should say no, but…how about a set of keys?"

"I'll get you a set before the end of the day."

"Sheriff? That was Mr. Katz." The dispatcher made a face. "Mona's being assaulted again."

"Fudge." The sheriff turned to Vaughn. "Sounds like the perfect opportunity for our newest employee to show us what he's got."

A domestic. Damn, he hated those. He strode toward the exit behind the dispatcher's station. "I'm ready. Let's hit it."

But when he looked over his shoulder, he saw the sheriff hadn't moved. Instead she watched him with a bemused expression. Meanwhile Clarissa had swiveled in her chair to follow his progress. She batted her eyes.

"Yeah, Deputy Fulton," she said. "Show us what you've got."

The sheriff made an irritated noise. "What I *meant* was, we can see him in action."

Clarissa popped an eyebrow.

"Watch him do his thing."

The other eyebrow came up.

"Gauge his level of experience." When Clarissa laughed out loud, the sheriff gave her head a disgusted shake. "Know what? Never mind."

Vaughn stared at them both in disbelief. "You're kidding me, right?" His gaze shifted from the sheriff to Clarissa and back again. "There's an *assault* in progress."

The sheriff pulled a set of keys from her pocket, but she hadn't taken more than two steps when the phone in her office rang. She held up a finger and veered toward her desk.

Vaughn shoved a hand through his hair. For God's sake, what would they do if someone called in a shooting, stop to take orders for lunch?

The sheriff reappeared. "That was the mayor. He's calling me in for an emergency conference. You're on your own, Deputy."

"Convenient," Vaughn muttered.

"You said you didn't need a wrangler. Here's your chance to prove it." She turned to Clarissa. "Give him the keys to his cruiser. Mr. Katz's address, too."

"Mr. Katz is at Ivy's. The calendar, remember?" Clarissa bit her lip. "You sure you want to send the new guy out there alone?"

"He can handle it." Sheriff Tate eyed his borrowed shirt. "As long as his arms don't go numb."

VAUGHN SHOOK HIS head as he steered the patrol car out of the courthouse parking lot. This call had to be some kind of initiation. No way anyone on the force would treat the report of an assault so casually.

The sheriff had it in for him. That much was clear.

Wherever you are, JD, I hope to hell you're back on the job tomorrow.

Then again, maybe he wouldn't be so damn touchy if he'd managed to sleep through the night.

His foster cat and her brood had kept him up. Some of that insomnia was his fault, though, since he'd hauled his ass out of bed pretty much on the hour to check that everyone was still breathing.

He followed the directions on his phone to the address Clarissa had provided. Twenty minutes after he started out, he pulled into a winding driveway marked by a sign that had him doing a double take. The *Dairy* in Millbrook Dairy Farm and Riding Stables had been crossed out and replaced with *Marry*, and in the corner someone had painted a long-lashed Holstein wearing a wedding veil.

He shook his head and pressed on the accelerator.

The right side of the driveway was crowded with cars parked perpendicular to a fence that bordered a small paddock. Behind the paddock stretched an endless expanse of green that hosted the occasional cluster of fawn-colored cows, their noses buried in the grass. Vaughn counted three large barns to the left of the driveway. Straight ahead loomed the house, an elegant A-frame with a sunroom jutting off the side. Beyond the house and barns shimmered a thin strip of blue that had to be the lake.

Damn, it was pretty here.

As Vaughn stepped out of the cruiser, a group of people spilled out of the barn nearest the house. When they caught sight of Vaughn, they started talking.

"You seriously called the cops?"

"About time they got here."

"You called 911? So help me, Larry, don't you ever ask me to pick up your gout pills from the pharmacy again. You're on your own, old man."

"Since when did we get a new deputy?"

"Cute, isn't he?"

Four women, a man and a pair of dogs made their way toward him. Three of the women were elderly. Two of them he knew. The Catlett sisters. What the hell did they have to do with this?

The man had to be in his nineties, and the fourth woman, a hot blonde leading the entire pack, looked to be around Vaughn's age. She wore jeans and muck boots, and behind her trotted the two dogs, side by side, a chubby brown-and-black mix and a gray schnauzer. The dogs' leashes trailed in the grass. Luckily neither dog seemed interested in taking a bite out of Vaughn.

The Catlett sisters and their friend, he wasn't so sure. Hazel and June offered him brash smiles while the other lady simply stared at his chest.

When the tall blonde reached him, she held out a hand. "I'm Ivy Walker," she said, voice friendly, expression curious. "Thank you for coming."

"Deputy Fulton." Vaughn started to put his hands on his hips, but his sleeves damn near cut off his circulation, so he let his arms fall to his sides. He nodded at the Catletts. "Ladies. What seems to be the trouble here?"

Ivy Walker's eyes widened. "You know Hazel and June?"

The lady with the gelled gray hair and plastic T-bones hanging from her ears tapped him on the shoulder. "No offense, dear, but do you need a few laundry pointers?"

Vaughn blinked, and struggled to reconcile that baby-doll voice with its owner, whose shoulders were wider than his. Like Hazel and June, she looked to be in her seventies, but he bet she could kick some serious ass. He looked down at the material stretched across his chest and cleared his throat. "This is a loaner."

June quirked her lips, which were the color of an avocado. "You'd be better off not wearing a shirt at all."

Hazel raised a hand and waggled her purple-tipped fingers. "I'll second that."

The old man shouldered his way forward, scowling. "You said this calendar would be family-friendly."

Hazel flapped a hand. "Considering the only photos we have of Mona are of her and Chance getting busy, that ship has sailed."

Vaughn barely resisted the urge to slap a hand to his face. What the hell was going on here?

Ivy Walker sent him a pitying look and patted

the old man's shoulder. "He's not here for the calendar, Mr. Katz. He's here to help you."

When the old man did nothing but stare and no one else moved, Vaughn clenched his teeth. "Does someone want to tell me where I can find Mona?"

The chorus started up again. Before Vaughn could holler for a time-out, Baby-doll Voice clapped her hands together. "Children, children," she called out, and surprisingly everyone quieted.

Mooooooo. As a unit, they turned to stare at a sleepy-eyed Holstein that had ambled up to the paddock fence to check them out. The model for the sign out front? When the ladies all waved at the cow, Vaughn rubbed his face.

Shaking down gangbangers on the streets of Erie never looked so good.

Ivy Walker took charge of the introductions. "That's Priscilla Mae," she said proudly, and it took Vaughn a moment to realize she meant the cow. "Deputy Fulton, this is Audrey Tweedy—" she pointed at Baby-doll Voice "—and Larry Katz. And apparently you know Hazel and June Catlett."

Larry Katz. He'd reported the assault. Vaughn pulled out his notebook. "Mr. Katz—"

The old guy frowned. "Any relation to Emerson Fulton?"

"He was my great-uncle."

"My condolences, Deputy. Your uncle was a

good man." Katz tucked his phone into the pocket of a plaid shirt that looked a lot like one Uncle Em used to wear. "And now I know where to find you if you don't take care of my Mona."

Vaughn scratched his jaw. Did the old man realize his words constituted a threat? When Katz's mouth adopted a Clint Eastwood curl, Vaughn had his answer. But at least they'd gotten around to discussing Mona. Who was she? Katz's wife? His daughter?

Hazel swatted Katz on the arm. "Lighten up, Larry. Mona's a slut and you know it."

"Enough," Vaughn barked. "I need to see Mona. *Now.*"

Silence, until a hot breeze pushed past, and rattled Audrey Tweedy's T-bone earrings. Wide-eyed, the five people facing him pointed.

Downward.

At the brown-and-black dog cozying up to the schnauzer.

Vaughn drew in a breath, held it until it burned then let it go. "Tell me what happened, Mr. Katz."

"What always happens when Mona and Baby Blue get together. They try to—" Audrey Tweedy flushed a raw steak–red "—get together. You know."

Yeah. He knew. Vaughn snapped his notepad closed and jammed it into his shirt pocket. Mona was in distress like Vaughn was in high heels.

"Mr. Katz," he said evenly. "Would you like to arrange for a vet to examine Mona?"

"You mean Wilmer Fish? Who's going to pay for that?"

"That would be your responsibility, sir. You can pursue compensation in court, but your failure to remove your dog from this situation won't help your case."

"Vaughn Fulton." Hazel glared. "Are you trying to talk him into suing us?"

Katz held up a palm before anyone else could interrupt. "You mean they can't be together? But they're friends."

"Friends with benefits." June nodded earnestly.

Ivy Walker stumbled away from the group and slapped at her knees as if brushing off dirt. Vaughn saw her shoulders shake and knew exactly how she felt.

"You can't have it both ways, Mr. Katz," he said grimly. "You need to either keep Mona confined, or accept that if she comes across one of her...friends, they may..."

"Get busy," Audrey Tweedy suggested.

Vaughn bared his teeth in thanks and turned back to Katz. "Has Mona been spayed?" When the old man nodded, he spread his hands. "Then maybe you should consider letting Mona be Mona."

He spent another fifteen minutes admiring the photos June Catlett had taken for the Pets Are

People, Too calendar they were putting together to raise money for the citizens' center. Even Priscilla Mae, a former Lilac Queen, apparently—*all righty, then*—had a place in the lineup.

"How about your cat?" Hazel poked at his biceps. "Play your cards right and we'll find a place for her, too." She beamed at Ivy, who'd recovered from her coughing fit. "She just had kittens."

"How sweet." Ivy studied Vaughn with new respect. "How many did she have?"

"Three," he said. "Two black, one gray. Want 'em?"

Ivy grinned. Vaughn sighed.

"Great idea, sis." June patted her camera. "Not Franklin would make an adorable addition to the calendar. Let's set up the shoot."

Audrey fingered a T-bone. "Not Franklin?"

"We thought she was Franklin but she wasn't," Hazel explained.

Katz curled his lip. "For God's sake, man. Name your cat."

"She's not my cat. And she can't be in the calendar. She's wearing a cast."

"What happened? You kick her?"

Hazel glared at Katz. "He would never do a thing like that."

"Know him that well, do you?"

"As a matter of fact, we do. When he was a child, he spent most of his summers right next door to us. So watch it, old man, or we'll put *you* in a cast."

Vaughn raised both hands, and his voice. "Nobody's putting anybody in a cast."

Katz grunted. "Wilmer Fish put your cat in a cast."

"She's not my—" Vaughn stopped and inhaled.

Ivy's gaze gleamed with compassion. And mirth. "What'd Wilmer say?"

"Her leg's broken. He figures she got hit by a car. She'll heal, but she has to stay off the leg for two weeks."

Ivy grimaced in sympathy. "You have her in a carrier?"

Vaughn nodded. He'd had to get one big enough for her and the kittens. Damn thing had cost him seventy bucks.

"We can still take a picture," June said. "Casts can be sexy."

"She's right," Hazel said.

Katz tugged at his sleeve and angled his wrist, showing Hazel a bandage on the meaty part of his palm.

"Put that thing away," she told him. "I have a boyfriend."

Audrey clamped her arms across her chest. "Please tell me you're not sticking with a name like Not Franklin. What about the kittens? Will they be Not Tom, Not Dick and Not Harry?"

Vaughn fought to keep his lips in line. "I'm

not planning on naming them. I'm not planning on keeping them." When the crowd around him sucked in a collective breath, he took a step toward his cruiser. "I don't do cats," he muttered.

June blinked. "But you have four."

Hazel tapped a finger against her grape jelly lips. "Don't worry. We'll name them for you."

"I'm not worried," he said.

But he was thinking he should be.

CHIN IN HAND, Lily glared at the spreadsheet the mayor had ordered her to update. Office supplies, gas, auto repair, training—he wanted current figures for every expense the sheriff's department incurred. No doubt because he intended to find somewhere else to cut.

Only, there *was* nowhere else. They didn't even have petty cash anymore.

The mayor was probably spending it on candy.

The back door squealed open and shut, and paper rustled. Fulton, back with their lunches. Clarissa, clapping her hands. Metal squeaked as she pulled out her desk drawer to get her purse.

Footsteps headed Lily's way. She had her hand on her glasses before she even realized her intent to remove them. *What is wrong with you, woman?* She let her hand drop and focused on her computer screen.

Vaughn strode into her office, bringing the smell of fresh bread and sunshine.

"Chicken," he said, and tossed the bag onto her desk.

"I asked for tuna."

"I meant you. I thought you said what's done is done. Why'd you throw me to the dogs like that? Or should I say, the Catletts?"

Lily turned a snort into a cough. *Busted.* Slowly she raised her head, fighting a smirk. Surprise stole the urge to smile when she glimpsed the humor in his eyes.

Just her luck. He could dish it out *and* take it.

"You're right," she muttered. "I'm sorry." She pushed to her feet. "Next time I'll let you know what you're getting into."

"I'd appreciate that. Though if we're going to be honest here, if I'd known what I was in for, I'd have gotten lost on the way over."

"I'd feel less guilty if you weren't such a good sport."

"Yeah," he drawled. "That won't work for me."

"Fair enough." She grabbed her purse, plopped it on top of a stack of folders and rummaged for her wallet. "So…" She glanced up. "How was it?"

"As painful as you meant it to be, but I believe we reached an understanding." He traded the bills she handed him for two quarters and a dime. "That calendar should be as popular as Mona appears to be."

"She did earn herself a reputation."

"So will I, if I don't get rid of this shirt."

Lily's smirk won out. "So what did you think of Hazel and June?"

"I already knew them. They live beside my uncle." He cleared his throat. "His house, I mean."

"I am sorry about Emerson. I should have said it sooner."

Fulton's gaze flattened. "I'm sorry you arrested him."

Lily stiffened. "I did what I had to do."

"He was dying," he said simply.

She wouldn't defend herself. It wouldn't do any good, considering the anger that simmered in his hard, dark eyes. She knew better than he did that not all of that anger was directed at her.

"What's done is done," she said.

"That apply to anyone else but you?"

For a long moment, neither of them spoke.

"Well," Lily finally said into the quiet as she gestured at the bag on her desk. "Thank you."

He gave a curt nod, and turned toward the door.

"You're not eating?" *Damn you, guilt.* The last thing she needed to do was connect with this guy, on any level. Especially a physical one, which meant she needed to stop checking him out.

Just in time, she averted her gaze from the enticing strain of biceps beneath his shirtsleeves.

He pivoted in the doorway. A hint of smugness flitted across his face, giving her the impression he knew exactly what she'd been thinking. "The mayor invited me to lunch."

Her knee jerked and banged against the desk. She swallowed a swearword. "Give him my best," she said cheerfully.

Fulton lifted an eyebrow.

"Never mind," she muttered.

"Nice glasses," he said, and left.

I hope you both choke. Lily poked at the bag containing her sandwich. Too bad her new deputy had taken her appetite with him.

CLARISSA MARCHED FROM one buzzing streetlight to the next, too frustrated to care about the darkness in between. Resentment spiked with every strike of stiletto on pavement. What was the use of offering to do someone a favor if you couldn't do it with a smile? But damn it, she'd been doing good deeds all day and her cheeks freaking *hurt*.

First her neighbor in the apartment above hers had needed help picking out a suit for his job interview. Then the elderly couple below had needed a ride to the grocery store. After lunch, JD had called from his sickbed to ask her to find the designer sunglasses he'd spent an entire paycheck on. When she wasn't on the phone or the radio, or running an errand for her grumpalicious boss, she was rifling through trash cans and walking the corridors of the courthouse, scanning the scuff-marked linoleum for JD's shades.

It might have been fun if she'd managed to re-cruit Vaughn to help. But he'd spent most of the afternoon with the mayor.

Which had nearly sent the sheriff over the edge. Hence Lily's fouler than foul mood.

In the end, where had Clarissa found the blasted shades? In JD's mail slot. Lily must have put them there then forgotten all about it. By the time Clarissa discovered them, she was mad enough to break the stupid things in half.

To top it all off, Lily had asked her to work late so they could finish three months' worth of ex-pense reports. That was what Lily did when she was upset—she worked overtime on top of her overtime, and every now and then Clarissa got to do it with her. It wouldn't have been so bad if Clarissa had thought to order more than one sand-wich at lunch, or if the vending machine had of-fered more than pretzels and chewing gum. Lily, who never seemed to eat enough for half a per-son, let alone a workaholic, never even noticed Clarissa's stomach grumbling.

Of course, she did have a lot on her mind. A lot of *man* on her mind. Clarissa doubted her boss was thinking about Vaughn Fulton for anywhere near the right reason, but still. She hadn't seen Lily so infuriated since the mayor informed them he was cutting their office supplies budget be-cause they used too much toilet paper.

Clarissa shifted the stack of books in her arms,

almost losing the entire pile when the library's air-conditioning unit kicked on. She passed the small garden built to screen the unit and breathed in the sweet, thick smell of honeysuckle. Her sour mood faded.

This was her final favor of the day, returning half a dozen hardback romances the clerk of the court had inadvertently left on one of the benches just inside the courthouse entrance. A quick text had ended up with Clarissa agreeing to take them back. Easy peasy. But if she hadn't had to work late, she'd have been able to take care of it in the daylight.

Hang in there, chickie. As soon as you get rid of these, you can head home, scramble yourself some eggs and see what's on BBC.

And tomorrow she'd tell anyone who asked for a favor to suck it.

She rounded the rear corner of the library and strode over to the heavy metal drawer built into the brick. Since all six books wouldn't fit inside at once, she set the stack down on the brick pavers. She scooped up the top two books, opened the drawer and slid them in. No satisfying *thunk* from the other side of the wall. Shouldn't there be a *thunk*?

She opened the drawer as far as it would go and peered inside. Nothing but black. She'd just have to trust the books had made it to safety.

She turned to grab the next two and almost

choked herself. Her scarf pulled taut, yanking her backward. She'd gotten it caught in the drawer.

Oh, this is freaking unbelievable.

Her heels wobbled on the uneven bricks as she twisted around to face the chute. She tugged lightly on the length of silk, but it didn't budge.

She swore again then remembered the LED light on her key chain. She reached into the front pocket of her capris and snagged her keys. She clicked on the light and aimed it into the drawer. One edge of her scarf had caught on the head of a screw. With her free hand, she reached for the fabric looped around her neck. Might as well pull the thing over her head so she didn't choke herself for real.

A small shape swooped at her from the right and something leathery smacked against her cheek. *Dear God, a freaking bat!* She shrieked and dropped her keys. They rattled down the inside of the drawer and instinct made her dive after them. When her chest smacked into the edge of the drawer she jerked backward, hissing with pain.

She didn't get far.

The other end of her scarf was caught.

She gulped down a half laugh, half sob and massaged the skin over her breasts. She'd have bruises in the morning. She'd also have a permanent hunchback if she didn't get to stand up soon.

Bracing her hands on her knees, she stared

down into the black maw of the library's drop box. The stretch of her beloved silk scarf kept the drawer open. She gripped the edge of the metal to take the tension off the fabric, and realized she didn't have enough slack to pull her head free.

She heaved a sigh. Time to play tug-of-war. Damn it, her one true piece of designer clothing and she was about to rip it to shreds.

"Fart!" she shouted, and a muffled version of her voice bounced back up at her. She wrapped a fist around each end of the scarf, drew in a breath and braced herself by spreading her legs and shifting her hips. She couldn't help snorting. Praise be she didn't have an audience, because she could only imagine what she looked like from behind.

"Evening." A deep, amused voice sounded directly behind her. "You seem to be having some trouble."

CHAPTER FOUR

CLARISSA GASPED AND squeezed her eyes shut. Her nerves went lax and she lost her grip on the scarf. "You think?" she said, as casually as she could manage. *Come any closer, buddy, and you'll get a stiletto to the crotch.*

The deep-voiced, shadow-lurking, could-possibly-be-a-killer stranger shifted closer. Goose bumps erupted across Clarissa's skin. Shoes scraped across brick as he moved into her peripheral vision. He showed her his palms, in the universal I-come-in-peace gesture, but considering he was so tall she couldn't maneuver her head back far enough to see his face, it did little to put her at ease.

The man was a freaking giant.

He bent forward and peered into the open drawer. White-blond hair gleamed in the halo of light cast by the nearest streetlamp and she caught a whiff of some spice—oregano?—before he shook his head and backed away. He made a humming sound and his palms rasped as he rubbed them together.

Thinking of her, or her predicament?

"Spaghetti or lasagna?" Clarissa blurted.

"What?"

"Quick, tell me what you had for dinner."

Out of the corner of her eye, she watched him scratch his chin. "A hell of a time to be thinking about food. I'm sorry to say, there aren't any leftovers."

"I'm not asking because I'm hungry. I'm trying to establish a bond between us so you won't kill me." She bit her lip. "Or worse."

Silence. She couldn't tell if he was grinning, or plotting nefarious deeds. If it was the deeds thing, she wished he'd get on with it because her feet were killing her.

"Spaghetti," he said solemnly. "And I promise to keep my hands to myself."

"I'd appreciate that," she said, and yanked. The scarf didn't budge. She readjusted her grip and yanked again, this time adding a growl for good measure.

Not even the hint of a ripping sound.

Damn. She'd certainly got her money's worth with this scarf.

"I could go inside and get a pair of scissors," the stranger offered.

"Don't you dare," Clarissa cried. "If anyone's going to ruin this scarf, it'll be me. Anyway, I thought men always carried pocketknives."

"I have a knife. I didn't think letting you hear it snap open would be the smartest thing to do."

He had a point. She braced a foot against the

wall and wrapped the silk tighter around her hands.

The giant grunted. "That thing rips free and you're going to land on your ass."

She relaxed her grip and rested her forehead on top of the drawer. "I guess you're getting quite the eyeful back there."

"Well, yeah."

She sighed, and lifted her hands. "I give. Your turn."

He reached in and grabbed her scarf below the knot, and with a flick of his wrist she was free. The drawer clanged shut and Clarissa stumbled backward. A hand on her elbow steadied her then fell away.

She straightened her spine with a groan, palms pressed to the small of her back, chin lifted moonward. "Thank you."

"You're welcome."

He sounded preoccupied. She dropped her chin and caught him staring at her chest. When she sputtered, he lifted his gaze to hers, looking more confused than embarrassed.

"These outdoor lights aren't as strong as they should be. Are those eyeballs painted on your scarf?"

"Nope." She glanced down and patted what was left of her favorite accessory. "They're boobs."

"I see." He cleared his throat. "Bet you really liven up the sheriff's office."

Her head jerked up. "You know where I work?"

"I am the librarian."

"You say that like it's synonymous with *mind reader*." She blinked. "Wait. You are?"

"Cozy mysteries."

"What?"

"Your favorite type of book." He held out an arm, indicating she should head for the parking lot.

"Second favorite." She stepped off the curb and started toward her car, then pivoted back toward the books she'd left stacked on the pavers. "I didn't get them all in."

"I'll take care of it."

They didn't speak again until Clarissa stopped at the driver's-side door of her Camry. She tipped her head. "We haven't met before. I'd remember the crick in my neck."

Even in the scant light cast by the streetlamps, she could see the red staining his cheeks. "I saw you at the diner once and asked about you."

"So you know my name."

"I do." He thrust out a hand. "Nice to meet you, Clarissa Dodd."

Clarissa disliked wimpy handshakes, and she liked to give as good as she got. She doubted, though, that her firm squeeze even registered to this guy whose hand was as big as his face.

"Nice to meet you, too..." She raised an eyebrow.

"Noble. Johnson."

"How appropriate. Thank you again, Noble

Johnson, for—" she pulled her hand free and flapped it over her shoulder at the scarf-eating death trap behind her "—that."

He jammed his hands into his pockets. "Romance?"

"No, thank you."

"I mean, is that your favorite genre?"

Oh. "It wouldn't matter anyway, because after tonight, it'll be books on escapism."

"Escapology, you mean." He jabbed a thumb at the building behind them. "We have a decent biography on Norman Murray Walters, if you're interested." When her cluelessness registered, his mouth drooped. "He was Australian. A contemporary of Houdini."

"Oh," she said, then added, "*Damn* it."

"Don't sweat it. You'd be surprised how many people don't recognize that name."

"No." She jerked open the knot in what was left of her scarf and yanked the fabric free of her neck. "My keys fell in the drop box."

He dug his own keys out of his pocket and held them up. "Good thing I can get into the building."

"My hero."

"No swooning necessary, but I wouldn't say no if you invited me out for a drink."

"If I say 'thank you, but no,' will you still get my keys?"

He made a pensive, humming sound. "If we'd been dating, you wouldn't need to ask that."

"Like one of those signs you see when you're driving? 'If you lived here, you'd already be home?'"

He beamed. "Exactly."

"Noble?"

"Yeah?"

"I'm too busy to date, and I need to get home." He hesitated then turned away with a shrug. "Wait," she said.

He swung back around, too quickly to hide the eagerness on his face, and she fought a wince.

"I just wanted to…" She twirled her index finger.

He frowned. "What?"

"You walk away and you're walking out of the light. You got a good, long look at my backside. It's only fair you return the favor."

A startled grin flashed. He turned and bent at the waist. Clarissa tipped her head and took *her* good, long look at a just-snug-enough pair of jeans.

"Satisfied?" he asked.

"Very nice," she said.

He straightened. "That mean you'll go out with me?"

"No." Clarissa poked her tongue against her cheek. "But I will be renewing my library card."

TUESDAY MORNING, AND JD was still out of commission. Lily had dropped in on him the afternoon before. He had no family in the area, but she'd done it more for herself than for him. One more minute spent behind her desk waiting for Fulton to return from his rendezvous with the mayor and she'd have started researching untraceable poisons.

And after Clarissa had spent most of the day hunting for the sunglasses Lily had tucked into JD's mail slot, Lily figured the least she could do was hand-deliver them. Her deputy had been grateful to see her. Even more so the ginger ale she'd brought, and the broth and crackers she'd fixed while there. It was plain the poor guy wouldn't be back to work for another day or two. He'd barely managed to sit up long enough to drink his broth.

Lily took the last bite of her banana just as the "gate" out front lifted and banged shut. When there was no subsequent click of high heels in the direction of Clarissa's desk, she hastily chewed and swallowed and swung back to her computer. The last thing she needed was Fulton walking in to find her staring at her own doorway, as if she couldn't wait for him to arrive.

Instead, it was Clarissa who appeared. Lily dipped her head and peered over her glasses at the lime-green canvas sneakers her dispatcher wore.

"A little early for those, isn't it?"

With a groan, Clarissa sank into the guest chair. "My feet are killing me. I couldn't even look at a pair of heels this morning without wanting to stab myself in the eye."

Lily dropped her banana peel in the trash. "Want to talk about it?"

"I met our librarian last night." Clarissa traced the yellow vertical stripes on her pencil skirt, which she'd paired with a short-sleeved sweater the color of a tangerine. With her lime-green tennis shoes, she looked like a citrus salad. "He asked me out."

"Then he has better taste than I gave him credit for."

The pleased surprise in Clarissa's eyes made Lily glad she'd said that out loud. Then Clarissa frowned. "Why don't you think he has good taste?"

"He likes bright colors as much as you do. Just not—" Lily floundered. "Not as coordinated."

"Well—" Clarissa shrugged "—I turned him down."

"Because of our new deputy?"

Clarissa's gaze sharpened. "Would that matter to you?"

"Hardly." *Shut up, Lily Anne. Shut up, shut up, shut up.* "Are you having second thoughts? About Noble?"

"I need a sanity check." She tipped her head. "He strikes me as the type to be looking for more than fun. You know I don't have time for anything but casual."

Lily winced as she reached for her coffee cup. "I'm sorry about keeping you up so late last night."

"Don't be. The truth is, you and I are just damn good together."

A throat cleared outside Lily's door. Fulton stepped into view, filling the frame. "Am I interrupting something?"

Clarissa winked at Lily, daring her to tease him with what he'd overheard. Lily gave her head a slight shake to indicate she'd pass. Besides being inappropriate, she didn't need Fulton taking any tales back to the mayor.

"Good morning, Deputy," Lily said, keeping it civil, ignoring the disappointment on her dispatcher's face. "Grab some coffee. We need to discuss collateral duties."

He nodded and disappeared.

Clarissa leaned in. "You going to assign him as school resource officer?"

"Hard to do when school's on summer break," Lily said dryly.

"Animal Control, then?"

"Too easy. He faced down the Catlett sisters, Audrey Tweedy and Mr. Katz, all at one time. He's proved he can handle the local wildlife."

Clarissa pushed to her feet. "I give up. Do whatever you want with him."

"Do I get any say in that?"

With a laugh, Clarissa turned toward the

door, where Fulton stood sipping a cup of coffee. "Sometimes it's more fun if you don't know what's in store," she said.

Fulton opened his mouth, glanced at Lily and wisely opted for another sip instead. Clarissa left and Lily waved Fulton into the now empty chair.

He had squeezed back into JD's uniform shirt. It was tucked neatly into his jeans, revealing his hip holster. His jaw was freshly shaved, and he smelled like a forest on a sunny day.

Lily scowled. "Can't you ask your mayor pal for money to buy a uniform?"

"He just scored me a flatscreen TV," he said mildly. "I don't want to take advantage."

She peered at him over her glasses, caught the glint in his eyes and wished he didn't make her feel like such a fuddy-duddy. "There's a spare rig in the back," she said. "I'll pull it out for you. A badge, too." She should have taken care of that yesterday.

"Thanks." He sipped his coffee, gaze steady on hers over the rim of his mug. "You sizing me up for a reflective vest?"

"What?" Lily blinked. Had she been staring at his chest? Fudge.

His lips twitched as he gestured with his cup. "Figured you had me in mind for crosswalk duty."

"I don't have you in mind at all, Deputy." When his smirk graduated to a grin, she regretted her words immediately. "What I mean is, I haven't decided on your collateral duty." She swiveled toward her computer and stared blindly at the spreadsheet she'd been working on. She had to stop caring that this man had the ear of the mayor. She had to get on with her job.

She hit a few keys. "Court security or records management?"

"You're giving me a choice?"

"I am."

"Court security, then." While she typed, he cradled his cup in his hands and scooted forward in the chair. "Listen. About this thing with the mayor—"

Clarissa appeared in the doorway. "Just got a call from Audrey Tweedy. The Petroskis are at it again."

Five minutes later, Lily and Fulton were headed south on Route 5, with Lily behind the wheel. Beside her in the passenger seat, Fulton took off his shades, polished them on his shirt and slid them back on. "What's the story?"

She flicked on her signal and changed lanes. "One of our old-timers, Jakub Petroski, owned a candy store on Buffalo Road. He passed away about six months ago. His kids arrived to settle his estate and we've had nothing but trouble since."

"You liked him."

She gave him the side eye. "Why do you say that?"

"You're talking. Can't be me. Must be him."

"Anyway," she said pointedly, "we get these calls once a week. When John and Sadie argue, they do it loudly."

"Anything more than words exchanged?"

With a shake of her head, she pulled into the driveway of a weathered brick Colonial with teal shutters, a columned porch tucked under a deep copper-coated gable and a chimney on either side of the house. A row of feathery spruces screened the property from the road. She never could understand why Jakub's kids were so eager to get rid of it.

She parked her cruiser and they got out.

Fulton rounded the hood. "How do you want to do this?"

Lily couldn't help a glimmer of respect. The last thing she needed on her team was a hotdogger.

"Wait here," she said. "JD handled these calls on his own. We don't want them to think we're here to do anything other than help."

He frowned, but nodded.

Lily grabbed her hat from the backseat and started for the house. She was halfway up the walk when the front door opened.

"Stop right there, Sheriff," John, a dark-haired, wiry man with the whitest teeth she'd ever seen, shouted at her through the screen door. "This isn't your business."

"It is when a crime's being committed," Lily responded calmly. "Let's start with disturbing the peace."

"That's bullshit. No way the neighbors can hear us. That bitch next door has been creeping around again."

He meant Audrey Tweedy. When the elder Petroski had realized he was dying, he'd begged Audrey to look after his flowers and shrubs until the house changed hands. The old woman had kept the masses of lilies and hydrangeas and irises looking lush. The rest of the property? Another story.

Lily glanced over her shoulder at Fulton, who was eyeing the shin-high grass and the newspapers littering the front porch. "The kids are in it for the money," he said flatly.

She nodded once. The Petroski twins had made it clear to JD that they couldn't sell the house and get out of Castle Creek fast enough. As far as Lily was concerned, they'd already taken way too much time.

She turned back to face the house. "We're just here to talk, Mr. Petroski."

"Come any farther and my sister's going to regret it."

Oh, fudge. This was new. "Want to tell me exactly what that means?"

Silence.

"Mr. Petroski," she shouted. "Can I call you John?"

"Only if you do it on your way off my property," he shouted back.

Beside her, Fulton grunted. "Funny guy."

Lily sighed. "I thought I asked you to wait by the car."

"This is the point where a show of force is appropriate."

She didn't say anything. He was right. And she couldn't help a swell of appreciation that he was there to back her up.

"Mr. Petroski," Fulton called. "Do you have any weapons in there with you?"

No response. A bumblebee droned by and leather creaked when Fulton shifted beside her. Lily tamped down a sizzle of desire. What was *wrong* with her?

The summer sun was gathering its strength. That was it. It was the heat. She adjusted the brim of her hat and grimaced as sweat trickled down between her shoulder blades.

"How about you, Miss Petroski?" she yelled. "Want to tell me what's going on in there?"

"My brother wants to sell the house to the old lady next door and I don't." Sadie was yelling down at them from an open upstairs window.

"What's wrong with the old lady next door?" The woman in question popped up from behind the hydrangeas that divided the yards.

Fulton had already dropped into a crouch, hand at his holster. Lily had one hand on her radio and the other on the butt of her gun. The instant she registered Audrey as a nonthreat, her knees went weak.

VAUGHN SWORE AND straightened out of his crouch. Did *no one* in this town mind their own business?

Jesus. The old lady could have been shot.

"Ma'am," he growled. "You need to step back."

Instead, Audrey Tweedy stiffened her lumberjack shoulders and faced her neighbors' house. "I made you a fair offer," she called. "Why won't you accept it?"

No answer. Meanwhile, Sheriff Tate was making shooing motions at Audrey. The elderly woman planted her bright white trainers wide, crossed her arms over her Go Army T-shirt and lifted her chin. She obviously wasn't going anywhere without a sumo wrestle.

The sheriff rolled her eyes and turned back to the house. "Mrs. Tweedy here said she heard you two threatening each other with knives. Is that true?"

"We only said that because she was listening in." Now John had his face pressed against the screen as he glowered at Audrey.

The sheriff sighed. "How about you two come out onto the porch? We can talk a lot easier face-to-face."

"Ha!" Sadie shouted. "You mean it'll be easier to shoot us."

"Nobody's getting shot here today," the sheriff said calmly, though she did cast a considering glance in Audrey Tweedy's direction. "I don't intend to let anyone get knifed, either."

"They need the money," Audrey said. The sheriff tried to shush her, but the volume on that baby-doll voice was cranked up to wake-the-dead. "I heard them. John owes five grand to his dentist and Sadie wants bigger breasts."

"Oh, my *God*," Sadie cried. "See what I mean?"

A thundering sound, like someone storming down a set of hardwood steps. "That's it! We're not selling!" Sadie shrieked from the first floor. "Not to her, not to anyone."

"Fine," her brother hollered back. "So we'll burn the goddamned place down to the ground!"

"Deputy Fulton," Sheriff Tate said through clenched teeth. "Please see Mrs. Tweedy safely inside her home."

Message received, loud and clear. Take the old woman away before someone does get hurt. He hoped to hell he wasn't going to have to man-handle the lady. She reminded him too much of his aunt Brenda.

When he began to weave his way toward her, maneuvering through chest-high shrubs laden with fat, round blossoms the same blue as the Popsicles he used to enjoy as a kid, the old lady

wagged a finger. "Now, listen, dear, I have no intention of moving an inch. I'm on my property.
I'm not breaking any laws."

Oh, yeah. Aunt Brenda all over again. Vaughn
lifted his left arm in a futile attempt to back her
up. "But you are, ma'am. You're interfering with
a police officer in the course of his duties. Now
you can go sit inside your house—" he reached
for the pouch at the back of the equipment belt
the sheriff had set him up with, pulled out the
cuffs and dangled them "—or you can sit inside
the squad car."

Audrey's eyes widened. She hesitated, then
gave a mighty sniff. "I had fully intended to
offer you two refreshments when you were done
here," she said crossly. "But I believe I'll keep my
bacon-wrapped shrimp to myself."

Vaughn watched her march across her yard to
her front porch. She stomped up the stairs, but
instead of slamming open the door, she turned
and dropped onto the top step. Fighting a grin,
Vaughn held up two fingers and pointed at his
eyes, then at her, then back at himself. Up went
her chin as she yanked at the hem of her T-shirt.

Too bad she was holding this against him, because that shrimp sounded good.

He pivoted back toward the Petroski house.
Oh, *shit*. The sheriff was standing in front of the
Petroskis' open screen door, staring down a big-
ass butcher knife.

Vaughn pulled his piece and ran.

The sheriff's hand never even twitched toward her pepper spray or stun gun. Instead she kicked out, and Vaughn heard a muffled thud as boot connected with bone. Steel clattered onto tile and the simultaneous high-pitched screech of pain could have been male *or* female. Mystery solved when a tall, thin woman collapsed against the screen door, both hands wrapped around her left shin. Sheriff Tate bent down and picked up the knife, seemingly unmoved by Sadie Petroski's wailing.

Or the fact that she could have easily taken a knife to the gut. Vaughn ground his teeth. He and the good sheriff were going to have to set some ground rules.

Scratch that. What the good sheriff needed was a refresher in defensive tactics.

"John Petroski," the sheriff hollered at the open doorway. "Come out onto the porch where we can see you."

"I was only showing it to you," Sadie sobbed. "I only wanted you to see what my dipshit brother's been waving at me." She rubbed her denim-clad shin as she sagged against the screen door, which had banged against the side of the house. "You bitch, you broke my leg."

"Your leg? What about my door?" Her brother stomped out onto the porch, wearing shorts but no shirt, a half-eaten peanut-butter-and-jelly sandwich in his hand. "Who's going to pay for that?"

With his free hand, Vaughn retrieved his cuffs. He climbed the porch steps and kicked several rolled-up newspapers out of the way. "Hands behind your back," he said to the brother.

Petroski stuffed the remainder of his sandwich in his mouth and complied. Vaughn holstered his weapon and fit the cuffs on the guy's jelly-smeared wrists.

Meanwhile the sheriff set down the knife, stepped on the handle and pulled her cuffs free of her belt.

"Didn't you hear me?" Sadie cried. "You broke my leg. Don't think I won't sue."

"Bruised it, maybe," the sheriff said. "But I didn't break it. Drop your leg and turn around."

"You're going to arrest me?" Sadie pushed upright, shoved her long red bangs out of her face and stomped her injured leg. "What the hell for?"

"Property damage," said her brother, through the remains of his sandwich.

"Screw you!" shouted Sadie. "It's my house, too."

Sheriff Tate fit her cuffs on a fuming Sadie. "Mr. Petroski, I need you to go with Deputy Fulton. He'll find someplace quiet where you can tell him your side of the story."

Vaughn led John Petroski down the porch steps and around the side of the house. Petroski was much calmer away from his sister. He admitted he'd brandished the knife at Sadie, then set it on the counter. She'd grabbed it and run for the door, shouting that she was going to "tell on him."

Jesus. "You two are how old?"

Petroski scowled, then jerked his head at the house. "What's she got coming?"

"Aggravated assault."

"Give me a frickin' break. I just told you, she wasn't threatening the sheriff."

"She was brandishing a weapon. That's called physical menace." When Petroski swore and kicked the side of the house, hard enough to dent the siding, Vaughn narrowed his eyes. "We going to have to put you in leg irons, too?"

"Don't you worry, Deputy. I've got him covered." Audrey Tweedy approached from the rear corner of the house, lip curled, eyes squinted. She carried a spray bottle of oven cleaner in one hand and a can of WD-40 in the other. "And you." She pointed the can at Petroski. "Stop putting holes in the house, or I'll drop my offer by ten percent."

Petroski snorted. "If anyone deserves to be arrested, it's this old bag. C'mon, man, she's trespassing."

Audrey lowered her weapon and grinned. "Sell me the house and I won't be."

They settled the Petroskis in the cruiser, escorted Audrey back to her own property and bagged the knife. Back at the station, Vaughn waited for a chance to pull the sheriff aside. She'd arrested both Petroskis for disturbing the peace and handled the processing and paperwork without any visible aftereffects from a situation that could have landed her in the hospital. Or worse.

Her attitude worried him. It also pissed him off.

The moment she returned to her office, a mug of coffee in one hand and a stack of paperwork in the other, he followed her in and shut the door. "I know you're smarter than what you pulled today. You have to be."

With slow and careful motions, the sheriff set her coffee on her desk and pushed her shoulders so far back it was a wonder she didn't topple over.

She had grit. He admired it, and he resented it. His job here wasn't going to get easier anytime soon, which made it damn inconvenient that every time he saw her he wanted to back her up against the nearest wall and practice his search-and-seizure skills.

"You don't know me," she said.

He sure as hell wanted to. "I won't get a chance, either, you keep taking idiotic gambles like that."

"Do I need to remind you who's the sheriff and who's the deputy here?"

He shook his head, and let his gaze linger on her chest. "Don't worry. I see the badge."

Her arms twitched, as if she wanted to fold

them over her chest. "Exactly what do you think I should have done differently?"

"How about drawing your piece when someone pulls a knife instead of rushing the house without backup—or any kind of weapon in hand? How about deploying pepper spray or using your stun gun so you can keep a safe distance until the offender's disarmed, instead of charging her like a long lost sister and hoping like hell she has no skills with the knife she's waving around?"

"Previous experience with the Petroskis gave me no reason to believe either would use a weapon."

"Civilians are not dependable. Angry civilians? Forget about it."

She shot him an odd look, then picked up her coffee and took a deliberate sip. "Don't you have a report to write?"

"You're not going to handle it?"

"You can tell Mayor Whitby I stand by my actions."

"Because it's the truth, or because you think that's what he wants to hear?"

"So you are reporting back to him."

Fulton curled his lip. "You're worried about your job. From what I've seen, you have reason to be."

She set down her coffee, dropped into her chair and jerked it close to her desk. "How about you let me worry about my job and you worry about yours?"

"My job? How about my ass? The kind of risks you take, you should add yours to the list, too. It'd be a shame if anything happened to all that heart-shaped perfection."

She shot to her feet. "Keep talking like that and you won't have to worry about your job for long."

"Oh, did I say something inappropriate?" Stone-faced, he yanked open the door. "Tell it to the mayor."

LILY GROUND HER teeth as she watched Fulton stride away. She barely resisted yelling at him, demanding who the hell he thought he was. With a growl so deep it made her cough, she flopped back into her chair. Bad enough she had to pander to the mayor, but did she have to put up with his sexist pal calling her cop skills into question?

She'd done what she needed to do. Getting possession of the knife had been her priority, and she'd achieved that. What had he expected her to do, shoot the woman?

She snatched up her coffee and swigged, not stopping until she'd emptied the cup. Which was a mistake because she burned the hell out of the roof of her mouth. With a *clack* she set the empty mug on her desk.

One thing she knew for certain—this wouldn't bother her so much if Fulton weren't so capable. As much as she hated to admit it, he was good police. JD couldn't have backed her up any better.

Fulton had handled Audrey Tweedy perfectly—
with respect, a touch of affection and just the
right amount of "don't mess with me."

Her office phone rang and though she wanted
to, she couldn't ignore it. She stood, scrubbed
her hands through her hair and scooped up the
receiver.

"Sheriff Tate."

"Minnie Landers won the pool."

Lily's chin sagged to her chest, even as she
grunted a resigned laugh. "Which one's Minnie?"

"You remember," her mother said. "Short. Fat.
Orange hair. Black pants coated with cat fur."

"Right. Minnie, with the tape roller."

"She gets a lot of use out of that tape roller.
She uses it to clean the Oreo crumbs out of the
bottom of her purse, and just the other day she
used it to trap a cockroach the size of a Nutter
Butter."

"Let me guess, Ma." Lily sat and propped her
chin in her hand. "You haven't eaten yet."

"We did. Lasagna. But no dessert yet. We got
tiramisu in the freezer. We had to take out Rosemarie's panties to make room."

Lily closed her eyes. She should let that go.
She really should. "Rosemarie keeps her panties
in the freezer?"

"She says the elastic lasts longer. You might
want to try it. Before you know it, you'll be going
through the change. You get a hot flash, you pull

a pair of panties out of the freezer and a nice roast for dinner and wah-lah. Not only are your nethers refreshed, but you got something to make sandwiches with for the rest of the week."

"Ma. I'm only thirty-nine."

"Like I said. Before you know it." Lily's mother waited a beat then huffed a sigh. "So ask me about the pool, already."

The smugness in that New Jersey voice made it clear her mother was going to enjoy this conversation a lot more than Lily would. "Tell me about the pool, Ma," she said evenly. "How much did Minnie win and why?"

"One hundred and twenty dollars. She guessed it would be more than thirty days before you called again and here we are, day thirty-one, and *I* had to call *you*. Fat Minnie gets the big bucks and I get the cold shoulder."

"Ma—"

"They asked me what I did to you. They said I must have done something terrible to make you neglect me like you do."

"We live a thousand miles apart."

"I know. It takes hours to drive. But it does not take thirty-one days to dial a phone number."

"That's true, Ma. I'm sorry."

"I told them about the time you got mad at me for not letting you go to the movies with that Robbins kid. Six months later, I was still cleaning flour out of my dresser drawers."

"Did you tell them about my driver's test, when you hid in the back of the SUV? You thought I'd made a rolling stop and popped up yelling for me to back up and try again. I've never heard someone scream so loud."

"I wasn't that loud."

"I meant the instructor."

A shrill ripping sound. Her mother had peeled back the top of a package of cookies. "So." Her mother sniffed. "This is going to be one of those conversations."

"I did mean to call, Ma."

"Just like you meant to tell me you're not coming for Labor Day weekend even though you promised?"

Lily winced. "How did you know?"

"A population explosion inside my head. My brain cells are breeding. I have so many more neurons firing now than when I married your father."

Lily dropped her head into her hand.

"Sudoku," her mother said. "You should try it. Also amaretto sours. I drink a few, watch TV, everything is amusing. Seems I'd better stock up for September, for when I'm sitting on the beach by myself."

"I have a temporary deputy I'm trying to break in."

"Is he cute?"

Lily lifted her head and stared at her doorway. "I didn't say it was a *he*."

"You didn't have to. You're very careful when you talk about men."

"Can you blame me?"

"You don't call, you don't visit. The least you can do is let me enjoy some long-distance match-making." She crunched on a cookie. "It's going on two years, baby girl."

"I know how long it's been."

"So tell me about this new man in your life."

"He's too young, too good-looking and very temporary."

"Oh, Lily Anne," her mother sighed. "He sounds perfect."

Lily knew better. Although as expertly as he'd handled Audrey Tweedy, she couldn't help wondering how he'd handle a woman in bed. How he'd handle *her* in bed.

Damn him.

She finally managed to end the conversation after ten minutes of listening to how Fulton would make the ideal transition man. But her mother's enthusiasm as she planned the resurrection of her daughter's love life failed to hide the hurt caused by Lily's change in plans.

Once again, she'd let someone down. No surprise, really. Practice made perfect.

CLARISSA HADN'T INTENDED to visit the library again. Not so soon, anyway. Yet here she was, two days later. But only because her mother had raised her right. Somebody did something nice for you, you thanked them. She hadn't necessarily meant you should do it in person, but Clarissa felt it was the proper thing to do.

Yeah, right. Her mother had also taught her not to lie. Especially to herself.

So much for that.

Noble's gesture had been beyond nice. Replacing the scarf half-eaten by the book drop could not have been cheap. But she couldn't let his thoughtfulness compromise her keep-it-casual rule. She'd find him, thank him, get her butt back to work and get on with her life.

She strolled past the checkout desk, peering as discreetly as she could into the office beyond, but didn't see anyone back there. He had to be here somewhere—she'd spotted his minivan in the parking lot. She passed a couple of shelves stacked with audiotapes and DVDs and found herself in the children's section, a generous square space padded with bright blue carpet and bordered by hip-high bookshelves.

The far corner of the square looked like it had been designed by Librarian Barbie. The focal point was a hot pink salon chair facing a semicircle of lime-green beanbag chairs and overstuffed purple pillows. It made her want to kick back with a kick-ass thriller. And eat. She wanted to eat.

Probably because the place smelled like bacon.

"That's me," said a deep voice at her back. "I had a BLT for lunch."

Fart. She'd been talking out loud again.

CHAPTER FIVE

THE NAPE OF Clarissa's neck tingled as she turned. Noble Johnson wore khakis and an orange T-shirt that read Librarian: The Original Search Engine. He'd pushed his shoulder-length blond hair behind his ears, and the faint shadow of a beard rode his cheeks. His massive hands settled on his hips as he grinned down at her.

Oh, my.

As appealing as he'd been in the dark, he was even better looking in the light. A liquid curl of desire heated her belly. She hoped to God there was a water fountain in the library, because she needed to put that fire *out*.

"A BLT?" she repeated stupidly, blinking to get her focus back. "Just one?"

"With extra bacon." He cocked his head. "You're here."

"I'm here." She fingered the ends of the scarf she'd found on her desk that morning. "I wanted to thank you for this."

"Nah. You wanted to see me."

She swallowed a laugh. "Actually, it was the library I wanted to see."

"Yeah?" His blue eyes lit up. "Have time for a tour? That way you can see me and my library at the same time."

"Can I come?" A young girl with long brown hair and half a dozen books under her arm popped out from behind him. She offered Noble a sly smile. "Last time you let Travis and me in the back, we each got an ice-cream sandwich and that was, like, forever ago. If they're still in the freezer, we should check the expiration date. See if they need to be thrown out or something."

"Uh-huh. Or something." Noble tucked the girl under his arm and winked at Clarissa. "Meet Grace Walker, Ivy's daughter. No one can make a chocolate-chip cookie like this kid. Seth's got it in his head that we keep nominating him to host poker night 'cause he knows how to make a sandwich. The rest of us know it's 'cause Grace here can bake like nobody's business. Right, kid?"

Grace mock-punched Noble when he gave her a noogie, but her face was flushed with pleasure. "I'm not really Ivy's daughter," she said to Clarissa. "My mom and dad got divorced. Ivy married my dad in March. Me and my brother and my dad all live at her farm now."

"Grace Elizabeth Walker." Ivy strode up wearing jeans, a pink shirt, riding boots and a disgruntled expression. She flicked her blond braid over her shoulder. "You most certainly are my daughter. Who but a mother would fuss at you for forgetting to feed the chickens at the same time she's sewing a button on your favorite shirt? You have plenty of room for two moms in your life, which is just as well, because I love you like crazy."

Noble rapped his knuckles on Grace's head. "Technically you're not my niece, but do you think that means I love you any less?"

Grace buried her face in Noble's side and shook her head.

"There you go, then," Ivy said gently. She winked at Noble and offered Clarissa an apologetic smile. "It's good to see you again, Clarissa. Grace, Clarissa works for the sheriff's department. She's the dispatcher. She's the one who contacted me after Cabana Boy got out of his stall and ended up downtown."

Grace lifted her head and rubbed her nose. "You work with Sheriff Tate?"

"I do."

"She doesn't like kids."

Clarissa wrestled a wince. "She does. She's just not very good with them."

Grace seemed doubtful. Clarissa couldn't blame her.

"We have to get back to the farm," Ivy said. "My daughter here—" she stroked a hand over Grace's hair "—has a riding lesson. Nice seeing you both."

Noble gave Grace another hug before letting her walk away.

Clarissa's throat pulled tight as she watched the pair leave. When she turned back to Noble, she found him watching her.

She smoothed her scarf. "I have to admit, you caught me off guard with this."

"I wanted to make sure you had a replacement." Red seeped into his cheeks as he studied the pattern on the scarf. "It was either cucumbers or screws. I figured summer—cucumbers..."

"You chose wisely."

He grinned in appreciation of her *Indiana Jones* reference. Something else they had in common.

Clarissa caught her breath. Something *else*? All they had in common was reading, and he did a lot more than she did.

A boy of seven or eight snuck up behind Noble. He pressed a finger to his lips, dropped to his knees and snatched at Noble's shoelace. When the lace pulled free of its knot, the boy snickered and leaped to his feet. Noble winked at Clarissa and, without turning his head, snaked an arm behind his back and grabbed the boy in a headlock. While his captive "struggled" to escape—twice he got loose, then immediately shoved his head back into the crook of Noble's elbow—Noble scrubbed his knuckles across the top of the kid's head.

Clarissa smiled despite herself. "You have a thing for noogies, don't you?"

"Worried I'll give you one on our first date?"

Noble raised his voice so she could hear him above the boy's giggling protests. "Let's go out so I can put your mind at ease."

"Shh." A middle-aged woman sitting in a nearby armchair rattled her magazine in disapproval. Noble dipped his head in apology and, without looking behind him, gave the kid a push. The boy ended up sprawled across two bean bags, laughing, arms pressed to his stomach. Noble grimaced another apology, then turned, picked up the kid and set him on his feet.

"You're going to get me in trouble," he said, and Clarissa rolled her eyes. "Go find your mom, okay?" When the boy headed for Adult Fiction, Noble swung around again. He caught Clarissa inching toward the entrance.

"What's your hurry?"

"I have to get back to work."

"Me, too. But we still have that whole noogie thing to put to rest."

"I'm not looking for anything serious right now." Or maybe ever.

"Neither am I," he said, throwing his arms up and out as if to say "we have a winner!" When her skepticism registered, he dropped his arms. "You want casual? I can do casual. I'll prove it." He swung around just as a tall woman in a sleeveless dress and flip-flops strolled by. He took two long steps to catch up with her. "Excuse me. Paula, right? Would you like to have a drink with me tonight, Paula?"

The woman responded with a blinding smile and an eager nod, and leaned in to say something Clarissa was too far away to hear. After a brief exchange, Paula headed for the checkout desk while Noble slowly turned, revealing a stunned expression. Clarissa didn't know whether to laugh or lash out.

She shouldn't care enough to do either.

"Nicely done," she said lightly. It was ridiculous, how much it bothered her. She had no reason to complain.

Or ache.

He'd been trying to make a point. Now there was little doubt he'd score.

THIRD DAY ON the job and Sheriff Tate was still looking at Vaughn like he'd taken a bite out of every donut in the box. He should have been at his desk, finishing his report on the Petroski arrests. Instead he'd followed Clarissa's example and ducked out at lunch. What he needed was some fresh, nonhostile air.

Okay, yeah, and he wanted to check on Not Franklin and her brood. He needed to find them a home. This cat-food-and-litter shit was expensive.

He let himself into his uncle's house, tossed his keys in the big flamingo ashtray he'd plucked from one of the boxes lining the hall and headed straight for the laundry room off the kitchen. A chorus of meows greeted him. He crouched in front of the carrier and smiled at the long-suffering expression on the mama cat's face.

"Hey, girl," he crooned. "Everybody okay?"

She lay on her right side on a bed of folded towels. Miracle of miracles, the cast on her back left leg remained clean and dry. The kittens whimpered and snuffled as they fed, minuscule paws pushing at their mama's belly. No need to scoop the litter box, and she still had food and water.

Now he could concentrate on getting his own lunch.

He had the fridge door open and was trying to decide between a fried egg sandwich and leftover chicken potpie from the diner when the doorbell rang. His stomach perked up. Maybe one of the Catlett sisters with another care package.

The prospect of not having to fix himself lunch had him jogging down the hall. But it wasn't a little old lady at his door. On his front porch stood a stranger, a lean dude maybe five years older than Vaughn, with swarthy skin and a ready smile.

The stranger extended his hand. "Vaughn Fulton? I'm JD Suazo."

The deputy on sick leave. Vaughn grasped his hand. "JD. Good to meet you. Come on in." Vaughn shut the door and led him to the kitchen. "Can I get you a beer? Or something to eat? I was just about to fix an egg sandwich."

JD's head swiveled from left to right as he catalogued the towers of junk choking the hallway. "No, thanks. I had an errand on this end of the county and figured I'd take a chance and see if you were home. You know, introduce myself."

"Glad you did. Feeling better?"

"Finally." He pulled out a kitchen chair and sat in a slouch. When he lifted his arms and laced his fingers behind his head, the left sleeve of his shirt slid up, revealing an eight-pointed compass rose tattooed on his tricep.

"I should be back on shift tomorrow," JD said. "Hey, cool clock you got there." He pointed above the sink, at a ceramic owl sharing a tree branch with two baby owls. "My mom likes owls, too."

"That and the cookie jar were the extent of my aunt's collection." Vaughn held up an empty glass. "Water?"

"Sure. Thanks."

Vaughn filled the glass at the sink and passed it to JD. "The sheriff said you were way overdue for some leave."

"Yeah, and don't think I won't take advantage of you while you're here. I'll help the sheriff get caught on up the administrative stuff, then I'm gone. Got a week to catch myself a pike. You fish?"

"Used to." Vaughn leaned back against the sink and crossed his ankles. "No offense, but you look like you need the break. The sheriff could use one, too."

"She's never *not* worked hard."

"It's affecting her judgment."

The deputy stiffened. "I heard about the Petroskis."

"Then you heard the sheriff almost took a knife in the gut." Vaughn watched as JD chugged his water. "Have you talked to anyone about that?"

"Reported her, you mean?" Slowly, JD leaned forward and set his glass on the table. "Listen, man," he said. "I realize Lily—Sheriff Tate— doesn't always err on the side of caution. But she's had it rough. She deals the way she deals."

Lily. Vaughn set his jaw. "Your sheriff went through a rough patch, so you all decide to cut her slack?"

"It was a hell of a rough patch, so yeah."

"That's no excuse for letting her get away with taking wild-ass chances that put her and any officer with her in danger."

JD shoved to his feet. "You don't know what you're talking about, so I suggest you back off."

"I do know. I've seen it." Vaughn took his time pushing away from the counter. "You notice something's wrong but you let it go because it's your family. It's the code. The job is hard as shit and nibbles at your soul day in and day out so everyone deserves to blow off a little steam, right?"

Vaughn shook his head. "That attitude gets people killed."

"I told you, man. Back. Off." JD's glare was hot enough to fry the eggs for Vaughn's sandwich. "She's lost more than you and I can ever imagine."

"So fill me in."

"Not my place. She wants you to know, she'll tell you."

Vaughn lifted his hands to his hips. "You two got something going on?"

"What? No. She's like a sister to me. Like you said. Family. She's a damn good cop, too. A little gung ho sometimes, but her badge is in the right place."

"You need to talk her into taking some time off."

After a moment, JD's lips twisted into a wry smile. "If you knew her better, you'd know you don't 'talk' her into anything." He nodded curtly. "Thanks for the water. I gotta hit it."

"Thanks for coming by."

JD turned toward the kitchen doorway, hesitated and turned back. "I have to ask…"

"The answer is no. I am not Whitby's snitch."

JD raised an eyebrow. "Good to know."

"You hadn't heard that rumor?"

"I've been home puking my guts out, remember?"

Vaughn grunted. But Lily had delivered soup,

so she'd had the opportunity to fill JD in. Which meant she hadn't shared her suspicions about Vaughn's role in her department. Interesting.

He pictured her fussing over JD. Sitting beside him smelling like cinnamon and sass and feeding him soup. Pursing those pretty pink lips and wiping his brow. Hugging his head to her just-the-right-size breasts.

Vaughn shook himself. What the hell was he doing, imagining the sheriff as Florence Nightingale? The woman was a ballbuster. A damn attractive one, but a ballbuster all the same.

"You okay, dawg?"

Vaughn jerked his gaze up to see JD watching him. "Sorry. What was it you wanted to ask?"

"What's up with your place? Where'd you get all this stuff?"

Vaughn explained about his uncle's plan to keep him in Castle Creek.

"We were all sorry to hear about his passing." JD exhaled. "You thinking about staying?"

"Too quiet here. And I have it too good in Erie. Gym's three blocks from my apartment. In those three blocks, I have my choice of four bars. Two streets beyond the gym? The hospital."

JD flashed a knowing grin. "Nurses?"

"Nurses." Vaughn held up his fist and they bumped knuckles.

"You know what? I think I'll take that beer after all."

"Right on. Hey, I got a shitload of repairs I need to make to this place. Got any recommendations? Plumbing, roofing, drywall, that kind of thing?"

JD nodded. "Yeah. I can get you some names." When Vaughn thanked him and turned to head back to the kitchen, JD stopped him. "You got the AC running?"

Vaughn shot him a look. "Damn right. It's eighty-eight degrees outside."

"You know you have a window open?" JD tipped his head toward the living room. "The Ensler kid's cutting the yard across the street. I can smell the grass. Plus I just heard something fall in there, like the breeze knocked it over."

"Don't tell me another cat got in the house." Vaughn brushed past JD and entered the living room, where he and Uncle Em used to kick back in front of the flatscreen and watch whatever sport was in season. His uncle used to kick back, anyway, in a shabby, hunter green recliner now buried under a mountain of folded blankets and battered aluminum TV trays. Vaughn always had to make do with the rose-covered club chair that had spent its entire life doing a time-out in the corner. For good reason, too, since the thing was about as wide as a box of crackers.

JD whistled behind him. "What are you going to do with all this..." He waved a hand at the chaos around them.

"Junk? Still trying to figure that out." He maneuvered his way to the windows on either side of the fireplace. Neither was open, but one was unlocked, the boxes underneath caved in.

Huh. "Someone was in here."

JD snorted. "How can you tell?"

"This is where I found the cat and I haven't been in here since. Somebody's been in here exploring."

"Exploring, or scavenging? Or maybe somebody dumped something they wished they hadn't."

"Why not knock on the door and ask me for it? Why break into a cop's house?" Vaughn turned to the window and flicked the catch closed.

JD shook his head. "That's not going to do much good if someone's determined to get in. You might want to invest in an alarm system."

"I have a better idea." Vaughn rubbed his hands together. "I'm going to invite everyone in. Offer it all up for free."

"You could have a riot on your hands."

"It'll be perfect. I can get rid of most of this junk without lifting a finger. Forget about a riot. You and I will be here."

"We will?"

"Name your price."

JD made a humming sound, then narrowed his gaze. "Dibs?"

"Done. I'll even throw in the owl clock." The cookie jar he'd keep for himself.

It seemed to Lily that she'd barely done a face-plant in her pillow before her alarm went off. "Oh, come *on*," she muttered. Morning already?

The buzzing persisted. She kicked the covers to the foot of the bed, pushed herself up and stumbled toward her alarm clock in the corner of the room. Halfway there, the sound finally registered. Not an annoying buzz, but the strains of a samba. *Clarissa*. After-hours 911 calls were routed to the dispatcher's cell, which meant Lily wouldn't be going back to bed anytime soon.

She rushed to her nightstand and snatched up her phone. "Tate here."

"A fight at Snoozy's." Clarissa never bothered with niceties in the middle of the night. "Two males, midtwenties, apparently inebriated. The altercation has moved to the parking lot. The caller spotted a knife."

Lily bit back a bad word. What was it with knives these days? "On my way. Have Fulton meet me there." She hung up and stripped off her T-shirt, wishing she could partner with JD on this. Especially since the buzz she was feeling was more about working with Fulton again than dealing with another idiot flashing a knife. But she couldn't take the chance that JD wasn't up to it.

Twelve minutes later, she whipped into Snoozy's parking lot. Fulton had beat her there, his red and blue strobes marking the lot as a crime scene. Her stomach dipped. This kind of drama was rare for Castle Creek, and now twice in one week? At least she had her chance to prove she wasn't the leap-before-you-look type Fulton believed her to be.

She swung her cruiser around to face his, her headlights helping to illuminate the semicircle of onlookers and the brawl they were cheering on. "Fudge," she muttered grimly. Two drunks were bad enough. Having to deal with an entire crowd was really going to suck.

She pushed out of her car as Fulton approached the men grappling against the grill of an over-sized pickup. A husky redhead in a T-shirt and shorts had a lean, dark-skinned man in a head-lock. An elbow to the gut reversed their positions. Lily didn't recognize either idiot.

Grunts and thumps and curses tore at the hot night air. The men's shoes scraped over the gravel in the lot and there was a ripping sound—the lean man's dress shirt had split under his arm. By-standers groaned and gasped and cheered. Several had their phones in the air, recording the brawl.

"Police," Fulton barked. "Break it up." He shifted around to the right of the pair and thrust out an arm, signaling the crowd to step back. Waiting for a natural separation, Lily knew. The two fighters were drunk, but they were still managing to land punches and at some point one would stagger back, or even hit the ground.

The good news? No sign of a knife, or injuries caused by one.

"Break it up," she shouted, then repeated herself in a deeper voice. Maybe the men would figure themselves outnumbered and give it up.

They never slowed.

Fantastic. They were going to have to do this the hard way.

The beefier drunk took a hit to the chin and reeled backward. *Now.* Lily rushed forward and grabbed him by the elbows. The man reeked of stale beer and garlic. With a roar, he lurched forward. Lily drove her left knee into the back of his and forced him to kneel.

"On the ground," she ordered. "Facedown." The moment he kissed pavement, she rested her knee on the small of his back and pulled her cuffs from her rig. "Hands behind your back."

A metallic snick brought her head up. Her gaze bounced along the line of bystanders until she identified the source of the noise—someone had snapped shut one of those stainless steel credit card cases. She shot Fulton a relieved smile and if he hadn't been trying to wrestle his own collar to the ground, he probably would have smiled back.

Beefy Guy was just sober enough to take advantage. Before Lily could cuff him, he bucked her off and lunged upright. He lowered his head and went into bulldozer mode, catching Lean Guy in the stomach and driving him into Fulton. All three went down hard. Lily sucked in a breath at the unmistakable thud of a head smacking concrete.

Fulton groaned. Lily pushed up onto her knees and bit back a yelp. Her left hip ached like nobody's business.

She staggered to her feet. Lean Guy lay like an overturned beetle on Fulton, legs thrashing, fists swinging as he battled Beefy Guy's hold on what was left of his shirt. Meanwhile Fulton held one hand to the back of his head, the other shoving at Lean Guy.

A skittering sound. An open jackknife skated onto the scene. With his left hand, Lean Guy slapped the ground beside him and clutched the knife. *Oh, no. Oh, God.* He thrust upward.

Lily dipped her shoulder and charged. She hit Beefy Guy from the side and knocked him off his feet. Fulton rolled, trapping Lean Guy beneath him. Lily stepped on Lean Guy's wrist and twisted the knife free, then strode back to Beefy Guy, who was on his knees, retching.

"Get up and you get pepper spray," she snarled. She closed the knife and shoved it into a pocket, pushed Beefy Guy onto his chest and cuffed him. When she turned to Fulton, he was hauling Lean Guy to his feet. "I'm sorry," she said.

He shook his head and winced. "Let's get these two in the patrol car."

Before one of them gets away again, he left unsaid.

Someone shouted and an engine gunned. From the shadowed portion of the lot, sounds of another scuffle drifted their way. A set of headlights blinked on and Lily squinted in the sudden light.

"That's him!" a male voice called from the crowd. "The guy who tossed the knife!"

The vehicle headed right for them. Lily shoved Beefy Guy at Fulton and stepped into the path of the oncoming lights.

"Lily! Get out of the way!"

She gripped her equipment belt and widened her stance. No way in hell was she letting this jerk get away.

The car sped up and Lily reached for her weapon. Before she could get her hand on it, someone grabbed her arm and yanked. She stumbled toward the curb as the car rocketed past, tires squealing. Lily couldn't catch her balance and landed on her hands and knees. Gravel lashed her palms. Behind her she heard the car speeding down the highway.

"*Damn* it." She stood and watched the taillights fade, then rounded on her deputy, ignoring the burn in her hip. "Why'd you let him get away?"

"Are you kidding me?" Fulton swore, stalked

away a few steps and stalked back. "Wait here," he growled.

He settled both drunks in the backseat, marched back to Lily and snatched at her hands. She swallowed a hiss of pain and shoved them behind her back.

"You hit your head on the curb," she said.

He swiped his hand across the back of his head and stared dispassionately at the blood on his fingers.

Lily put a hand to her radio. Fulton tried to stop her and she moved out of reach. "Not negotiable."

He swore again. She ignored him.

As she radioed for the rescue squad, one of Snoozy's waitresses came running over with a towel and a bag of ice. Fulton thanked her, wrapped the towel around the ice and pressed it to the back of his head. When he grunted, Lily winced.

"I'm so sorry, Sheriff." The server—Gina, Lily thought her name was—addressed Lily but kept her eyes on Fulton. "Is there anything else I can do? Get you a drink? Some aspirin?"

"The sheriff could use some antiseptic for her hands."

Fulton wandered over to the cruiser and leaned against it. The lack of color in his face made Lily grateful she'd called the squad.

Gina's gaze was more wistful than concerned. "Is he going to be okay?"

"He'll live." If only to lecture Lily. She'd be sure to return the favor.

"Forget about that antiseptic, Gina," she said. "I need to start asking questions." And she'd keep asking, until she found out who was behind the wheel of that car. Probably too much to hope that Snoozy had surveillance cameras.

Half an hour later, she was still questioning witnesses when Fulton pulled her aside.

"You should call JD. Have him come help you out." He nodded at the rescue rig. "They're taking me in for X-rays."

"I'm surprised you agreed to that."

"You don't want me on the job if I'm not one hundred percent, do you?"

She bristled. "Was that a crack?"

"It was a question. But now that you mention it, what the hell were you thinking?"

"You're right. I should never have let that jerk get hold of that knife. I let myself get distracted."

His head reared back as if she'd taken a swing at him. When he spoke again, it was through clenched teeth. "I'm talking about the fact that you deliberately stepped in front of a moving vehicle. Why would you take that kind of risk?"

"It would have paid off if you hadn't interfered."

"We're supposed to be a team. You know what a team is, right? People who work together?"

Slowly she closed her notebook and clicked her

pen so the ink wouldn't dry. "I saw an opportunity and I took it."

Fingers clenching his duty belt, he leaned in close. "With no regard for safety. Not yours, and sure as hell not your partner's. You have some kind of death wish?"

"If it had been JD instead of me, would you still have a problem?"

Someone tittered. Lily glared at the remaining witnesses, who huddled in a circle comparing videos. The bar owner hovered in front of the entrance, his thin face and handlebar mustache droopier than ever. Snoozy wanted them gone so he could lock up and go to bed. She didn't blame him. But neither she nor Snoozy would be leaving until every last witness had been questioned.

"I'm committed to my job," she told Fulton.

"Keep thinking you're invincible and you will be committed."

"Cute. Don't you have an ambulance to catch?"

He tried to stare some sense into her. She was immune. To him, anyway.

"Go get your head examined." She rapped him once on the arm with her notebook. "And take tomorrow off. If the doctor gives the okay, I'll see you at the station on Sunday."

THE FOLLOWING MORNING, Lily trudged up the diner steps. Coffee. She needed coffee. She *wanted* to go back to bed, but duty called. So she'd settle for coffee.

She hoped it did the trick. After she'd booked the two drunks, she'd barely slept. Instead she'd spent what little was left of the night replaying the moment she'd stepped in front of the car. Not her finest hour. What if instead of stopping, the driver had swerved to miss her and ended up hitting innocent bystanders?

Her left eye started to twitch as she tugged on the diner door. It took three tries to get the thing open and she got it on the third only because someone pushed while she pulled. The sudden lack of resistance sent her staggering. Wrought iron dug into her back as her hands grappled for purchase. Thank God for the railing because without it, she'd have ended up a hood ornament on a late-eighties Lincoln Continental.

"Sorry about that, Sheriff." Audrey Tweedy adjusted her lime-green purse and squinted up at Lily's every-which-way hair. "Looks like you've had a rough morning already, dear. And your face is so pale." She tsk-tsked. "You know what your problem is?"

"Lack of sleep." And a ridiculous compulsion to prove herself to a man she'd have to deal with for three months, max. A man who made her more nervous than a first offender called before a judge.

But only because that man had an in with the

mayor. It didn't have anything to do with his being hot. Though he was. Hot. Massive-bonfire-on-a-summer-beach kind of hot. Not to mention over a decade younger than she was.

"Lack of sleep is not the reason." Audrey rummaged in her mammoth bag and produced a can of Vienna sausages. "It's lack of protein. Here you are, dear. Have at it."

Someone pushed against the diner door Audrey was blocking. She never batted an eye.

"Take it," she said. "It'll put the color back in your cheeks."

Lily levered away from the railing, accepted the sausages and smiled weakly. "Thank you."

She waited. Audrey beamed. The person behind the door knocked.

Lily pointed over Audrey's shoulder. "I need to get in there," she said. "I'm on a food run." She'd arranged for one of the reserve members to stay overnight at the station to keep an eye on their guests. Now she owed everyone breakfast.

"Have Marcus whip you up some steak and eggs. No protein, no pep, is what I always say."

By the time Lily made it inside Cal's Diner, she was prepared to arrest anyone who got between her and her coffee. It was early, but it was Saturday, which meant the place was packed. Lily wedged herself in between two stools, one the color of mustard, the other the color of ketchup, each supporting the backside of one of the half-dozen old-timer regulars. After exchanging hellos and apologizing for jostling a glass of orange juice with her elbow, she caught the waitress's attention with a wave just this side of panicked.

"Rachel."

The thin, brown-haired teen hurried over, wiping her hands on her black apron. Her smile revealed a smear of bubblegum pink lipstick on her teeth. "Hey, Sheriff. What can I get you?"

Less than sixty seconds later, Lily was sipping at her best hope of getting through the day. Rachel rang her up then leaned over the counter.

"I met the new deputy," she whispered, fanning her face. "Is he single?"

Lily blinked. Rachel couldn't be more than eighteen. Anyway, how was Lily supposed to know whether Fulton was involved?

Fudge. She really wanted to know whether Fulton was involved.

The old man to Lily's left adjusted his ball cap and pushed at his yolk-smeared plate. "He's available."

Rachel's brown eyes glittered. "How do you know?"

His buddy to Lily's right tugged at his wiry beard. "Heard it from Hazel Catlett. Ran into her and her sister at the SaveMore. They were standing with the sample lady, taking names of all the single gals comin' in."

Lily choked on her coffee. "They're trying to set him up? But he's going back to Erie."

"Erie?" Rachel spoke the word in a reverent whisper. "I wouldn't mind moving to Erie. Where does he live? Along Bayfront, do you think? Could you imagine waking up to a view like that every morning?"

The man with the beard chortled. "The lake, or the man?"

Rachel flushed, peeked over his shoulder and scuttled away. The old man smothered his chuckle with a big bite of biscuit.

Lily pulled in a quick breath. Rachel hadn't said where she'd seen Vaughn Fulton, but suddenly Lily knew. She turned, and sure enough, Fulton sat alone in a booth by the window, working on a stack of pancakes. He had a mild case of bed-head and his gray T-shirt looked like it had been grabbed off the top of his laundry basket. He glanced up, caught her staring and toasted her with his fork.

The buzzing started in her hands. It traveled up her arms and spread throughout her chest, warming her insides better than any cup of coffee.

No. *No.* Not him. Not anyone, ever again. But especially not him.

CHAPTER SIX

LILY EXHALED AND eased her shoulders out of their hunch. Ten steps had her standing beside the empty bench seat across from Fulton.

"May I?" Without waiting for his nod, she slid into the booth. Not easy to do with her hands full.

He swiped his napkin across his mouth and eyed the can of sausages she set on the table. "I'd prefer flowers."

"The florist isn't open yet."

He gave her a once-over as he scooped another forkful of pancake. "You look like you got as much sleep as I did."

"I was expecting you to call after your visit to the ER. How are you?"

He shoved the bite into his mouth. She waited, but he chewed that forkful, like, twenty-seven times, and the moment he swallowed, he had his coffee mug at his mouth.

Lily sat back. "See, the way you're avoiding my question makes me think there's something really wrong with you."

"I have a big-ass headache," he admitted. "Other than that, I'm good."

"No concussion?"

"No concussion."

She curled her hands around her cup and forced herself to hold his gaze. "You probably expect me to say I'm sorry for last night. But I won't apologize for trying to apprehend an offender." She ignored a ripple of guilt. "That's my job."

"Screw the apology." He turned his fork sideways and halved a sausage patty. "Worry about dissension in your ranks."

Her hands jerked, and coffee slapped wetly against the sides of her to-go cup. "There was no dissension in the ranks until you came along and stirred it up."

"It was there. No one wanted to call you on it."

"My people know better than to fear reprisal."

His fork clanked onto the edge of his plate. "It's not fear of reprisal that keeps your people from speaking out. It's fear that what they have to say might send you over the edge."

She drew in a sharp breath. "You don't know what you're talking about. I'm fine. My people know I'm fine."

"You had a crisis," Fulton said. "I don't know what it was, but I do know you haven't moved on."

"So you're a therapist, too?"

"I can be. You're welcome to check out my couch, anytime."

She snapped upright. "That's neither funny

nor appropriate." Enticing, though. An image of the two of them stretched out on a black leather sofa had her heartbeat slowing to a thick, syrupy throb.

Lily Anne, you are a hypocrite.

"Order's ready, Sheriff," Rachel called from behind the counter.

Fulton pushed away his plate. "You're understaffed. Something happens to you, who's going to pick up the slack?"

Lily bristled. She opened her mouth to tell him she knew exactly what she was doing, thank you very much, when someone was suddenly standing beside her. Someone who smelled faintly of citrus and ash. Her stomach sank as she looked up to see Burke Yancey grinning down at her, the exhaustion in his face and the wrinkled state of his navy shirt and pants making it obvious he'd just come off shift. Running a hand through his shaggy hair, he gave Lily a lingering look.

"Morning, Sheriff. You're a sight for sore eyes."

"I doubt it," she said. A loud screech had her peering around him. Four of his fellow firefighters were pulling two tables together and the way they were stumbling around, she'd be surprised if they didn't all end up falling asleep in their eggs. "Rough night?"

His grin slipped. "Someone torched that abandoned gas station out on Route 5, past the vineyards. It was a bitch to put out. No one's got the energy to man the grill, so Cap's buying us breakfast."

"Anyone hurt?" Fulton asked.

Burke shifted, glanced from Fulton to Lily and back again, then held out a hand. "Burke Yancey."

Fulton gripped Burke's hand. "Vaughn Fulton."

"He's our newest deputy," Lily said.

Burke's gaze narrowed. "You didn't mention you'd hired someone."

He said it as if they'd talked just that morning. "I haven't seen you to tell you."

"I have an easy fix for that." When Lily remained silent, he angled his body toward Fulton. "What do you think of Castle Creek?"

"I have fond memories of the place." Fulton pulled his wallet from his back pocket. "I used to visit my aunt and uncle during the summers. But I won't be staying."

"He prefers the city," Lily said.

"Yeah?" Burke stared down at her. "The country has everything I could ever need."

Fulton thumped his wallet onto the table and gulped the remains of his coffee.

"Wait." Burke snapped his fingers. "Fulton. Your uncle was Emerson, right? We helped him out with a chimney fire a couple of years back. Sorry you lost him, man." When Fulton nodded his thanks, Burke dipped his knees in a now-I-get-it gesture. "It was you with Lily at the fight last night. Word is the sheriff here—" before Lily could slide out of range, he gave her shoulder a quick rub "—charged right in and broke things up before anyone had a chance to get hurt. Good for you, Lil. I hope your deputies take a page out of your book."

Heat crept up Lily's throat as she met Fulton's contemptuous gaze.

"Hey, how about that dinner you owe me?" Burke grinned. "Next Saturday night? I'll take you to Mama Leoni's and we'll drink a toast to Castle Creek's badass sheriff."

Maybe it was good Burke was standing right beside her because her cheeks were on fire. Any moment now, they'd spontaneously combust. "I'm on duty then," she said tightly.

"Okay. All right. We can talk later, after I get some shut-eye. Good to meet you, Fulton."

"Yancey."

Lily lifted suddenly heavy hands to her coffee cup. *I hope your deputies take a page out of your book.* Fulton was right, damn him. She was acting like her decisions would have no consequences.

No way she'd have wanted any of her people to step in front of that car.

Fulton watched her, his mouth grim.

"You could say 'I told you so,'" she muttered.

"And distract you from your guilt?"

She leaned forward, the cup scraping across

the table as she tucked it against her chest. "Listen," she began, "there's something—"

"Sheriff?" Rachel hailed her again, pointing at the bags beside the register.

Lily sagged. If she didn't get a move on, the food would be cold.

Kind of like the vibe she was getting from Fulton.

CONVERSATION STOPPED WHEN Lily walked into the station early Sunday. Clarissa, JD and Fulton stood in a circle in front of the dispatcher's desk, Fulton in his uniform, JD and Clarissa in jeans. Clarissa had dressed up her denim capris with lime-green sneakers and a matching sleeveless turtleneck, but her face didn't reflect the vibrancy of her outfit.

Lily didn't call mandatory meetings often, and when she did, the topic tended to be on the dreary side.

She set the bakery box on Clarissa's desk. "Help yourself, guys. Cinnamon rolls from the diner. Freshly baked."

Clarissa whimpered. "It's that bad?" She trudged around her desk and slumped into her chair.

JD was already reaching for a napkin. He nudged Fulton with his elbow. "Better grab one now, dawg, before whatever she has to say ruins your appetite."

"I'll wait." Fulton crossed his arms over his chest, hesitated and dropped them again.

Lily caught her breath. He was nervous. For *her*. Warmth loosened her limbs, then she bit the inside of her lip. Since Fulton was tight with the mayor, wouldn't he already know what she had to say?

She curled her fingers around her equipment belt. "You all know what happened at Snoozy's Friday night. I took a risk that could have gotten my partner hurt, not to mention innocent civilians. I believed doing my job was more important than any injury I might sustain, but I was wrong. Deputy Fulton tried to tell me I was setting a bad example. That didn't sink in until I realized that if any of you had pulled that same stunt, I'd have put you on suspension."

Cardboard rustled as JD helped himself to another roll. Clarissa slapped his hand and he almost fumbled the pastry.

"What?" He lifted his shoulders. "I eat when I'm stressed. So sue me."

"You're a pig."

"And I got the badge to prove it."

Fulton gave them both a quelling glance. "Go ahead, Sheriff."

Lily nodded her thanks. "I owe you all an apology. I want to be the example you should follow, not the example you shouldn't. Most of you know my history." She stared at the wall behind Clarissa, determined not to meet Fulton's penetrating gaze. "But we've all suffered in some way or another, and I promise I do know that personal tragedy is no justification for making poor choices on the job. I ignored that for a while. Consider me wised up."

Silence, until JD broke it by brushing his hands together. When he failed to get rid of the stickiness, he snatched up Clarissa's water bottle, tipped some liquid onto a napkin and swiped at his palms. "Are you suspending yourself?" he asked.

Lily had expected the question. She just hadn't expected JD to ask it. "I will if you'll cover my shifts."

JD scowled. "The mayor didn't suspend you?"

"The mayor asked me to step down."

Clarissa gasped. Fulton folded his arms and looked down at the boots he'd crossed at the ankles. JD simply stared.

Dullness settled behind Lily's breastbone.

"JD?" she prompted quietly. "You have something you need to say?"

"Yeah." He tossed aside the napkin and pushed to his feet. "One of the kids in Clarissa's building asked if he could have your vest because he'd heard you were too tough to worry about stopping bullets."

Lily's stomach dropped.

"Tattletale," Clarissa scolded.

Lily held up a hand, saw it shake and grabbed

back onto her belt. "I'm sorry to hear that. I am glad you told me, though. Mayor Whitby and I already agreed I'd spend some time out in the community emphasizing our commitment to safe practices. I'll make it a point to hold assemblies at all three schools."

Clarissa twisted the cap on her water bottle. "Does that mean you're not stepping down?"

"It means I asked the mayor for another chance. I'm asking the same of you." Finally she found the courage to meet Fulton's gaze. "You have my word. No more unnecessary risks." How ironic, considering she'd once worried Fulton would prove to be the devil-may-care kind. She uncurled her hands from around her belt and forced a smile despite the stabbing ache as blood surged back into her fingers. "Are we good?"

Ten minutes later, after a hug from Clarissa and a fist bump from JD—which was so much more than she'd expected—Lily and Fulton were alone in the station.

She studied his face. "You look better today."

"You mean I don't look like I just crawled out of my laundry basket?"

She tried for an amused huff, but it came out sounding more like a grunt of pain. She swung away and headed for her office.

He followed. "You said no more risks, but that was a pretty big one you just took."

"Let's hope it pays off."

"It will."

She sank into her chair and rolled up tight to her desk.

Fulton lingered in the doorway, uniform shirt clinging to his defined torso when he raised his arms to the door frame and leaned in. Good God, the man was gorgeous.

"You should be proud of yourself," he said, "for putting it all out there."

"You mean, for admitting you were right." She gave her head a shake. "Just because I accept it doesn't mean I don't resent it. And I'm not suicidal, by the way. I just got carried away."

He remained silent.

She dropped her gaze to her desk and shifted papers, searching for something to focus on besides her deputy's physique. "I thought you were going to get a new shirt."

"It's on back order."

Lily sighed. She didn't have to look up to know he was smirking. "Shouldn't you be out on patrol?"

"I wanted you to know." He dropped his arms and moved a step closer. "Whitby hasn't offered me your job. He realizes he won't find anyone more dedicated than you."

Lily leaned back in her chair. "You mean he knows you're not interested."

"Not in the job, no."

Even as her pulse started to bounce and her

skin erupted with hot pinpricks of pleasure, she set her jaw. "You need to stop with the innuendos," she said. "I feel like they're some kind of consolation prize. Your way of saying you're sorry I screwed up."

"You're right. I shouldn't joke. I apologize."

"It's about time you took a turn," she muttered. When Fulton gave a deep chuckle, her stomach flipped. *No backsliding, Lily Anne.*

Inspiration struck. "Aren't you still angry I arrested your uncle?"

He cocked his head. "I'm beginning to believe there's more to that story." Without waiting for a response, he spun away, then turned back. "If you're not busy next Saturday, you should come check out my junk."

Lily felt her eyes stretch wide. "Excuse me?"

Fulton coughed. "I meant trash. Scrap. Castoffs. All the odds and ends that got dumped at my uncle's house before he died. Everything's free, and it all has to go. Spread the word. It'll do you good."

Lily slid her glasses into place, the better to enjoy the red tinting Fulton's ears. "How do you figure that?"

"The sooner my house is empty, the sooner I can head back to Erie."

A sudden tightness behind her lids had her batting her eyes. *Damn it.* Why should she miss him? He was arrogant and nosy and bossy as heck.

He was also kind, funny and too damn perceptive for anyone's good.

"Besides," he continued. "You haven't met Not Franklin."

"Not Franklin?"

"The cat who turned out *not* to be the neighbors' tom Franklin."

Lily fought the urge to bounce up and down in her seat. She'd been dying to see the kittens. "*That's* the name you're saddling her with?"

"No sense in giving her a name when whoever adopts her will only change it." He shifted. "So, you'll be there? Or do you have a date?"

"I don't date."

"Not even the firefighter? The one who calls you *Lil*?"

She pushed her glasses farther up her nose and turned to her computer. "He has a hard time taking no for an answer."

"So do I. When it comes to doing a good deed, that is."

Lily shot him a wry glance. "Fine. I'll be there."

"Great. One more thing."

"You need me to bring a pickup."

His face lit up. "You have one?"

"Nope."

"Okay, then." He walked up to her desk, braced his hands and leaned in. Lily told herself to move away, but he smelled *so* good. Like licorice. And damn it, she didn't even *like* licorice.

His dark chocolate gaze held hers. "What were you going to tell me?" he asked softly. "At the diner, just before the server called you up to the counter?"

"I don't remember," she lied.

He reached out and trailed a finger along the underside of her jaw. She braced herself against the long lick of heat that burned away the moisture in her mouth.

"Maybe it'll come to you by Saturday," he said.

She tried not to watch him walk away, but he did have a very fine butt.

And she was only human.

MONDAY EVENING, CLARISSA was headed home after running errands—mostly her own, which made for a welcome change—when the synchronized flash of blue lights yanked her attention to the library's parking lot. She slowed her Camry, then with a stab of guilt checked her rearview mirror. No one behind her, praise be.

Noble and JD stood talking under a streetlight. When Clarissa spotted the bandage on Noble's head, she hit the brake. Too late to turn into the lot, but hanging a U-turn was easy enough to do. She cringed when her tires squealed.

Why hadn't anyone called her? Yeah, she had the night off, but did that mean she had to be completely out of the loop?

First thing in the morning, she was writing a freaking memo.

Absently she waved at JD, who was just pulling out of the lot. Things had been awkward at the station all day, but Lily's apology the morning before had gone a long way toward helping everyone breathe better.

Noble waited for her under the light, shifting from one foot to the other. Anxious to get home, no doubt. She shouldn't keep him. But surely he wouldn't mind a little friendly sympathy?

Her heels snapped a quick rhythm across the pavement as she cursed herself for not taking two seconds to do a makeup check. No, she wasn't going to date the man, but a girl still liked to look her best. Noble, on the other hand, looked...

"Awful," she said when she reached him. "You look awful." She studied the stark white patch on his temple, frowned over the lack of color in his cheeks and scanned the bloodstains on the shoulder of his T-shirt. With a noisy swallow, she jerked her gaze away. "Shouldn't you be on your way to the hospital?"

He crooked a grin, the appreciative gleam in his eyes doing dangerous things to her heart rate. "It's only a flesh wound."

"Points for the *Monty Python* reference, demerits for being such a man." She shoved her hands into the pockets of her cherry-print halter dress. "What happened?"

"Worried?"

"Curious."

"Harsh." Noble scratched his chin and circled around behind her. She twisted her head left, then right, to see what he was up to. The man had to have one hell of a headache. Surely he wasn't in the mood to check out her ass?

But he didn't pause behind her to enjoy the view. Instead he ended up on her left, away from the light, eyes narrowed in thought.

"Let's make a deal," he said. "I tell you what happened, you agree to go out with me."

She flapped a hand. "All I have to do is call JD to get the story."

"He can't tell it as well as I can."

Her gaze fell to his T-shirt, which read Check It Out. She'd be happy to, if it weren't for all that blood. She lifted her chin. "What about Paula?"

"She didn't appreciate my sense of humor."

That should not have made her feel like popping open a bottle of champagne. "You should be home in bed."

"I'll rest better knowing your answer."

Since she had her nose in the air anyway, she gave a sniff. "I'm not a big fan of extortion. Besides, I can guess what happened. No one believed you when you told them a supposedly adult female got stuck in the book depository, so you felt you had to re-create the event. You hit your head in the process." She leaned forward and poked him in the biceps. A very thick, very rigid bicep.

"Serves you right," she said breathlessly.

"Wrong. I didn't tell anyone."

"Really."

"I do have half a brain. Making jokes at a woman's expense is not the best way to get into her—"

"Pants?"

Even in the dim light, she could see his cheeks go ruddy. "I was about to say 'good graces.'"

"I apologize for the assumption."

"Yeah? You know how to make it up to me."

"I told you before." Clarissa smoothed her skirt, wishing their hushed voices and the fireflies and the smell of honeysuckle weren't making this encounter so damn romantic. "I don't have time to date. Anyway, I don't think we'd be a good match. I like to keep things casual. You're more a long-term kind of guy." She motioned with her head at the vehicle parked at the end of the lot. "The minivan gives it away."

"My other ride's a pickup."

"Extended cab?" When he nodded, she gave him a what'd-I-tell-you? look.

He regarded her thoughtfully, no trace of sulk in his expression.

Moonlight streamed through the leaf-fringed branches of middle-aged oaks, brightening the spaces neglected by the streetlights. His light blue

T-shirt gleamed in the shadows and her belly fluttered madly, like one of those game booths blowing a whirlwind of dollar bills.

"You did that on purpose," she said. "Moved away from the light, so I wouldn't see the blood."

"Seemed the right thing to do." His teeth flashed white. "What guy wants to turn off the woman of his dreams?"

Clarissa blinked. *Pay no attention to that tingle in your chest, chickie.*

Yeah, that really wasn't working for her.

"Okay," she said. "I'll go out with you. Spill about what happened here."

"I must have hit my head harder than I thought. Did you just say yes?"

She fought a smile. "Technically, I said okay."

His T-shirt stretched as he inhaled. The tingle in Clarissa's chest moved south. *Stop that.*

"Great," he said. "Good. A deal's a deal, so here's the story. I was in the office, getting ready to close up for the night, when I heard banging. I went out front to find some kid trying to pry the cash box out of the copier. Not surprisingly, when he saw me he ran. I started to give chase but tripped on the rubber mat and ended up head-butting the umbrella stand."

She grimaced in sympathy. "Why didn't you want to tell me?"

"It's not the most flattering story."

"You could have lied."

"I wouldn't do that." He frowned. "You're not planning on lying to me, are you?"

"I'm not planning on doing anything to you." But she wanted to. Oh, how she wanted to. She backed toward her car. "I hope you feel better. Call me when you figure out where we're going for our date."

"I think you're looking forward to this more than you're letting on."

"I think you might have brain damage."

He chuckled, then jolted forward. "Wait. I don't have your number."

"Yeah," she said. "I think you do."

HE HADN'T EXPECTED to see lights. Not at this time of night. Only one person would be inside the station so many hours past quitting time, which meant his crap-fest of a day was finally about to take a turn for the better.

A bolt of anticipation had his blood sizzling. He wanted to see her in something other than a uniform. He wanted her naked. He wanted her in bed with him, naked.

Damn it. When had attraction turned to need?

He walked up to the windows and peered in through a gap between the blinds. Lily stood over a bucket in the center of the room, lowering a dripping mop into the wringer. She bent forward and pressed down hard on the lever, then lifted the mop and slapped it onto the floor. She worked the mop like she'd cleaned the floor hundreds of times. She probably had.

While still in uniform, no less. Jesus, had she even gone home?

He stepped farther into the light so he could find his key. Castle Creek's sheriff's department was so small that unless they had someone tucked away in a holding cell, the station wasn't manned 24/7. Since the two jackasses from the bar the other night had been transported to the Erie jail, Lily was alone.

A hell of a far cry from the twenty-four-hour crowd he was used to at the Erie PD, but exactly what he needed right now.

He rapped twice on the door before letting himself in. No key had been necessary. Lily swung around, eyes wide, hands fumbling the mop handle. The heavy, lemon-pine scent of an industrial cleaner hung in the air.

"What are you doing here?" she asked. No, not asked. Demanded.

Vintage Lily Tate.

She was breathing hard, and sweat gleamed on her forehead. She'd been working her way toward the booking area in the back, so she'd already mopped half the station. He stroked his gaze over her toned biceps and she tensed.

Don't be a dick, Fulton. She'd already warned

him once for flirting. Did he want to find himself out of a job because he couldn't keep it clean?

Hell, no.

But it wasn't like he could help it. Not anymore.

Eyes back on her face where they belonged, he twirled his key ring around his index finger. "I left my Ray-Bans in my cruiser."

"That seems to be going around."

"When I came to get them, I noticed the light." He motioned with his head toward the exit. "You left the door unlocked."

She stacked her hands on the end of the mop handle. "Do you really think someone would be silly enough to break in here?"

She was an experienced law enforcement officer, fearless and in prime condition. And if all else failed, she could incapacitate an attacker by irritating the hell out of him. Still, his gut soured at the thought of anyone putting their hands on her. Friend *or* foe.

"Why risk it?" he said, and could have kicked his own ass at the thickness of his words.

Her eyes shuttered. "This isn't Erie."

"You're telling me."

"If you're unhappy, why stay?"

"I made a promise."

"Admirable." She lowered the mop handle back into push position. "You have your shades, and I'd like to get back to my cleaning."

"Maybe I was looking for a little peace and quiet, too."

"Sorry I ruined it for you."

"You didn't. You're an undemanding person. Too undemanding, sometimes."

"Meaning?"

He eyed the wet floor around her. "Meaning you have a hard time asking for help."

"Let me guess. Somebody wants something from you."

"A lot of somebodies."

"I'm not going to add to your list." She ran a hand through her hair, must have realized it was sticking straight up and started to pluck at her bangs. When she met his gaze, she scowled and dropped her hand. "I can handle this myself," she said curtly.

"You want me to leave."

"It wouldn't hurt my feelings."

He bit back a smile and crossed his arms. "Indulge me first. Tell me what you're doing here."

"Mopping."

No shit. "Most people watch TV or make a sandwich when they have trouble sleeping."

She rolled her eyes and pushed the mop into motion again. The longer he watched, the pointier her chin became and the harder she worked the mop. The closer she pushed it his way, too.

When the tips of the strings lashed the toes of his boots, he grinned and stepped back.

"How long are you planning to be here?" he asked.

She stopped again, and gulped air. Small strands of hair stuck to her cheeks. "This is a great workout, you know."

"You trying to Tom Sawyer me?"

She smiled, and it did something to the inside of his chest. It was rare, that curve of her lips. At least, it was rare to have it aimed in his direction.

"No sense in trying," she said. "It's hard to kid a kidder."

"I'd call you on the insult, but I'd rather not get the business end of a mop upside my head. Why are you the one doing the cleaning? Budget cuts?"

"It was either this or hold bake sales. As much as I love a good cookie, I bake about as well as Clarissa does goth."

He laughed. "Yeah, hard to picture her in black. What do you have left to do?"

"Bathrooms." When he made a face, she chuckled and pushed the mop at him. "If you take over here, I'll take toilet duty."

"Deal."

She headed toward the closet, for cleaning supplies, he guessed. Before she could disappear into the back, he spoke up. "I don't have as much pull with Whitby as you think, but I could say something about finding room in the budget for a janitor."

"If you have that much pull, I'd appreciate it if you'd ask him to get a move on with your replacement."

Okay, that hurt. "You still resent me."

"You think?" She tucked a spray bottle under her arm, grabbed a bucket of supplies and shut the closet door. Outside the entrance to lockup, she hesitated. "Actually, my resentment got lost in all the guilt I feel for nearly getting you run over. Thank you, by the way. For pulling me out of the way."

It shocked the hell out of him that she didn't choke on the words. He dipped the mop in the bucket. "You're about the only person I know who doesn't want something from me. Besides my absence, I mean."

"Want to talk about it?"

"Two words. Mayor Whitby." When she flinched, he held up a hand. "Nothing to do with your job."

"What, then?"

"I ran into him at the store."

"You mean he tracked you to the store."

"Probably. He wanted to make sure I was aware of his pet project."

Lily was nodding. "He's planning a clubhouse on the lake. He asked you for money for that? Knowing what he pays his deputies? Talk about shameless." She pointed at the floor by his feet. "Pay attention, Fulton. You missed a spot."

"Not only do you not want anything from me, you're the only person who doesn't care whether I like you."

"Not true. I want a clean floor. And I like you just fine—as a deputy."

"I know the real reason you arrested my uncle." He glanced up as he squeezed the mop dry. "You're not saying because you want me to believe you're a hard-ass. But I know the old man was begging to be arrested. I know because I met his girlfriend today. Delia. I stopped her for speeding and she told me Uncle Em wouldn't have approved of me giving her a ticket."

Lily smiled and leaned back against the metal door. "Sounds like Delia."

"She told me they'd been falling all over themselves, trying to get arrested. Indecent exposure standing in line at the bank, groping in a rowboat at the lake, sex in a parked car behind the hardware store." He exaggerated a shudder. "I've seen some disturbing things, but that would have landed me with PTSD."

"Glad I could save you the trauma," Lily said dryly. "In the end, your uncle got his way. Ending up in the 'joint,' as he called it, was one of the few remaining items on his bucket list."

"Why let me believe you bullied him?"

She shrugged.

"Let me guess. You're petrified someone might like you. Might want to get close to you."

Her exhale was impatient as she straightened and gestured with the spray bottle. "Why do people bother to ask questions right before providing their own answers?"

"It pisses you off that I've discovered your creamy marshmallow center."

"You've discovered no such thing."

"Give me time."

"You are unbelievable."

With a grin, he started to mop. "I get that a lot."

"I have toilets to scrub and that's bound to be a lot more fun than listening to your nonsense."

"Nonsense? What are you, eighty?"

Silence. He glanced up, and as soon as he got a look at her face, he realized his mistake.

Damn it.

"I'll dump the bucket when you're done," she said stiffly. "Feel free to lock the door behind you."

She turned and stabbed at the keypad, then disappeared behind the battered metal door.

Vaughn sighed. That bonehead maneuver would take a lot more than a bucket of bleach and a mop to clean up.

Peace and quiet, what he'd told her he wanted. The joke was on him, because he'd never get another moment's peace. Not while he was in Castle Creek, working for the woman he was falling for.

How the hell had this happened? He was a career-first kind of guy. Yeah, he'd had his share of relationships, but only one had come close to making him want to consider any kind of long term. They'd lived together for half a year, and that had put an end to the whole commitment experiment. Women were into the uniform and the whole protector thing, not so much the crazy-ass hours and the occasional trip into head case territory.

Lily was different. She understood the demands of the job. Hell, she relished them. But that was nothing compared to how dedicated she was, not just to her job but to her people. Yeah, she had a smart mouth and a stubbornness that could make a man grind his teeth to powder, but she was also fearless and compassionate. It had shaken him, to find out she'd been doing his uncle a favor by arresting him. Yet she'd never defended herself, and he suspected that had more to do with preserving his uncle's dignity than anything else.

All that sour and sweet, wrapped up in a package that had started to make him ache at night.

Vaughn closed the station door behind him and headed for his cruiser. Damn it, he was sounding like a jackass. What if this was all about the challenge? About the fact that he had even less experience with rejection than he did with commitment?

Lily Tate wasn't immune to him. That much he

knew. Whenever she was around him her breathing went out of sync, like she'd lost track of her inhales and exhales.

Or maybe she was just fighting not to go all Hulk on his ass. All he knew was that when she'd stepped in front of that car, time had slowed to a crawl, and the images that had flashed across his brain had been all about what might have been. With her.

THE FOLLOWING SATURDAY, Lily stood beside the open trunk of her patrol car and stared across Vaughn's dandelion-studded front yard at the man who both infuriated and charmed her. Early morning August smelled like dried grass, lake perch and leftover charcoal from someone's barbecue. The air, which the heat had yet to thicken, echoed with thumps and laughter and the clanging of metal on metal as Vaughn helped a long-haired guy in a sleeveless hoodie maneuver a bed frame into the back of a faded red pickup. The Catlett sisters, in maxi skirts, sandals and brightly patterned tunics, stood on either side of Vaughn, alternately singing out orders and fanning their faces.

The fanning had nothing to do with the heat.

And for God's sake, when had she started thinking of him as Vaughn?

He wore an olive-green pair of cargo shorts, leaving his muscular legs bare. Throw in mussed-up hair, a barely there beard and a dark gray

T-shirt that sweat had already plastered to his powerful chest and it was no wonder the ladies were looking woozy.

Lily could do with a cold drink herself.

As Vaughn handed Hazel an armful of the webbed straps he and hoodie guy would use to tie down the bed frame, JD came out onto the porch carrying two boxes with an old-fashioned kitchen mixer balanced on top. Instantly the Catlett sisters went into divide-and-conquer mode. Hazel continued to "help" Vaughn by swinging the straps like a showgirl's feather boa while June clutched at JD's forearm and guided him to the opposite side of the truck bed, taking short, careful steps as if he were walking with both eyes closed.

JD wore his jeans and black muscle shirt well, but his appearance didn't do dastardly things to her blood pressure like Vaughn's did. Though, heck, she was already lusting after one employee, why not make it two? JD loaded the boxes into the truck, spotted Lily and waved. She managed a feeble wave back, saw Vaughn was turning her way and practically dived into her trunk.

She rolled her eyes at herself. At least she had an excuse for acting like a bonehead. The week had been a long one. And the remark Vaughn had made about her age still stung. Which was ridiculous. She *had* sounded like a fuddy-duddy. Sexy it was not, fussing at a man while wielding a mop. She'd made things worse by pouting, though. Forget eleven years older. She was acting like she was eleven years old, period.

Lily was digging out the boxes from the back of the trunk when footsteps thudded across the grass. She straightened as Vaughn jogged the rest of the way to the car.

"Hey. Thanks for coming." He shoved his shades off his face, peeled off a glove and took her hand, then with a grimace, released his grip and swiped his palm down the side of his shorts. "Sorry about that. Although if you stay, it won't be long before you're just as sweaty as I am. Need any help unloading? Wait. Why are you unloading? You're supposed to take stuff home with you, not add to my collection."

She was still fighting the image of the both of them sweating. Together. "Umm…"

JD appeared behind Vaughn. "The lady with the red hair's asking for you. She doesn't appreciate my packing skills."

Hazel joined them at the bumper. "No, she doesn't appreciate your pants. Not as much as Vaughn's shorts, anyway."

Lily could relate.

"Don't keep your buxom young customer waiting, sweet cheeks." Hazel patted Vaughn's shoulder and peered into the trunk. "What do we have here?"

Lily placed two boxes in JD's outstretched

arms. "Subs and croissant sandwiches from the diner."

"And Marcus's apple tarts. I can smell 'em." JD exchanged an awkward high five with Hazel, who gestured for Lily to hand over the box of tarts.

"This was nice of you." Vaughn lifted a Tupperware container of fruit, and after Lily snagged a bag of paper plates and napkins, he slammed the trunk closed. "You thought of everything."

Lily did her best to rein in her smile. Was she beaming? She had a terrible feeling she was beaming. "I figured if you didn't have to stop and fix lunch, you might get more done today."

"Did you." Vaughn surveyed her uniform. "You know, I was hoping to see you out of that."

Lily gasped. "Excuse me?"

"I haven't seen you in civilian clothes yet."

"I'm on duty."

"Are you ever off duty?" A smile flirted with his mouth. "Any chance I'll get to see you in a pair of jeans someday? Maybe even a skirt?"

Lily clenched her fingers around the thin plastic handles. "I can stay and help out," she said primly, "but as soon as a call comes in, I have to go."

"I appreciate the help." He leaned in. "I'd appreciate it more if you had fewer clothes on."

She stepped back and glared at him, even as longing gathered in her belly. "We talked about this. Are you *trying* to get slapped with sexual harassment charges?" When Hazel and JD abruptly stopped their conversation behind Vaughn, Lily dialed it down to a whisper. "Because I will break out the cuffs."

"Promise?" He let loose a smirk, but a moment later, his expression lost all trace of humor.

Probably because her face had flushed cherry-red. She could feel the burn.

He winced. "Okay, here's the thing. When I'm nervous, I flirt."

"What?"

"You make me nervous. You do realize you're gorgeous, right? And I'm not just talking looks."

Lily stared. A thank-you hovered on the tip of her tongue, but she couldn't work her lips.

With a wink he turned away, and in a mock drill-sergeant voice barked at Hazel and JD to get moving. Lily, meanwhile, talked herself out of tearing open the package of paper plates so she could fan her own face.

CHAPTER SEVEN

GET IT TOGETHER, *Lily Anne.* She had no time for empty flattery. She was there for two reasons, and two reasons only. To promote teamwork and to help Vaughn Fulton finish what he'd come to Castle Creek to do. The sooner, the better.

She trudged across the yard behind the others, keeping her gaze carefully averted from Vaughn's backside.

From behind them came the rumble of approaching engines. They all turned to watch a pickup and a minivan park at the curb. Half a dozen people popped out.

"More customers," Vaughn said, with such glee that if he hadn't been holding the fruit, he'd have probably been rubbing his palms together.

"I'll take that." Lily reclaimed the container. "Anything I can do inside?"

"Check on the cats, would you? They're in the laundry room." He started toward the latest batch of treasure hunters while Hazel and JD went into the house. "After that, June can find you something to do."

By the time Lily had stashed the fruit in the

fridge, next to the sandwiches, she understood why Vaughn was desperate for this free-for-all to work. There was stuff *everywhere*. Boxes and bins and stacks and piles—how could he live like this? Underneath the tantalizing smell of coffee lingered a mustiness mixed with…what was that, engine oil? Once Vaughn had cleared out the house, he'd have to bring someone in to clean it.

Then again, she'd seen firsthand that he knew his way around a mop.

It didn't take her long to find the laundry room. She opened the door tucked into the corner of the kitchen and found Jared Ensler on his butt in the middle of the floor, a trio of kittens tumbling over each other on a towel between his knees while mama cat remained watchful in an oversized carrier nearby. Lily made a sympathetic noise when she spotted the cast on the cat's rear leg. Jared's head jerked up.

"I came to meet the new additions," she told him cheerfully. "Mind if I join you?"

Jared shook his head and turned his attention back to the kittens, but Lily could feel him watching her out of the corner of his eye. She plopped down beside him, carefully scooped up a black ball of fur and held it against her cheek. The kitten mewled and nuzzled her skin.

"How sweet," Lily breathed.

"They're right at two weeks." Gently, Jared detached the gray one from his jeans and set it back on the towel with its playmate. "They just opened their eyes. In another week, their ear canals will open and a week after that, their baby teeth will start to show."

"You know a lot about cats. Do you have any at home?"

Jared shrugged, but Lily recognized the pride behind the movement.

"We used to," he said. His voice thickened. "A kind of cream-colored, orange-ish cat. Scottie named him Friendly. We had to put him down 'cause he got cancer."

"I'm sorry to hear that." She blinked, her eyes suddenly damp. "Where is Scottie?"

"He had to stay home 'cause he didn't finish the dishes."

"Bummer." Lily cringed. Did anyone even say "bummer" anymore? Probably no one popular. "You two still working toward a new Xbox?"

Jared flashed a grin that revealed a wayward eyetooth. "Our dad got addicted to *Call of Duty*, so he hooked us up with a new one. Now we're saving for a dirt bike."

Lily barely refrained from asking if they'd cleared that with their mom. "So are you here looking for stuff to sell?" When he shrugged again and looked away, she frowned and handed him the kitten. "Not alongside Route 5, I hope."

"If I say no, do I get another twenty?"

"Don't push it, kid."

He plucked at the ragged threads sprouting from a small hole in the knee of his jeans. "Actually, I'm hunting roosters and eagles."

"You mean collectibles? Like salt and pepper shakers?"

Jared snorted a laugh. "Nah, I'm talking coins. You know, French rooster? American eagle? Gold bullion?"

"No, I don't know, but I'm impressed that you do." When he blushed, she smiled gently. "You have reason to believe there's something like that here?"

"I heard Mrs. Yackley talk about how she lost her collection. She had like, dozens of coins." His eyes went bright and he pulled up his knees. "I was thinking, if she'd dropped some stuff off here, maybe the coins were inside. You know, like in the pockets of a coat, or stashed in the false bottom of a box, or something. So I asked and she said yeah, she'd brought over some junk. She said if I found her coins, she'd give me a prize."

"If you find her coins in all this chaos, you'll have earned a reward."

"I know, right? Mrs. Y even put it in writing." He pulled a wrinkled piece of paper from his back pocket and held it up. "See?"

Lily squinted, and wished she'd brought her readers with her. "Is it me, or is it dark in here?"

"It's not you. I read that kittens' pupils are slow

to dilate and contract. You're supposed to keep them away from bright lights."

Lily's head snapped around. Vaughn stood in the doorway, arms crossed, expression unreadable. Not Franklin meowed an earnest welcome and Lily pressed a hand to the ache in her chest. When she realized what she was doing, she dropped her chin and pretended to brush something from her tie.

If a smirk had a sound, Vaughn made it.

One by one, Jared positioned the kittens against their mother's belly then got to his feet. "I've already been through the stuff in the living room," he said to Vaughn. "Okay if I start looking in the dining room?"

"Sure. But don't try to move anything heavy by yourself. Find anything weird, you let me know. Same thing if anyone acts pushy or creeps you out. Cool?"

"Cool." Jared waved into the carrier. "'Bye, kitties. See you later. I gotta get back to work now."

As Jared scurried from the room, Lily stood and swiped at her cheek.

Vaughn touched her forearm. "You okay?"

"Cuteness overload," she muttered. She palmed the moisture from her other cheek. "The kittens are going, too?"

He exhaled. "When they're old enough. It wouldn't be fair to keep them cooped up in my apartment. Plus they're shooting my grocery budget all to hell."

"And Not Franklin?"

"I'll find her a good home, too."

"Take her back to Erie. You could check on her during the day, like you do now." The chagrin on his face made her smile. "Oh, yeah. You're busted. Talk about wanting people to think you're a hard-ass."

"She has a broken leg," he said gruffly. "She needs care."

The black cat meowed again, green-gold eyes locked on Vaughn.

"Seems to me she needs you. Maybe you could take her and one of her kittens, too, to keep her company?"

"Maybe." He crossed to the carrier, crouched and stroked the cat under her chin. When a contented purr eased into the silence, Vaughn glanced at Lily over his shoulder. "You'd make a good mom."

"Nice try, but I'm home even less than you are. Anyway, I'm not much of a cat person."

He gave Not Franklin one last pat, secured the wire door and stood. "I wasn't talking about cats."

Shock gave Lily's bones a cold, hard shake. She could have sworn she heard them rattle. "Then you don't know what you're talking about."

"You do it without realizing. JD, when he was sick. Clarissa, whenever she second-guesses herself. You've been trying to convince Whitby to cut back on the candy, and just now, with Jared, you couldn't have been more encouraging. If that's not mothering, I don't know what is."

So that's how he saw her. As the wipes-runny-noses-and-nags-about-vegetables-and-sets-curfews type. Yes, he was a flirt. Big deal. How much of that was pure charm and how much was sucking up to the boss? Did she really believe that nonsense about making him nervous?

Nonsense? What are you, eighty?

Hurt squeezed her throat, making it hard to breathe. She did her best to tamp down the sensation because it was ridiculous. So ridiculous she was tempted to throw herself into the role and ask if he'd remembered to put on clean underwear that morning.

When Vaughn frowned, Lily swallowed a bitter sigh. "Go with your strengths," her father had always told her. Apparently all his strengths had been wrapped up in a chunky barista named Rosalie. She'd led him to Winnipeg and they'd never heard from him again.

But that was beside the point.

"Keep making that face and it'll freeze that way," Lily said, and reached up to pat him on the cheek.

He caught her wrist and pulled her closer. "Don't," he said softly. "If you want to touch me because you're curious, or needy? Go for it. I'm here for you." The wry heat in his eyes faded and he released her. "But if you're trying to convince us both you're not into me, then it's hands off."

She remained silent long enough to get her breathing under control. "I plead the fifth."

"An admission in its own right," he whispered, and the brush of warm breath against her neck sent need shuddering along her nerve endings.

She backed toward the door, fighting the false sense of intimacy. Fumbling for normalcy.

"Speaking of Jared…" *Oh, fantastic.* Whose voice was that? Lily forced herself to inhale, and felt the deep ache of her lungs inflating. "What was that about people creeping him out?"

Vaughn considered his answer. Or maybe he was buying time.

"Just a precaution." Rubbing his chin seemed to help him come to a decision. "I'm hoping this open house helps me get rid of all the crap my uncle saddled me with, but there's something else. Someone's broken in at least once to look for something. I figure they broke in before I got here, too, which is how the cat got in. I thought if I opened my doors to the town I wouldn't have to worry about intruders anymore."

Lily frowned. "Jared's adventurous, but I've never known him to do anything dishonest. Did you hear what he said about Mrs. Yackley's coins?"

"Yep. It is possible someone else is searching for them."

Lily tipped her head. "You didn't report any break-ins."

"Because I can handle it on my own."

"Really." She gave him a dirty look. "You can say that, after all the grief you gave me for having that exact same attitude?"

He rolled his eyes to the ceiling. "There's no bigger zealot than a convert."

"Fine." She tucked her fingers behind her rig at the small of her back. "If you don't get rid of everything today, you may want to consider hiring someone to haul the rest away. You have a family to think of now, you know."

He shot her a startled glance. "Yeah, I guess I do." He reached around her and opened the door, his expression pensive. One step brought him close enough that she could feel the heat radiating from his chest, and it was all she could do not to curl into it.

"Lily..." he began, his voice constricted.

A noise at the door, and a choked exclamation. *"Lily!"*

She jerked at the rebuke and turned. Burke Yancey stood there looking as if he'd caught her playing with matches.

"Burke." Lily heaved an inward sigh. "What are you doing here?"

"I was on my way to the station," he said. Which made sense, considering he was wearing his firefighter T-shirt and work pants. He was also clean-shaven and smelling of limes, though the tightness of his mouth made it look as though he'd been sucking on them.

"Fulton," Burke said stiffly.

"Yancey," Vaughn replied, with that spoken-smirk thing again.

Lily kept her attention on the firefighter. "Were you looking for me?"

He nodded, his blue eyes lasering in on Vaughn. "I saw your cruiser outside. We never did get to talk about our date."

Here we go again. "We can talk now." Lily's smile felt stiff as she aimed it at Vaughn. "I know you have a lot on your plate. After Burke and I are done, I'll track down June and see how I can help."

Vaughn hesitated then gave her a curt nod. The moment he disappeared, Burke rounded on Lily. "I'm getting the impression we're already done."

Finally. "Burke. We never got started."

"Because you wouldn't give us a chance."

Her mother's gallbladder would explode if she knew Lily was rejecting not only a solid wage earner, but also a public protector with good looks to boot. But Lily's job was more than enough.

She would *make* it more than enough.

"I'm sorry," she said. "But I have made it clear. I'm not interested in being anything more than friends."

"But Wonder Boy out there." He jabbed a finger in the direction of the hallway. "You want more with him. What, I'm not young enough for you? Guys your age don't do it for you?"

When Lily blanched, he swung around and stomped out of the room.

She followed slowly, hoping Burke would stomp his way right out the front door. But no, that would be asking too much. Vaughn had been heading back their way, probably to ask them to take it outside, when he and Burke ended up chest-to-chest.

Avid onlookers crowded the doorways along the hall. Burke plucked a small notepad out of his back pocket, licked a finger and started flipping pages.

"You know how many fire codes you're violating here?"

Vaughn pressed a palm against the staircase. "I'm guessing at least one, since we're blocking the exit."

"This is not a joke, Deputy. One evaporated gallon of gasoline has the equivalent energy of fifty pounds of dynamite. How many gallons of flammables are you storing in this house? It's an arsonist's wet dream."

Lily flinched. There were kids in the house. "Language," she murmured.

"You're right." Vaughn straightened. "Fire is no joke. My uncle left behind cans of paint and thinner, and I came across a couple of containers of gasoline, but I got rid of all that first thing."

"Glad to hear it. Now I got another question for you. You know the absolute worst place for a fire to start in the home?" Burke pointed at the stairwell behind Vaughn. "You got all kinds of combustibles stacked under there."

"I'll get those moved right away."

"I should shut you down." Burke made a sweeping gesture with his notebook. "Get these people out of harm's way."

Disappointed moans and exclamations of outrage filled the corridor. Jared poked his head out of the dining room, spotted Lily and stared at her beseechingly.

Fudge.

She moved to Burke's side. "Won't you please reconsider? He's planning to move these boxes, and most of the rest of the…collection will probably be gone by the end of the day, anyway."

Vaughn shook his head. "The last thing I want to do is endanger anyone. If Burke thinks I should ask everyone to leave, I will."

The hostility in the firefighter's expression clung tight. "This whole idea was irresponsible. Your uncle should have known better."

"B. Yancey. VHS tapes." Hazel pulled up the flaps of the box she was leaning against, picked out a tape and pursed her lavender lips. *"Mighty Morphin Power Rangers,"* she said, and squinted down the hallway. "Burke Yancey, did this come from you?" She pointed to the two boxes beneath it. "And these?"

Burke paled. He scanned the faces lining the hall and shoved his notebook back into his pocket. "Smoke detectors functioning?"

Vaughn nodded. "Checked 'em the day I arrived."

"I'd like to inspect the other floors. See if there's anything else you need to worry about."

"Appreciate that."

They shook hands. Vaughn pointed out the door to the basement, Burke marched into the depths and Lily huffed a sigh of relief.

A low-pitched beeping sounded behind them. They turned to watch two teenage boys slink through the front door, one of them carrying a metal detector. Someone else who'd heard of Mrs. Yackley's coins?

Vaughn shook his head at the teens, who were elbowing each other and snickering as they aimed the detector at a curvy blonde in a short skirt. "Guess I'd better go nip that in the bud."

As she watched Vaughn walk away, Lily caught the gaze of Paige Southerly, the mayor's assistant and onetime girlfriend. Paige shifted a stack of paperbacks from her right hip to her left and strolled up to Lily. "So. You and the new deputy, huh?"

"No." Lily fought the urge to bite her lip. Was

her interest in him that obvious? "It's not like that." And it wasn't, even if she was starting to think she might want it to be. "Besides the fact that he works for me, he's much younger than I am. I would feel desperate."

"No, you wouldn't. Not at first." Paige set her books on a nearby box and shoved the sleeves of her lightweight cardigan up her forearms. "It's after the affair's over, when he's hanging out with women even younger than he is. That's when you feel desperate."

Lily grimaced. "I'm sorry. That was thoughtless of me."

Paige waved away her concern. "Rick wasn't too young for me, he just wasn't right for me. It was awkward after the breakup, working with him, but I didn't want to lose my job, too. I'm good at it. He'd be lost without me."

"We all would," Lily said.

Vaughn closed the front door behind the metal-detector teens and started past Paige and Lily on his way to the kitchen. Paige snagged the sleeve of his T-shirt. "You haven't by any chance come across any bags of candy or business swag, like those rubber coin holders you squeeze at both ends to open?"

Vaughn rested his hands on his hips and Lily had to rip her gaze away from the enticing play of muscles under his shirt. "I've seen a crap-load of pens and partially used notepads, but I couldn't tell you where," he said.

Paige's mouth turned down at the corners. "If you do find a stash of candy and office supplies, give me a shout, would you?"

"You bet."

"Vaughn Fulton, you get your butt in here." Hazel's voice floated down the hallway from the kitchen. "You know better than to leave a sandwich half-eaten. And why isn't there any fruit on your plate?"

He made a face. "You two should come grab a sandwich." He nodded at Lily. "You especially, since you brought 'em."

"Vaughn Fulton!"

With a roll of his eyes, he disappeared down the hall. Paige retrieved her books and headed toward the office. "I have time to search one more room. Mind giving me a hand?"

Half an hour later, after rifling through too many boxes to count, they still hadn't found what Paige was looking for.

"I'd talk smack about the mayor for going through your desk," Lily said, "but never in a million years would he give away candy."

"No, it was me." Breathing heavily, Paige pushed her dark blond hair away from her cheek. "Rick tore his desk apart looking for someone's business card and read me the riot act for not keeping him organized. I waited for him to leave, grabbed a box, marched over to his desk and started emptying drawers. That was two weeks ago and the only thing he noticed missing was the candy. I would have put it all back after I'd had a chance to cool down, but one of the clerks saw me with the box and offered to bring it over here. The mayor may not have missed anything, but there's an item or two I'd like to have back." She stood and stretched. "Lesson learned. I need to get home and let my dog out."

Vaughn came into the office as Paige was leaving. He thanked her for coming, and once she was gone, gave Lily a mock scowl. "You couldn't have talked her into taking more than a measly stack of paperbacks?"

"It's not like I'm working for commission," she said tartly.

"Good point. Speaking of pay, why don't you come get something to eat? You'll be glad you did if you get called out. I'll even share the last apple tart."

"No way I can refuse an offer like that," she said lightly. But as she followed him out of the room, Paige's words haunted her.

It's after the affair's over, when he's hanging out with women even younger than he is. That's when you feel desperate.

CLARISSA HADN'T BEEN on a date in a while. A long while. Not even the hurry-let's-get-naked kind of date. She missed sex, but she didn't miss the stress and disappointment and nasty surprises that came with dating. Not that it mattered, because if she ever hoped to dig herself out of the massive hole she'd gleefully flung herself into, she had to stick to her long-term plan.

It was dark inside that hole. Dark, and scary as hell. That made it easy to refuse those forever kind of invites.

Or it had, until Noble Johnson came along. Noble, with his spaghetti breath and lame jokes and intimidating size that made her feel safe and secure. Which was *not* a good thing because she had no intention of relying on anyone other than herself. And she *definitely* wasn't straying from her it's-all-about-me course.

Depending on someone else was like expecting the rain to hold off because you forgot your umbrella. Either way, you were doomed to disappointment. And if your hair didn't end up wet, your pillowcase did.

She set down her menu, folded her hands and stared across the table at her date.

Still. For the first time in a long while, Clarissa yearned to hold hands. To cuddle on the couch and share suggestive glances over the produce in the grocery store.

"I know what you're thinking," he rumbled without lifting his gaze. "Not the best-looking man I've gone out with. His nose is too big, his ears stick out and that shirt is so bright it makes his suit want to run screaming back into the closet."

Clarissa took a leisurely sip of her water. "I never noticed that your ears stick out."

"But the nose thing, right?"

"Meh." She offered a one-sided shrug. "I've seen bigger."

Suspicion narrowed his eyes as he regarded her over the top of his menu. She hid a smile and skimmed her gaze over the broad, broad shoulders of his gray suit jacket and the Caribbean-blue polo shirt he wore beneath it, then let it linger on what the open collar revealed—the lightly tanned hollow of his throat and the chaotic pulse that beat there.

"I'm nervous," he said gruffly. "You're only giving me one shot at this."

"I'm nervous, too. That I won't make it worth your while."

"You already have."

His words hit like a second glass of wine. Her spine relaxed, and she stopped second-guessing her outfit. She'd wanted to impress him, not tease him, so she'd bypassed anything with a low-cut bodice and settled instead on a grape sleeveless sheath she'd paired with chunky strands of multi-colored beads.

"You look like Mardi Gras," he said, and picked up his menu again.

Clarissa adjusted her glasses and studied her date's lowered head. Waited. In vain. He was totally focused on the page, trailing a finger down the section of entrees and muttering something that sounded like "marsala."

That was it? That was all he had to say? That she resembled a festival associated with binge drinking and naked breasts?

She was used to more intimate flattery. She was used to being the recipient of gravel-voiced whispers praising her hair and her lips and her—

Her shoulders met the back of her chair with a quiet thump. *Face it, chickie.* She was tired of what she was used to hearing. The words were the same and so was the sole objective—to gain admission to her bed. Noble's only motivation was to score a second date. Assuming he enjoyed the first one.

"Thank you," she said belatedly. "For the compliment."

Noble raised his head. "I'm sorry?"

"Your shirt is just right."

He flushed, and fumbled for the wine list.

While Noble placed their orders with a server in fabulous black heels—dear Lord, her feet must cry out for mercy at the end of every shift but that didn't stop Clarissa from craving a pair of her own—another server walked by with fresh-baked rolls. Clarissa barely refrained from plucking one from the basket as it passed.

There weren't many high-end eateries in Castle Creek, but Mama Leoni's was one of them. The restaurant was renowned for its extensive wine list, its manicotti and its yeast rolls, which were nearly as famous as the cinnamon rolls at Cal's Diner. Quietly, Clarissa hummed along with Dean Martin as "That's Amore" wafted out of hidden speakers while other diners talked in muted voices and silverware clinked against white ceramic plates. Maroon velvet wall hangings, gleaming wood tables and chandeliers dimmed to a quiet sparkle imbued the interior with a cozy glow.

Their exquisite-taste-in-footwear server walked by with someone's dessert and Clarissa nearly fell out of her chair. She whipped around to point out the towering slab of chocolate cake and the lust on Noble's face—aimed at her and not the cake—had Clarissa feeling a glow more carnal than cozy. It stretched from the top of her updo to the tips of her polished toes.

She pushed at her glasses. "You shouldn't look at me like that."

He gave her a lazy once-over. "You look like that—" he gestured at his face "—I look like this."

Clarissa swallowed. This was not going to end well.

Her jewelry clattered against the tabletop as she leaned toward Noble. "You're a lovely man, and I'm flattered by your interest. But I have a five-year plan and there's no room for romance. I'm not throwing down a challenge, I'm being honest. I don't do relationships."

"How many guys have had a problem with that?"

"What guy *would* have a problem? No-strings-attached sex? They were all over that. Literally." He didn't move a muscle, facial or otherwise, and she rolled her eyes. "Fine. So one or two figured they could change my mind. They were wrong. I got out of a bad marriage two years ago and I'm still paying for it, and I don't mean emotionally."

The server arrived with their wine. Noble remained silent while he went through the ritual of sampling then approving the Shiraz. The moment the server moved away, Noble pitched forward.

"Five years? It's going to take that long to erase the debt your asshole husband left you with?"

"The five years includes saving enough to get me where I want to go."

His face fell. "You're moving out of Castle Creek?"

"Not moving. Traveling."

"I see." He exhaled and picked up his wineglass. "To freedom, then."

Hot tears pricked at her eyes and Clarissa blinked furiously. He'd packed all her hopes and dreams into one word. The right word.

How had he known?

She pinned on a smile and returned his toast. "To freedom."

She couldn't bring herself to meet his gaze as she sipped. The wine coated her tongue with a slightly bitter richness that according to the label was supposed to carry overtones of blackberry and smoke, but Clarissa could taste only expectations.

Noble's expectations. She set down her wine and reached for her water.

"Tell me about freedom," he said. "Where will it take you first?"

"I haven't decided. I have a long list."

He tilted up the bread basket. "Name one place on your list and you can have your choice of roll."

"There's only one kind in there." She helped herself and shot him a coy glance. "Buy me dessert and I'll name two."

"Deal."

"England," she said. "More Yorkshire than London. I was a huge Gothic romance fan when I was a teen and I promised myself that someday I'd wander the moors."

"Wearing a pair of stout boots and carrying a walking stick."

She smiled. "Stopping at a local pub with low ceilings and stone floors and ordering bangers and mash."

"And a pint of Black Sheep."

"My fantasy usually runs to cider."

"What's next on your wish list?"

"Greece."

His gaze skimmed her bare arms. "You'd have to set aside one suitcase just for sunscreen." He traced the design on the wine bottle's label. "How long have you had a second job?"

"What?"

"When I called to set this up, we had a hard time agreeing on a night to go out. You weren't playing hard-to-get, so…" He shrugged. "Any place I might run into you?"

"Not unless you need a motel room some night in Erie. I work the reception desk at a Red Roof Inn." When his eyes flickered, she bristled. "What?"

"I know what it's like, is all. On the weekends I help out with a buddy's greenhouse business while he finishes up his final tour with the Army." He reached out and tapped a finger on the back of her hand. "You can't be getting enough sleep. I mean, how much obligation-free fun are we going to be able to have if you're always tired?"

She couldn't help a smile, even as regret tumbled through her. "I think we both know there won't be a second date."

"We do?"

"We're not even halfway through our first and you're already worrying if I'm getting enough sleep and how safe I am in that motel after dark."

He grunted. "You have a third job as a psychic?"

"This is supposed to be casual."

Noble shifted in his chair and threw his arm across the back. The movement put him off-center, so he looked ready to fall over. His suit jacket gaped open, revealing what looked like a grape-jelly stain on his shirt.

Clarissa fought the compulsion to lunge across the table and hug him.

"These guys you invite into your bed," he said. "They don't worry about you at all? Do they even bring their own condoms?"

So much for the hug. Clarissa shoved at her water and it pinged against her wineglass. Shiraz sloshed onto the table. "This." She threw down her napkin and the textured ivory turned red as it soaked up the spill. "This is what I swore to avoid."

"What, becoming the victim of common decency?"

She jerked to her feet. "I'll find my own way home."

"Like hell." He stood and thrust a finger at something behind her.

She turned to see their server with a full tray in her hands and pained curiosity on her face. Clarissa gave her a moue of apology.

"Don't you even want your eggplant rollatini?" Noble demanded. "It's exceptional. They chiffonade the basil."

Whatever the hell that meant.

"Fine," Clarissa snapped. "I'll take my meal to go. Please."

"Wrap mine up, too." Noble pushed in his chair and set his credit card on the tray. "We'll wait up front."

With a courtly sweep of his arm, he indicated Clarissa should go first. Head up, chin almost as high as her level of embarrassment, she led the way to the restaurant lobby. The server rushed toward them from the kitchen, a white plastic take-out bag in one hand and a credit card slip in the other. Noble signed the slip, thanked the server and opened the door for Clarissa.

She took two steps away from the entrance and swung back. "I'm so sorry," she said.

Without a word he headed for his minivan.

Clarissa followed at an awkward trot, barely able to keep up with his giant strides. She couldn't blame him for being angry. She'd embarrassed him. She'd embarrassed herself.

She was smart enough to know the sabotage had been inevitable. Caring about someone meant giving up her dreams.

And she could care about Noble Johnson. She could care a lot.

He pressed the button on his key fob. A cheerful double beep mocked the misery of an evening her defensiveness had ruined. A rush of wet heat behind her eyes warned that she was about to add to her humiliation.

Noble strode around to the passenger side. Another press of his key fob and the rear passenger door slid open, albeit with a creaking reluctance. He set the bag of food inside and turned, the yellowish glow from the streetlight behind him spilling over his shoulders. Out of a pale granite face, Nordic blue eyes glittered down at her. He was a good foot taller than she was, with muscles that would put a professional wrestler's to shame, and his jaw was rigid with fury. Yet it wasn't fear that had her swallowing. It was regret.

"Please forgive me," she said huskily. "Creating a scene in there was completely uncalled for. I'd feel so much better if you'd let me pay for my meal."

"You have no idea how this dating thing is supposed to work, do you?" He shifted closer. "I don't want your money."

Clarissa blinked. He didn't sound angry. Why didn't he sound angry?

"Noble," she said, faltering. "Are you...turned on?"

CHAPTER EIGHT

NOBLE PLANTED A palm against the minivan, to the left of Clarissa's head, and leaned in. "That was one of the sexiest damn things I've ever seen," he said, voice ragged. "You acting all condescending, throwing down your napkin like the challenge you pretend not to be. I'm going to kiss you now. You don't want my mouth on yours? Back away."

"Condescending?" she gasped. "*Me?* You're the one who—"

He pivoted his body so she was squeezed between him and his ride. The sudden press of his hard chest pulled a squeak from the back of her throat.

Wait was Clarissa's one clear thought, even as a belated thrill ran through her. Eyes wide, she watched his mouth approach. He didn't hesitate, didn't tease. Just took.

His lips were warm and firm and her eyes fluttered closed. Her gentle giant? Wasn't. His fingers tunneled into her hair, yanking in the process, and she yelped into his mouth. He groaned an apology and helped himself to her tongue. *There* was that heady taste of blackberries. Maybe she could learn to like Shiraz after all.

She slid her hands around his waist to his back, under his suit jacket. Beneath her palms, his shirt was damp with sweat. Her heart pinched at the same time her legs turned to water.

Oh, chickie. You are in so much trouble.

He ate at her mouth like a man starved and it was all she could do to keep up. When he finally dragged his face from hers they were both breathing harshly, eyes at half-mast, lips wet and raw. He gently disentangled his hands from her hair and when she realized he was shaking, she nearly reached for him again.

She stared at his thick wrist and the black scrunchie compressing the crisp, white-blond hairs. Absently, she raised a hand to the back of her head, where a slight bulge in her hair marked where the hair elastic used to be. The bobby pins were gone, too. So much for all the time she'd spent on her updo.

"How did that get there?" The sight of her scrunchie on his wrist unnerved her. His wearing it seemed…intimate.

He followed her gaze, pulled the band free and held it out. "I didn't want you to lose it."

"Thank you," she said. She scraped her hair into a ponytail, uncomfortable with the weight of his gaze. Reveling in the weight of his body.

"You look shell-shocked," he said. "Because

you weren't ready, or because you didn't expect to enjoy it?"

"Because I wasn't ready."

"I did warn you."

"And because I didn't expect to enjoy it that much."

When a pair of headlights swept over them, he shuffled back a step. "Next time, I won't warn you," he said.

"Next time?"

"Everyone deserves a second chance and I've decided to give you one."

"How generous of you."

"Isn't it?" He grinned. "Wherever we end up during take two, feel free to make a scene."

She swallowed a rebuke and trembled a laugh. "You're not what I expected, Noble Johnson."

He yanked on the door to close it. "I keep telling the guys I have depths."

"The guys?" She turned toward him, instinctively seeking his heat despite the warm summer air. "What guys?"

"Poker buddies."

"And what do they say about your depths?"

"That they hold more than their fair share of methane."

She made a face. "You have no idea how this dating thing is supposed to work, do you?" She poked his chest and pressed her shoulder blades back against the minivan. Yes, she was shameless. "And is that why you don't mind me making a scene? So word will get back to your poker buddies that you had a date?"

"I believe I made it perfectly clear how I feel about your dramatic side." He canted his head. "Need a reminder already?"

"As a matter of fact—" she lifted onto her toes, palmed the back of his neck and tilted his head downward "—I do."

LILY HESITATED AT the curb outside Vaughn's house, just as she had that morning. What did she think she was doing? He would see right through her excuse. Recognize the real reason she'd come back.

She was lonely. And worried. And as fickle as it made her, curious about what he'd been about to say before Burke Yancey walked into the laundry room.

What she really needed to do was go home, take a shower and go to bed. She'd snagged that sandwich at Vaughn's house but she'd only managed two bites before getting called downtown. A fault in the overhead sprinkler system resulted in the flooding of Eugenia Blue's dress shop. Lily had spent the rest of the day consoling a tearful Eugenia, mopping up water and helping her salvage what they could of her high-end merchandise.

Fresh, Lily was not. Still she wasn't in the mood to go home. She couldn't shake the image of Eugenia's face, or the misery in her eyes, which Lily suspected had more to do with the absence of the shop owner's on-again off-again beau Harris Briggs than with the disaster area her business had turned into.

And that made Lily wonder if Vaughn could use a dose of plain, old-fashioned sympathy.

Slowly she crossed the yard, every step a rebellion against common sense. But even if he weren't awake, even if she didn't get to see him, the rhythmic buzz of crickets and the sweet scent of honeysuckle were lovely, nostalgic distractions from the fact that she'd end her day in a house that echoed.

She wasn't even halfway up the sidewalk when he came outside and loped down the stairs. He'd changed into a pair of jeans and a soft white T-shirt—probably had taken a shower, too. She stopped. Not feeling fresh was sure to translate to not smelling fresh.

He hadn't bothered to turn on the outside lights, but the streetlamps cast enough of a glow that she could see his one-sided smile. "I was wondering whether you were going to come in."

"You've had a long day. I didn't want to disturb you." She took a step back. "And I just realized I smell like sweaty socks."

"Your pants are wet. What have you been up to?"

Briefly she explained about the dress shop.

Vaughn grimaced. "I'm sorry to hear that. At

least come sit on the porch for a minute." He slid a thin box from his back pocket and gave it a shake. "Come over here, little girl, and I'll give you some candy."

She laughed at the familiar bright pink-and-white box glinting in the light. Good & Plenty. "That explains why you always smell like licorice."

"My uncle got me hooked on these when I was a kid."

"I'm not a big fan."

"Try some." He shook the box again. "Your tastes may have changed."

His words sounded like a dare. She heaved a sigh and walked up, her hand out. He shook a small pile of the pink and white capsules into her palm and raised an eyebrow. She selected a pink one, put it on her tongue and bit down.

"No." She turned and spit it out, picked up his hand and emptied the rest of her stash into it. "Still not a fan."

"I can see that." He tossed the candy into his mouth and made *mmm-mmm* noises as he chewed.

She shook her head. "Any sign of your intruder?"

"No." He returned the box to his back pocket. "But my foolproof plan? Wasn't."

"What do you mean?"

"Someone unlocked the window in the downstairs bathroom."

"What are you going to do?"

"Lock it."

"But don't you want to know who's looking for what?"

Vaughn ran a hand over the back of his neck. "Between the job, the house and…some other stuff, I don't have the energy for a stakeout."

The phrase *some other stuff* made her feel lonely. And protective. And idiotic.

"Why don't you set up a camera? You may not catch them in the act, but—"

His shoulders straightened. "But I'll get them on tape. Or digital, or whatever."

"You can borrow what you need from the department. JD can set you up."

"Good idea. Thanks, Sheriff." He bent down and pressed his lips to her cheek.

Lily stilled.

The summer dark was lively. Tiny flashes of neon lit the way for chirrupy crickets and buzzing frogs, and somewhere nearby a dog barked and a car radio throbbed, but every noise and pulse of light in the entire neighborhood paled in comparison to what was happening inside Lily's chest.

She should back away.

Her muscles refused to cooperate.

Vaughn's mouth trailed a heady warmth from her cheek to her jaw. "I'm grateful for your help today," he murmured.

"If this is the way you thank people, I think I need to stop doing you favors."

"You think too much."

That gave her the strength to lean away. "That's a line. You think I'm so needy I wouldn't recognize that's a line?"

His eyes gleamed out of the shadows. "I think you're looking for any excuse to avoid intimacy."

"This is not something you're just finding out."

"No. But I thought you were getting used to the idea."

"Because we mopped together?" she sputtered.

"Because earlier today we admitted we want each other."

"I have to go."

He caught her hand as she swung away. The simple touch sent heat spiraling up her arm.

"You know," he drawled, "I could get called back to Erie any day now. Any minute now, my phone could ring. You and I…we might never see each other again."

She tugged her hand free. "Let me guess. We should seize every opportunity to express our feelings for each other."

"Right on." He eyed her warily. "Unless those feelings will lead to violence." When that didn't get a reaction, he narrowed his gaze. "Aren't you curious?"

"Extremely. But it's not worth the risk. Anyway, it's not as if you're going off to war."

He snorted. "You've never patrolled the lower east side."

"This leave of absence is about more than your promise to your uncle, isn't it?"

A shadow drifted across his face and she held her breath. If he insisted on share and share alike, she'd simply walk away. Instead he slogged over to the porch and sank down onto the steps. Rested his forearms on his knees and dangled his hands in between.

"I'm being investigated," he said. "By IA."

Lily sucked in a breath and plopped down beside him, her back against the wooden spindles that climbed each side of the stairs. "What happened?"

"My partner. Faith. She happened." He wiped his mouth, as if wanting to rub away the taste of her name. "She was a good cop. An honest cop. But the discrimination, the sucky pay and the repeat customers we hauled to booking got her down. She made some bad choices, including getting engaged to a cop on the take. After that, she stopped making good choices, period. I'm not trying to excuse her, just…she had two kids and a bad influence whispering in her ear about giving them a better life. When I realized what was happening, I tried to talk her into turning herself in. She couldn't face the fallout."

"She put you in a terrible position."

He shrugged. "Her boyfriend got suspicious, figured we were having an affair and bugged our patrol car. When he heard me start to bring her around, he decided to be the first to work a deal. Set me up as the snitch. Things got tense."

"You mean you were being threatened. That's why they sent you away." She folded her arms and leaned forward, pressing against her knees. "Your unit just turned on you like that?"

"The whole damn division turned on me."

"You didn't do anything."

"I would have." He leaned back on his elbows and stretched out his legs. "I waited too long as it was."

"So they're gathering evidence against the fiancé?"

"Yeah. They'll call me when they're ready for me."

Lily balanced her chin between her palms. "You should sound bitter."

"Because of what my unit did?" He shook his head. "That's on me. I was senior. I should have caught it sooner. Turned her around sooner."

"I get that. But you wouldn't be fighting this guilt if Faith hadn't gone on the take in the first place."

His lips quirked. "Every single person who's

heard this story has tried to talk me out of that guilt."

"Which probably makes you want to hold on to it that much tighter."

He hummed in agreement. They sat silently for a while, the honeysuckle-scented dark curling around them. Emboldened by the shadows, Lily let her gaze drift over Vaughn's rumpled hair, his muscled biceps and chest, his flat belly and strong thighs.

She gripped the tops of her knees as she pictured herself sliding along the step, bracing her hands on his shoulders and easing onto his lap. Digging her nails into his skin. Pressing the ache between her legs to the hot hardness between his.

A shimmering warmth burst inside her and spread outward. She opened her mouth in a vain attempt to steady her breathing. If only she were wearing a skirt instead of her uniform. Something silky and sheer. And short, so she wouldn't have to tug much to pull it up over her—

"See anything you like?" he asked softly.

She jerked upright and smacked her head on the railing. "The stars," she gasped. "They're so bright."

His deep chuckle should have ticked her off. Instead it made her shudder. First with need, then self-reproach.

Still a hypocrite, Lily Anne.

She straightened. She should leave the poor

man alone. He had to be exhausted. Still, she couldn't bring herself to pop the cozy bubble they'd created. She slid her palms up and down her thighs. "You must be looking forward to being back on the job."

He remained quiet. Thinking about his response, or trying to figure out why she wasn't willing to get physical? No. He wouldn't sweat it. There were too many women out there who *would* be willing.

"Yeah. I do want to get back out on the street. And despite everything, the Erie PD is more my family than my own is."

He crossed his ankles with a jarring thump, and Lily ached for him. She knew what it was like to yearn for a closeness that always seemed just out of reach. Then again, she'd probably be closer to her mother if she actually followed up on her plans to visit.

He turned his face toward hers, and his gaze roved her features. "That troubled expression of yours have anything to do with me?"

"Mostly me. A little you."

"Maybe someday you'll tell me more." He must have sensed she wanted to squash that hope like a bug because he didn't give her a chance to respond. "What made you want to be a cop?"

"My grandfather was one."

"So he inspired you to be a cop, just like him?"

"Not just like him. Not anything like him, actually." She shifted on the step. "You know that stereotype of a country cop who parks his car in a secluded spot, checks in every hour with a bogus status and spends the day napping and eating junk food? And when he pulls someone over, it isn't necessarily because they did anything wrong but because he's in the mood to ruin someone's day? That was my grandfather. He could be a sweetheart, but when he and my grandmother were on the outs, he could also be a bastard."

"Napping and eating all day, huh? I wouldn't mind trying that for a while."

"He was three hundred pounds when he died."

"Whoa. Well, I'd say you've more than redeemed your family name." When she gave a skeptical grunt, he twisted around to look up at her. "What?"

"That's awfully nice of you, considering everything I've put you through."

"I'm a nice guy."

"Okay, nice guy. Your turn. What inspired you to wear the uniform?"

He turned away again and gazed toward the house across the street. The windows were all dark except for the last one on the left. Behind the blinds a random fluctuation of light indicated someone was watching late night TV.

"I knew from an early age I wanted to be a cop," he said. "We had a lot of crime in our neighborhood. My parents owned a little hole-in-the-wall pizza place and my dad offered free meals to the local police so there'd often be one or two cops hanging around." He missed those days, before his folks became rich and snooty.

"And you decided to do your part to make the neighborhood safer."

"I was also a bit of a rebel."

"You." This time she had to fake her gasp. "I don't believe it."

Across the street, the light from the television vanished. Somewhere, an AC unit kicked off. The neighborhood quieted.

Time to go, Lily Anne.

She stood, and winced at the stretch of over-worked muscles. Keeping her back to the railing, she slowly worked her way down to the cement path. "If you could change anything about your job, what would it be?"

"That's easy," he said. "I already put in for a transfer to our detective division. If I stick with patrol too long, I'll end up behind a desk."

"And your parents win?"

He sat up. "What do you mean?"

"Your face, when you talked about your parents and being a cop. I got the impression they don't approve."

He exhaled. "They insist I can do better."

"God save us from well-meaning parents."

"Sounds like you have two of your own."

"Just one. But it feels like two."

He pushed to his feet and descended the two steps to the sidewalk. "She didn't want you to be a cop?"

"Actually, she's okay with the cop thing. She'd just rather I work for a department with a bigger dating pool. Go figure."

One corner of his mouth kicked up as he tucked his hands under his armpits. "Your Jersey accent gets stronger when you talk about your mom."

"I don't have an accent."

"My ass. That's like saying the Catletts don't wear makeup."

"Shh." She smacked his arm. "They'll hear you."

She squinted through the dark at the house next door. No sign of little old ladies, though they could be on the other side of the plank fence, spying through a knothole.

The thought creeped her out, and made it easier to finally head back to her cruiser.

FRAYED BANDS OF violet and orange filtered softly through the gray as dawn crept up and over the lake. Lily drove with her window down, enjoying the peach-scented breeze tossing hair she rarely more than finger-combed, anyway. The morning chill blew goose bumps across her arms, but she knew in a matter of hours, she'd be grateful for her short sleeves.

She crested a hill and spotted the reason she

hadn't had time for her morning coffee. He was leaning against the door of his cruiser, arms crossed, designer shades riding the end of his nose. When she stopped beside him and lowered the passenger-side window, he pushed away from his car and bent to peer into hers.

"You break it, you buy it," she drawled.

Vaughn rested his arms on the door and raised both eyebrows.

"Stop looking at me like that," she said. "And why are you even wearing sunglasses?"

With a heavy exhale, he opened the car door and dropped into the passenger seat. "Good morning to you, too."

She grinned as she lifted her foot off the brake. "It's not my fault the thing broke down."

"Thanks for coming to get me," he said grumpily. He fastened his seat belt, tucked his shades into his shirt pocket and raised the window. "The tow truck's coming, but I haven't had my coffee yet."

"Me, either. When we get to the station, I'm buying."

She could feel his frown. "Sometimes I think you enjoy scrounging for supplies and working extra hours just to keep things—" He half turned in his seat and stared her down. "Son of a bitch. That's it, isn't it? The more indispensable you are, the longer hours you need to keep and the less time you have to think about whatever happened in your past that no one wants to tell me about."

"It wasn't a *whatever*. It was a tragedy. And no one has said anything because it doesn't have anything to do with you."

She lowered the window the rest of the way, needing the blast of air to cool her resentment. Needing the noise, too, to drown out her passenger.

She'd been actually looking forward to riding with this jerk?

"You're right," he said, almost shouting so she could hear him over the sound of rushing air. "I'm a dick. I'm sorry. For being passive-aggressive, but not for caring about you."

Lily raised the window and tugged her hair back down over her left ear. Her hands flexed on the steering wheel and she shifted in her seat. Decided to go for it, despite being low on caffeine.

"Okay, can we just…clear the air?"

"Good idea." Vaughn turned to face her again. "You first."

"Me?" she squealed. "Why me?"

His grin was grudging. "That's an octave I don't think I've heard from you before." He went quiet then, and when Lily glanced his way and saw that his eyes had turned dark as a pocket, she knew exactly what he was thinking.

God save her.

"Fine. I'll go first." Her gaze slid to his mouth

before darting back to the road. "You were going to kiss me yesterday. That would have been bad."

"No, Lily. It would have been good. Very, very good."

She slapped a palm against the steering wheel. "*How* do you know it would have been good? How can you go all dreamy-eyed and low-voiced when you don't even know what kissing me would be like?"

"Is that an invitation?"

The rising sun dripped yellow light across the rows of grapevines bordering both sides of the road. Even before the brightness climbed the windshield, she felt its warmth. Then the pitch of the road changed, the tires humming loudly over new pavement. Like a warning.

Her heart had basically been in storage for two years. Wasn't it time for some fresh air?

"Lily?"

A glance at the speedometer had her easing off the accelerator. Too fast. Much like whatever was happening between her and Vaughn.

"I want to say no." *You haven't felt this rush in so long.* "Or if I say yes, I want to blame my subconscious for it." *Get to the point.* "The truth is, I do want to kiss you."

He muttered a swearword. "You couldn't have told me this last night?"

"Last night I smelled like gym socks."

"Pull over."

She shook her head. "I promised my crew. No more poor decisions on the job. Besides, we're on patrol. A special mission for the mayor. He's expecting us. His lake property is attracting a lot of litter and even a campfire or two and—"

"Lily."

"Vaughn. You know I'm already in hot water with him. What if someone from the town council happens to drive by while we're making out on the side of the road? I haven't even had my coffee, for God's sake."

"Okay, then. You'll make your poor decisions off the clock." He said something under his breath and shifted in his seat. "And at the end of our shift we can look forward to getting off together."

A blast of sparkling heat streaked through Lily, and she jerked the wheel. Gravel pinged against the undercarriage. She bit back a filthy word and maneuvered the car back onto the road.

"Stop that," she growled. "We were talking about a kiss."

"There are all kinds of kisses."

Oh, dear God. She was floundering for a comeback, her brain sputtering on empty, when she spotted a flash of lavender on their right.

"What is that?" She leaned forward and squinted through the windshield. Sucked in a breath and hit the brakes. "Vaughn."

He was already shoving out of his seat belt. "Jesus," he breathed. "It's a kid."

CHAPTER NINE

"OH, NO," LILY CHOKED. "Oh, God."

The child—a girl, judging from the scraggly ribbons of butter-blond hair shielding her face—lay unmoving on her side, her back to the road.

Vaughn was out of the car and running before she'd come to a complete stop. Lily slammed the cruiser into Park and sprinted after him. He squatted beside the girl, smoothed the hair from her face and touched two fingers to her neck.

Lily dropped to her knees in the grass slick with dew, panic burning a hole in her lungs. When Vaughn finally nodded, she gently palmed the girl's back and allowed herself one quick sob of relief as she felt the unmistakable rise and fall.

"Pulse steady." Vaughn scanned the girl from head to toe. "No sign of trauma, but we'd better not move her until the EMTs take a look." He raised his head. "Good eye. We almost drove right by her."

The hint of torment in his voice made her reach out. He met her halfway, and they briefly clasped fingers before turning their attention back to the girl who lay silent between them.

Vaughn shifted to his knees, leaned forward and stroked the girl's cheek. "Hey," he said gently. "Wake up, cupcake."

Her face and neck were pink from sun exposure, her jeans and lavender T-shirt wrinkled and damp. Her clothes were a size too small, and her tennis shoes had seen better days.

"She looks to be about seven or eight." *Elodie would have been seven*. "Where did she come from?" Lily jerked her chin toward the distant glass-front house situated above the vineyards. "I know not from there. The owners don't have any children."

"Got a jacket?"

With a nod, she stood. "I'll have Clarissa send the rescue squad and find out if anyone's reported a missing child."

She strode toward the cruiser, shaking fingers pressed against her lips. When she'd first spotted the girl, she hadn't had any idea whether she was alive or dead. With Elodie she'd known. One dread-filled glimpse and she'd simply been able to tell. It hadn't stopped her from hoping. But hope hadn't lasted long.

After radioing Clarissa, she popped open the trunk and grabbed the navy hoodie she kept there. A gleaming black pickup truck crested the hill facing her and slowed as it approached. Lily lifted a concrete arm and waved it by. The engine growled with disappointment as the truck sped away.

Lily hurried back to the child's side and covered her with the hoodie. The fabric reached from her neck to her shins. "Rescue's on the way."

Vaughn nodded and continued to stroke the girl's face. When his eyes went soft, Lily knew she'd woken.

"Hey, there," Vaughn said, his voice a placid mix of cheerfulness and reassurance. "What's your name, cupcake?"

A grubby hand appeared from beneath the sweatshirt. The girl shoved at her hair and rubbed at her eyes, and her lower jaw dropped to make way for a sleepy yawn. She blinked at Vaughn and pushed up onto her elbow.

"I'm Deputy Vaughn, and this is Sheriff Lily."

The girl swung her chin toward Lily, and her walnut eyes went wide. "I'm surrounded," she whispered.

Vaughn dropped his head to hide a smile, but Lily noted the real fear in the child's eyes. Slowly she raised her hands. "You know what? I think I'll go stand over there, and give you a chance to talk with Deputy Vaughn. He's had a rough morning. I'm sure he could use a friend."

The girl watched closely as Lily moved away several paces, though Lily was careful to remain within hearing range in case Vaughn needed anything. The girl rubbed her nose with the back of her hand and pushed to a sitting position.

"Easy." Vaughn put out his hands, as if to prop her up. "How are you feeling? Are you hurt?"

She shook her head.

"Cold?"

A nod.

"Can I help you put that sweatshirt on?"

She considered, then offered another nod.

With deliberately unhurried motions that reminded Lily of Mayor Whitby, Vaughn eased the hoodie over the child's head, helped her find the sleeves and rolled them up a good half-dozen times before her hands poked through. She struggled to her feet and yawned again.

"Feel like telling us your name?" Vaughn remained on his knees, but straightened his back. "Or should I keep calling you cupcake?"

The girl's gaze locked onto his equipment belt. "You going to cuff me?"

"No. What makes you think I would do that?"

She shrugged and rubbed a knuckle over one eye. Her lips started to shake. "I said I had to g-go to the bathroom," she whimpered. "He stopped the car and let me out and before I was finished he d-drove away."

Lily clenched her teeth together while Vaughn's nostrils flared. *What kind of man would*—her head jerked toward the road. The black truck.

The girl's father? Had Lily chased away the man responsible for dumping a child on the side of the road?

"Who did?" How Vaughn managed to keep his voice calm, Lily would never know. "Who drove away?"

Her eyes darted from Vaughn to Lily and back again. "Lenny. My mom's boyfriend."

Lily took a step closer. "What does Lenny drive?"

"A big blue car."

Panic started to wind its way through Lily, leaving cold in its wake. What if they weren't able to identify this child? What if something had happened to her mother?

Vaughn gave Lily an odd look as he rose. He brushed at the grass stains on his knees. "What was your mom doing when Lenny drove away?"

"I think she was sleeping."

"When did this happen, cupcake?"

She tucked each hand into the opposite sleeve and crossed her arms. "My name is Miranda."

Vaughn gave a solemn nod. "Can you tell us your last name?"

She rolled her eyes. "I am almost in the second grade."

Lily smiled, even as her heart contracted. She risked moving a few steps closer. "So that makes you what, seven years old?"

"Uh-huh. My last name is Oakes. *O-a-k-e-s.* My middle name is May."

"That's pretty," Lily said. "Were you born in May?"

She shook her head. "November."

Vaughn took up the questioning. "Do you live here in Pennsylvania?" A nod. "Do you know your address?"

"We don't live in our house anymore. We live in an apartment."

"How about your old address? Maybe your neighbors know where your mom is."

"Mr. Wilkinson might. My mom said he made it his business to know everything." She coughed. "May I have something to drink?"

"I'll get you some water." Kicking herself for not thinking of it sooner, Lily hurried back to the cruiser and grabbed a plastic bottle of water from the cooler in the trunk. Miranda would probably be hungry, too. She took a quick inventory of the lunch she'd packed herself—turkey sandwich, dill pickle, banana—and returned with the water in time to hear Vaughn repeat his earlier question.

"When did Lenny drive away?"

"Yesterday."

Lily squeezed her eyes so tight, orange lights exploded behind her lids. She blinked them open and saw that Vaughn's eyes had gone hard.

He gave himself a moment by turning in a slow

circle, as if inspecting the ground. "You slept here last night?"

Miranda accepted the bottle of water Lily had opened for her and swallowed several mouthfuls. When she lowered the bottle, water dripped from her chin and made dark blotches on the hoodie. She pointed down the road toward a grove of pine trees.

"Over there. I got up because I heard a noise. I started walking again, but I got tired."

"Is that where Lenny dropped you off?"

With a shake of her head, she lifted a foot to show him her mud-encrusted shoes. "I walked a lot. Miles and miles, probably."

He reached out a hand and lightly touched her hair. Miranda didn't flinch. "You're a brave girl," Vaughn said.

"Just hungry. Got any cupcakes?"

"Not on me, but I can get you one."

"In the meantime," Lily said, "how about a turkey sandwich? Or a banana?"

Miranda unlaced her arms and flopped them so that the sleeves drooped over her hands. "I like bananas."

"Me, too." Vaughn gave Lily a surreptitious thumbs-up. "Why don't we all head over to the squad car? You can sit on something more comfortable than the hard ground while you eat your banana. Sound good?"

Miranda looked doubtfully toward the cruiser. "Am I under arrest?"

"No, Miranda." Lily kneeled and gestured at her sleeves, wanting to roll them up again for her. The little girl hesitated, then turned and walked to Vaughn, arms extended. Vaughn shot Lily an apologetic glance. She bit the inside of her cheek, frustrated by the sting of rejection it was ridiculous to feel.

"We are taking you to the police station with us," she said huskily, "but only because we want to help."

"But how will my mom find me? She won't know where to look for me."

"You let us worry about that. We've got your back." Vaughn finished with her sleeves and guided her toward the car. "Let's get you that snack."

Miranda balked. "I just remembered. I'm not supposed to talk to strangers." Her liquid gaze traveled from Vaughn to Lily to the squad car. "And I'm never supposed to get into their car."

Lily mentally applauded the girl's absent mother. "I bet your mom taught you that you can trust the police."

Miranda nodded. "And firemen," she whispered.

"Right." Vaughn tapped the gold five-pointed star over his left shirt pocket. "We're police and we have badges. So you can trust us."

Finally Miranda agreed to sit in the car, but

only if they left the door open. She sat sideways, thin legs dangling above the grass as she chewed dainty mouthfuls of banana while Vaughn kept an eye out for the rescue squad and Lily entered notes on her smartphone. After Miranda finished the banana, she painstakingly rolled the peel into a tight ball and tucked it into the hoodie's front pocket. Lily's throat swelled.

She looked down at her cell, then back up at Miranda, and gave herself a mental eye roll. Slowly she strolled toward the car. "Miranda, did you have a phone when you got out of the car?"

The little girl shook her head.

Fudge. "Do you know your mom's phone number? Or a relative's number?"

"She taught it to me, but I can't remember." She drew up her knees and wrapped her arms around them tight enough to leave marks.

Lily itched to haul her into a hug. "That's okay," she said. "We'll figure it out."

Vaughn backed away from the shoulder and joined them on the far side of the cruiser. "The ambulance is here."

The vehicle's engine rumbled loudly. Miranda shrank against the backseat as the ambulance maneuvered to a stop just beyond Lily's patrol car.

"That's for me?" she asked, in a small voice. The rear doors banged open and she jumped. "But I thought we were going to the police station. I don't want to go to the hospital."

"You may not have to. Let's see what these guys have to say, okay?"

Lily watched, impressed, as Vaughn coaxed Miranda into the rear of the ambulance. Vaughn and the two EMTs made a game of it—she'd point to a piece of equipment, they'd tell her the name and she had to guess whether or not it was real. Considering they were using words like *burbledrome* and *ferfflekemper*, it wasn't hard for Miranda to figure out which names they'd made up.

But the girl's smile disappeared when the verdict was announced—Miranda was dehydrated enough that the EMTs wanted to take her in. She slouched on the ambulance's shiny aluminum bumper, chin to chest, arms crossed, refusing to move.

"Don't you want to feel better?" Vaughn perched beside her and patted her grass-stained knee. "Take a shower, wash your hair, put on some silly jammies, eat a cupcake and watch cartoons?"

"I don't have any jammies."

"You don't have a cupcake, either, but I promised I'd get you one, right? What kind of silly jammies do you want?"

With a wince, Lily mirrored Miranda's pose and leaned against the hood of her cruiser. One thing being a parent taught you—never make a promise to a kid if you weren't sure you could deliver.

Miranda peeked up at Vaughn through her tangled blond hair. "I like unicorns."

"I'll see what I can do. In case they don't have unicorns, what's your favorite color?"

"Purple," she said immediately.

He glanced up at Lily and she had to smile at the smart-ass gleam in his eyes. Apparently he knew a thing or two about kids.

"So," he said, "you'll go to the hospital and let the nurses spoil you rotten?"

"Will you go with me?" she asked in a tiny voice.

Vaughn lifted an eyebrow at Lily, and she nodded.

As one of the EMTs hopped from the back of the ambulance, the other winked at Miranda and patted the gurney. Vaughn lifted the little girl up and over the bumper, then climbed in after her. The first EMT shut and latched the door and headed for the driver's seat. Gravel crunched as the vehicle pulled away.

Stiffly, Lily pushed away from the hood of her car and tugged her keys from her pocket. The hospital was the very last place she wanted to be, and she had a hard time relating to kids. Little girls especially had the ability to make her want to crawl into a corner and weep.

Still, she wished, harder than she'd wished for anything in a long time, that she was the one Miranda had asked to go with her.

Two hours later, Lily parked in the hospital lot, drained the rest of her takeout coffee and called Vaughn on her cell.

He picked up right away. "Where are you?"

"In the parking lot."

"Come on up."

"I'd rather you come down."

He exhaled. "Is this you being bossy, or you being nervous about hospitals?"

How did he *do* that? "How do you know I'm not just being lazy?" His silence was one big eye roll. "Fine." With a *thump*, Lily dropped her head back against the headrest. "I have a thing about hospitals."

"Sorry to hear it. That sucks. Get your ass up here."

She jerked upright, scaring an old man who was limping past the car. He stumbled to the left, sent her a scowl and lurched into motion again.

"I need you to stay with Miranda," Vaughn said. "If I don't produce a pair of unicorn jammies and a cupcake soon, she's going to start crying. I don't like it when they cry."

"Women often cry when you're near?"

"This time it won't be tears of gratitude."

Lily made a rude noise and reached for the ignition. "I'll run your errands for you."

"I'm the one who made the promise."

"Fine." She pulled her keys from the ignition and clutched them tightly. "What's her room number?"

Ten minutes later, Lily met Vaughn outside Miranda's hospital room. The orange and green stripes on the walls, the oversized daisy decals on the floor and the huge half-moon fish tank that doubled as a reception desk were all painfully familiar. So were the smells of pine cleaner and Play-Doh, and the sounds of children's cartoons. And that incessant mechanical beeping.

As Vaughn closed Miranda's door behind him, Lily was gritting her teeth so hard her jaw ached.

His gaze roved her face. "You okay?"

Suck it up, Lily Anne. This isn't about you.

"Fine. What's the story?"

"They've admitted her. They want to keep her overnight for observation."

"How'd she take it?"

"Better than I expected." He scowled. "The EMTs were right about the dehydration, and she's underweight. Maybe she or her mother suffered some recent trauma. Maybe she's been neglected. As far as how she ended up on the side of the road, either the boyfriend forced the mom to leave the kid behind…"

"Or the mom slept through it and when she wakes up, she's going to be some kind of freaked out." Lily nodded at a wide-eyed kid wearing Batman pajamas. He was pushing a rolling IV, keeping his head turned toward her and eyeing her gun until he disappeared around a corner.

She wrapped her hands around her equipment

belt. "JD asked the city police to check out Miranda's old address. Told them to talk to Mr. Wilkinson. The number associated with the address is no longer in service, so Clarissa's trying to identify her cell phone provider."

"Anybody call CWS?"

Child Welfare Services. Lily nodded. "I did," she said huskily.

Vaughn squeezed her shoulder. "They fed her breakfast, so she shouldn't be hungry. I'll be back as soon as I can. Anything I can get you while I'm out?"

She tossed him her keys. "My turkey sandwich from the trunk."

After watching him stride away, she slunk into the room. The happy-face curtains were closed, so the light was dim, brightened by occasional flashes of color from the muted TV mounted just below the ceiling in the corner. Miranda was sleeping on her side under a yellow blanket, hands stacked beneath her cheek. Someone had brushed her hair, and the blond strands lay like scattered silk on the pillow. Lily reached out, then curled her fingers and turned away. She eased into the cushy recliner across from the TV, leaned her head back and watched a soundless SpongeBob SquarePants flip Krabby Patty burgers.

Her stomach growled, and Miranda woke. Lily hoped her smile wasn't as feeble as it felt.

Four episodes of *SpongeBob SquarePants*, three

rejected offers to play Go Fish and thirteen que-
ries about Vaughn's whereabouts later, Lily's cell
rang. She answered as if letting it go to voice mail
could very well mean the end of the free world.

"Tate here."

"Everything okay?" asked a deep voice.

She glanced at the bed, where Miranda was
eating her lunch off a tray, eyes trained on Lily.
She didn't smile, but she didn't stick out her
tongue, either.

Lily pushed upright. "Everything's fine," she
said. "Miranda's eating macaroni and cheese,
I'm finishing up a granola bar from the vending
machine and we're both—" she turned her head
and spoke in a whisper "—wondering where the
hell you are."

Vaughn grunted. "I'm sorry. You're going to
have to hang out a while longer."

"Why?" she almost whimpered.

"A real domestic this time. A woman in the
apartment complex on Seneca called it in. I'm on
my way there. Not sure what I'll find, so I wanted
to give you a heads-up."

She stood and winced at the stiffness in her
muscles. "JD going to back you up?"

"He's on his way."

"Keep me posted."

"Will do. Oh, and Sheriff?"

"Hang in there," he was probably going to say,
or "keep your chin up," or some other silly plati-

tude that was certain to make him feel better than it would her. "Yes, Deputy?"

"Excellent turkey sandwich." He disconnected.

Lily stared at her phone. "He ate my sandwich." The jerk.

"When is Vaughn coming back?"

Slowly, Lily turned to Miranda, bracing herself for a tantrum. "Not for a while, I'm afraid. He had to go make sure someone is okay."

"Is he going to arrest anyone?"

"Possibly." She thumbed through her contacts until she got to Clarissa's name. "You can ask him when he gets back."

"You're leaving?"

Lily's head snapped up. Had that been alarm she'd heard?

What do you think it was? Just because she doesn't like you doesn't mean she wants to be alone.

"I have things to do back at the station," she said carefully. "I was going to ask a friend of mine to come keep you company."

"Like eating?"

"What?"

"One of the things you have to do. Is it eating? Because Vaughn took your sandwich?" The girl's hair fell in her eyes as she rummaged on her tray and held up her pudding. "You can have this. Chocolate isn't even my favorite. That way you don't have to go."

Lily took a moment to let her heart melt, then slid her phone back into her pocket. "Thank you, Miranda. That's very sweet of you. You keep the pudding, though. I'll have Vaughn bring some more, since he ate my sandwich."

"Does that mean you're not leaving?"

"That's right. I'm not leaving."

Miranda smiled, revealing a gap between her front teeth. She peeled back the plastic wrap, shoved her spoon in and hesitated. "Lily?" Her voice trembled.

Lily moved to the bed. "What's wrong, Miranda?"

She gave a huge, wet sniff. "Did he eat my cupcake, too?"

WHEN VAUGHN WALKED into the hospital room, he felt like a husband sneaking into the house after playing all-night poker. But no one screamed or sobbed or threw a frying pan at his head.

Talk about anticlimactic.

Hands in his pockets, he stood at the foot of Miranda's bed. She was fast asleep, both arms flung over her head. He stared at the sweet purse of her lips and the steady rise and fall of her ribs, and a wistful warmth spread to every corner of his chest. He transferred his gaze to Lily, who sat sideways in the recliner, legs draped over one arm.

The good news? She was asleep, too.

The bad news? He had to wake her.

After setting the box and bag on the bed, he moved to the chair, braced his hands on the arms and leaned in, taking in the soft swell of her cheek, the thick curves of her lashes, the slight bump in her nose. And her scent. Cinnamon. He inhaled, and a quick shudder of need pushed him away again. He stepped back and murmured her name. Again, louder this time.

She shot upright, blinking away sleep. He grinned at the flush that stained her skin, and she glowered.

"Don't look at me like that. It was either fall asleep or shoot the TV." She glanced at Miranda, then at the dark beyond the window, then back at Vaughn. Her eyes narrowed. "What time is it?"

"Nine."

"Nine?" She launched from the chair, winced at its squeaking protest and peered again at the bed. Miranda lay oblivious. Lily passed a hand over her forehead. "Where have you been?"

"The domestic got complicated. Then I had a report to write, then I got another call, a complaint about noise at the public landing. A bunch of teens decided to spend their Sunday night skinny-dipping."

"I assume alcohol was involved."

"Yeah." He scratched his chin. "About that…"

"Oh, no," she groaned softly. "And you had my car."

"I cleaned up the worst of it. I'll take it home with me and finish up first thing in the morning."

She studied his face and nodded her thanks. "I'm sorry. I shouldn't complain. You've had a long day, too."

Back away from the female. Keep your hands where I can see them, and back slowly away.

He obeyed his conscience, if only because Lily wouldn't respond well to finding herself yanked into a full-body clinch.

He cleared his throat. "Everything okay here?"

"Fine. Well, other than an unhealthy addiction to inane cartoons and chocolate pudding. She slept most of the afternoon. Couldn't even talk her into a game of Candy Land."

The defeat in her voice just about wrecked him.

"Come with me." He jerked a thumb at the door. "I've got a sandwich for you out in the car." When she screwed up her face, he held up a hand. "It's in the trunk. No possible cross-contamination with teen puke."

She blinked up at him, the bruises under her eyes making his chest ache. "What, was it too heavy to carry inside? One of Snoozy's meatball masterpieces, maybe?" She pressed a hand to her stomach. "Actually, that sounds good."

"You need to take a break, even if it's a short one. Let's go for a walk."

Her head had already taken up a slow wag.

"I'm not leaving her alone. I'm not letting her wake up alone. I promised."

"Lily—"

"I'll stay with her," said a quiet voice.

They both glanced over at the doorway.

A middle-aged nurse with close-cropped black hair stood just inside the room, a rolled-up magazine in her hand, a yellow insulated lunch tote tucked under her opposite arm. Her dark blue scrubs hung loosely on her body, as if she'd recently lost weight.

"I don't mind," she said. "I just got off shift, so no one will be looking for me. Don't take too long, though, because there's a queen-size bed with fresh sheets calling my name." She moved into the room, her eyes on Miranda's thin face. "Still, I don't mind pretending not to hear it for another thirty minutes or so. Especially for this sweet baby." She glanced up. "I'm Nadine, by the way."

Vaughn didn't give Lily a chance to argue. He grabbed her hand and flashed a smile at the nurse. "Thanks, Nadine. We'll be back in twenty."

As soon as the elevator doors closed behind them, Lily flexed her fingers. "You can let go now," she said. "I won't make a break for it."

He heard the amusement in her voice, but he heard a trace of wistfulness, too. Because she wanted to stay with Miranda, or because she liked holding his hand? That second thought sent his gut into a queasy little free fall.

Don't be a dick. This isn't about you.

Reluctantly he released his hold. "Fine," he said. "But don't think I won't haul out the cuffs."

"Don't be ridiculous," she said briskly, and just like that, Sheriff Tate was back.

When they stepped beyond the automatic double doors, she lifted her face to the night sky and breathed deep. "I can smell the lake," she murmured.

He stared at her profile in the shadows, at the sweet shape of her ear, partly covered by strands of dark hair lifted by the breeze. At the imperfect slope of her nose and the rosy lure of her lips.

He wanted her. Good God, how he wanted her.

He wanted to taste her, sink into her, make her shudder and scream. He wanted her to care. Not the you-look-tired-so-take-the-day-off kind of care. He wanted the you-look-tired-so-here's-a-hug-and-by-the-way-I-can't-live-without-you kind.

Easy, jackass. You're losing it.

"What happened to your nose?" he blurted.

She touched it with her fingertips. "Depends on who's asking. I used to make up something badass, like—" She rounded on him, the light in her eyes an unsettling mix of ruthlessness and glee. "I was in the city chasing a drug dealer when the scumbag ran up to the roof. He jumped a gap between buildings and made it. I jumped the gap and didn't. But I managed to grab his leg, and as I crawled up to the edge of the roof, he kicked me in the face. No way I was letting go. Not until I'd yanked him off the roof and had him dangling by an arm. Then I let go."

Vaughn whistled softly. "That is pretty badass. Though you might want to ease up on the *Law and Order* reruns." He took her arm, pulling her out of the way of a woman in a wheelchair holding a newborn. An elderly man pushed the pair toward an SUV with a Welcome, Baby balloon tied to the passenger-side mirror.

"I'm over there," Vaughn said, indicating the far corner of the lot. He stepped off the curb and Lily followed.

"When I was a kid," she said, "I dreamed of becoming a famous actress. I don't seem to have the talent for it, though, because only the drunks buy my drug dealer story." She popped a shoulder. "The truth about my nose is nowhere near as exciting. This girl I knew in elementary school said my nose needed fixing, so she took a pair of pliers to it."

"Jesus."

"I know, right? If the real story got out, not even the kids would take me seriously."

"Your secret is safe with me." He looked both ways before guiding her across an access road and toward the cruiser he'd parked under a street-light.

"Safety first?" she teased.

"If we eat in the dark, you might get my sandwich by mistake." He saw her expression and grinned. "And yes, I know I behaved badly, but I'm about to make it up to you." He popped the trunk and grabbed two plastic bags. He closed the trunk again, covered it with a beach towel from one of the bags and pulled two hoagies from the other.

The hearty scents of tomato and oregano drifted into the night air, and Lily's eyes went wide. "You *did* go by Snoozy's."

"By rights we should be drinking beer with these, but we'll have to make do with water." He dug farther into the second bag and produced two bottles.

Paper rustled and plastic crackled as they unwrapped their sandwiches and twisted the caps off their water bottles. They stood face-to-face, each with a hip leaned against the cruiser's trunk, and dove into the best meatball-and-mozzarella subs Vaughn had ever tried—including the ones his parents used to sell.

Lily managed half. She wrapped the remainder in the paper, rested her butt on the bumper and watched a group of smokers mingle in a nearby courtyard while Vaughn polished off his entire meal.

"That was kind of you," she said. "Thanks."

He doubted she'd think so in a moment. "I have an ulterior motive. It's time you told me what this is all about."

"This?" She pushed off the trunk and turned to face him.

"Lily." When she remained mute, he touched a finger to her temple and curved it around behind her ear, tucking away a strand of hair. "First, you can hardly bring yourself to step foot inside the hospital, then it's like pulling teeth to get you to leave. This is about more than Miranda. I've seen the photo on your desk."

"My daughter." She swallowed and pushed her hands into her pockets. "Elodie. She was five when that picture was taken."

"What happened?"

"So, what, the sub was a bribe?" When he didn't react, simply looked at her, she took a shuddery breath. "You don't need to know."

"After all we've been through? I deserve to know."

She collapsed into herself, like a poorly pitched tent. "You must have heard something."

"I'd rather hear it from you."

Sirens sounded in the distance. An ambulance, rushing toward the emergency entrance. Her lips trembled. "I missed the signs."

Shit. "Cancer?"

"Not those kind of signs. My husband was… unstable."

Vaughn had a bad feeling. The you're-not-wearing-a-vest-and-a-perp-just-pulled-a-gun-on-you kind of feeling.

"What happened?" he asked again. He dreaded the answer, but needed to hear it.

"He—my husband—was convinced I was turning Elodie against him. She seemed more comfortable with me, and even though that's normal, for a child to favor one parent over the other, Garrison didn't handle it well. One morning when I was out on shift, he left a letter. Wrote that he needed some alone time with Elodie so he could repair the damage I'd done. It was October, but he didn't even let her get dressed. Just put her in the car in her nightgown and started driving."

Her voice was shaking, her lashes wet with tears. Vaughn ran a hand over his face. He wanted to pull her close, whisper that it would be okay, but of course it wouldn't, and he doubted she'd welcome a hug from the man forcing her to relive the tragedy that had cost her a family.

"A drunk driver killed them," she said, her voice strangled. "Ran a stop sign and plowed right into Garrison's car. They all died at the scene. I told everyone that Garrison had been taking Elodie to shop for her Halloween costume, but that wasn't true. He was taking Elodie, period. He was taking her away from me."

"And you blame yourself because you didn't see it coming."

"I let her down. Garrison and I had problems. I wanted to work them out, for her. It was my fault. She died because of me." When he opened his mouth, her expression turned fierce. "Don't you dare say it wasn't. You don't know. And I don't want to hear it."

She stood there vibrating, hands jammed in her pockets, shoulders rigid, and Vaughn had never felt more helpless. "What do you need from me?"

"I want you to say it. The truth. No one else would. I need you to agree. I need you to tell me it was my fault."

"Even if it was your fault, I would never help you punish yourself."

"You asked me what I needed." When he shook his head, she choked out a protest. "Then—" She ripped her hands free of her pockets and lurched forward. Her fingers scrabbled at his shirt as she thrust her chin upward and pressed her lips to his.

CHAPTER TEN

VAUGHN SUCKED IN a shocked breath. He inhaled Lily's moan and his mouth got smart and took over the kiss.

Warm. Soft. Sweet.

Damn, she tasted good.

He gripped her elbows and the heated silk of her skin almost gave him vertigo. Sharp jabs of pain in his belly—her fingernails dug into his abs and he couldn't have cared less. His breathing roughened as his lips rubbed over hers. He gripped her shoulders and took her tongue and the kiss went wild, their teeth clicking, bodies pressing, and all the while she made the kind of sounds that echo forever in a man's fantasies.

Pleasure was one endless, ball-tightening ripple.

Until she jolted back down onto her heels and backed away. Eyes wide, she pressed an unsteady palm to her lips.

Meanwhile Vaughn's lungs screamed for air and his dick screamed for release. "Don't tell me," he said tightly. "That wasn't supposed to happen."

She shook her head, still touching her lips.

Anger spurted. Unfair? Yeah. Understandable?

Who the hell cared? All he knew was he wanted to shove her hand out of the way and take her mouth until bliss sizzled away every last compulsion she had to blame herself for her family's death.

As if she could read his mind, she dropped her hand and stumbled back a step. "I was going to say thank you. I was upset and you…made me feel better."

"Bullshit. The sandwich made you feel better. The kiss made you feel alive."

"I can't help being a cliché. I haven't kissed a man since my husband died." She slapped her palms to her cheeks. "I owe you an apology. *God.* I can't believe I did that. And on top of everything else I've done. If Whitby found out, he'd have you sworn in by morning."

"No one saw us." Vaughn worked his jaw, fighting to find the words that would convince her to give him—*this*—a shot. "Lily."

"Sheriff, to you. That's all I can be to you. This job is all I have."

His brand-new shirt felt two sizes too small and he was sweating like he was back at his parents' restaurant, pulling pizza after pizza from a six-hundred-degree brick oven. "Your job is all you've let yourself have."

"I don't want your advice."

"I know what you want." He raised an eyebrow. "Even if you don't."

Her expression reflected both disgust and resignation as she shook her head. "What I want is to drop the subject and go back inside."

LILY SPENT THE rest of the night in Miranda's hospital room. Mostly she paced, replaying the kiss, scolding herself both for initiating it and for not letting it go on longer. She should have let herself enjoy it, because she'd never get another chance to.

Monday morning after breakfast, Nadine returned to check on Miranda and managed to find a volunteer willing to stay with the little girl until either Vaughn or Lily could get away from the station. When the pretty volunteer showed up with a Barbie puzzle and two helpings of chocolate pudding, Miranda never even glanced up as Lily headed for the door.

Guilty conscience quieted, Lily went home to shower and change. An hour later she walked into the station, her stomach writhing with nerves. Not only did she have no idea what to say to Vaughn, but she also wouldn't know what to say to Miranda if they failed to find her mother.

Clarissa had her head down, taking notes as someone spoke into her headset, when Lily approached. JD leaned over the counter, reviewing something—a map, it looked like—with a man in a baseball cap. Vaughn was headed her way, a folder in his hand and a stern expression on his face.

She licked her lips and moved away from Clarissa's desk. When he stood in front of her, her knees dipped in entreaty. "I'm sorry about last night."

He shook his head. "Don't be. We both said—and did—things we shouldn't have."

"You're not mad?"

Confusion replaced severity. "Why would I be mad?"

"I took advantage of you. I know you're especially sensitive to that."

A laugh broke free of his throat. JD glanced over his shoulder, and Clarissa thumped her desk, demanding quiet while she was on the phone.

"It was mutual," Vaughn said. "But I get it. You think I'm too young for you."

"Too young for me?" Lily scowled. "What is this, reverse psychology?" Looking past Vaughn's shoulder, she finally registered that Clarissa was waving madly from her workstation. She hurried over and Clarissa covered her mike. "Miranda's mom. Says her name is Heather Oakes."

A quick glance at the counter showed the door closing behind their visitor. "Put her on speaker." Lily folded her arms and clutched her elbows.

Vaughn appeared beside her, and gave her a thumbs-up.

He was acting as if the kiss had never taken

place. She should be relieved. Instead she wanted to pout, and the realization of how ridiculous she was being made her glad for Vaughn's sake that he seemed good with putting last night behind them.

Clarissa gave her a nod.

"Mrs. Oakes? This is Sheriff Tate of the Castle Creek sheriff's department. How can I help you?"

"I-it wasn't me," Heather Oakes whispered. "It was Lenny. I swear, I had no idea." Her voice was so low and thick, Lily could barely interpret the words. "I never thought he could do anything like this. Never in a million years."

"Anything like what, ma'am?"

"D-did you find her? Did you find my daughter?"

Lily exchanged glances with Vaughn. He nodded his agreement. The woman's distress sounded authentic.

"Your daughter is missing?" Lily asked calmly.

A shocked silence, then the woman heaved in a rattling breath. "You mean you haven't found her?"

"Mrs. Oakes, can you tell us what happened?"

When Heather started to cry, great, gulping sobs that ripped in and out of her throat, Lily's own throat ached with empathy. "I f-fell asleep," the woman sobbed. "Lenny—he's my boyfriend—he's always wanted it to be just the two of us. It's not that he doesn't like her. He just doesn't have any patience, you know?"

"What did Lenny do?"

"He—he drove away," she wailed. She started to cough, and when she spoke again, she'd reverted to a choked whisper. "He said he let her out of the car to go to the bathroom and he just left her there. She walked behind a pine tree and he *left* her there."

"Mrs. Oakes, where are you?"

"Please tell me you found her. Please tell me you have Miranda. She's only seven."

Something was clattering. Lily looked down to see a pair of scissors under the hand she'd rested on Clarissa's desk. She rolled her fingers into a fist and shoved it into her pocket.

"Hello?" The speakers resonated with panic. "Did you find her? Is she okay?"

Lily tried to swallow, but a hot mass of sorrow clung to the back of her throat.

Vaughn squeezed her elbow, which should have calmed her, but instead reminded her of the way he'd held her last night.

"This is Deputy Fulton, Mrs. Oakes. Can you tell us where you are right now?"

"I can't talk long. He locked me in the basement but he'll be back. I'll get away as soon as I can, but please, please tell me you found my little girl."

"We did find her, Mrs. Oakes." Vaughn's voice was tight. "Yesterday morning."

"Oh, thank God. It was Lenny. If only I hadn't fallen asleep. I never would have let something like that happen if I'd been awake."

"Tell us where you are and we'll send someone to get you."

"I—I don't know. Is Miranda there? Can I speak to her? Is she all right?"

"We took her to the hospital," Lily said. "She was dehydrated, so they kept her overnight for observation. She'll be released soon. Meanwhile CWS is arranging a temporary home for her."

"Child services?" Heather practically spit the words. "You're turning my baby over to child services?"

"We had no choice, Mrs. Oakes. We haven't been able to locate any relatives. Miranda's safe, which means that right now, we're more worried about you. Are you in danger?"

"No. Yes. I—I don't know. He's holding me *hostage.*"

Briefly Vaughn tightened his grip on Lily's elbow. "Did you see a weapon?" he asked.

"You mean like a gun?" Heather started to hyperventilate. Once she had herself under control, she whispered an apology. "No gun. But he does have a knife."

Clarissa made a soft noise of protest.

Lily pulled away from Vaughn, laced her fingers behind her neck and started to pace. "Is there anything at all you can tell us to help us find you?"

"We drove for hours. He wouldn't let me out of the car…" Footsteps pounded in the background. "He's coming," Heather whispered anxiously. "I have to go."

The line went dead.

Lily rounded on Clarissa. "What can you do?"

"Now that we have a cell number, we can ask the provider to ping her phone. It's an emergency, so we don't need a warrant. I'll make the call. Hold on."

Lily turned to Vaughn. "Her emotion was genuine."

He nodded. "Some of it. But she didn't ask how Miranda was doing until the very end. Didn't express concern that she'd been out all night. She spent most of the time convincing us it wasn't her fault."

"She's scared she'll lose her daughter," Lily said. "That doesn't mean she abandoned her."

"Her cell pinged off a tower in Pittsburgh." Clarissa made a face. "I'm sorry, that's all they can tell us. Her phone is off now."

"She said they drove for hours." JD raised his eyebrows. "But it's only two hours to Pittsburgh."

Clarissa took off her headset. "Maybe he drove around to confuse her?"

"No." Vaughn gave his head a shake. "She didn't

say anything about wearing a blindfold. And did you notice when I asked about a weapon?"

Lily inhaled. "She's the one who mentioned a gun."

"And right after that she had trouble breathing." Clarissa lifted halfway out of her chair. "She was buying time."

JD punched Vaughn lightly in the shoulder. "Good call, dawg."

"She didn't maintain her whisper, either," Vaughn said.

"She wouldn't have allowed herself to get so upset if she was truly scared about making too much noise." Lily ran a hand through her hair. "You're thinking she was in on the decision to leave Miranda behind."

"Afraid so."

Clarissa looked from Lily to Vaughn and back again. "But she was so upset."

Lily turned and settled hard against the desk. "Because she changed her mind."

"That's my guess," Vaughn said grimly. "They got high, ditched the kid, holed up somewhere for the night and when Heather Oakes woke up sober…"

"She realized she'd made a terrible mistake and called to make sure someone went looking for her daughter." Lily rubbed at her temple.

"That's assuming an awful lot," Clarissa said.

Vaughn squeezed the back of his neck. "Unfortunately, I've seen shit like this before."

Clarissa handed Lily a cold bottle of water. "You two make a good team."

When Lily struggled to open the bottle, Vaughn took it from her, twisted off the cap and handed it back. "Yeah," he said. "We do."

JD scratched his head. "That thing about buying time. What's that about?"

"Getting Miranda back." Lily picked at the label on the plastic. "If Lenny had a gun and Heather knew it, and the court could prove Heather knew Lenny was unstable, she'd never get Miranda back." To Clarissa, she said, "Do me a favor. See if she has a record."

"On it." Clarissa rolled back up to her desk and started typing. "Couldn't she just say she didn't know he had a gun?"

Vaughn shook his head. "Still works against her. If she doesn't know her boyfriend well enough to know whether he has a gun, then why bring him around her daughter?"

"That makes no sense." Clarissa looked up from her screen. "There are lots of people out there who don't know what their family and friends are hiding."

No one spoke. They all stood, tense and still, waiting for Lily's reaction. The only sound in the room was the tick and whirr of the government-issue clock on the wall above them.

"But those other people are not being scrutinized by the court," Lily said crisply, and the spell was broken. When Clarissa shot her an apologetic glance, Lily made a let-it-go gesture and turned to JD. "Any luck identifying Lenny?"

He lifted his shoulders in an awkward shrug. "Still got a couple of feelers out there, but we don't even know what kind of car he drives. *Blue* won't cut it. The Oakeses' old neighbor, Mr. Wilkinson, had never heard the name Lenny before. Said he must be a new one."

"Heather Oakes is not in the system," Clarissa said. "What now?"

Lily set down her water and helped herself to a squirt of the hand lotion on her dispatcher's desk. "Now that we know where they're headed, and we have a general description of the car, we can put in a request for toll-booth footage."

"Will do." Clarissa swiveled back toward her array of screens.

Lily exhaled as she rubbed the lotion into her hands. "If Heather knows where she is, she's not saying. If she is in danger and we call her back, we could push Lenny into doing something drastic."

"Can't call her back if her phone's off," JD said.

Vaughn nodded. "So we wait."

CLARISSA SLID THE spinach salad across Lily's desk. The sheriff looked as unsettled as her dispatcher was feeling. Which was good, actually, because Clarissa could use the distraction. Tamping down a pesky swell of guilt, she folded her arms. "Did something happen between you and Vaughn? And before you ask how I can tell, *everyone* can tell. You're sitting on opposite sides of the office but that's not stopping the sparks from flying." She patted her French twist. "Every now and then I have to duck so my 'do doesn't catch fire."

Lily turned back to her computer. "Everything's fine. Thanks for the salad."

"Oh, no, you don't. I made sure to ask for extra bacon. The least you can do is confide in me."

Lily snatched up a pen, leaned back in her chair and made a face. "I kissed him."

"Oh, my God, that's freaking *awesome*." Clarissa scooted onto the edge of the desk. "Tell me more."

"It's not awesome, and there is no more." Lily hesitated, and her cheeks reddened. "Well, the kiss was awesome, but it was a terrible mistake and it won't happen again. I was frustrated." She raised a hand. "And no, not that kind of frustrated."

"I get it. You're sad for Miranda. You're lonely, too, and yes, sexually destitute on top of that. But why do you say it was a mistake?"

"He works for me."

Clarissa smirked. "In more ways than one."

When Lily glowered, she spread her hands. "I'm just saying. What can it hurt? He won't be around for long and you could stand a little fun. It makes the sucky stuff so much easier to bear."

"You know what makes the sucky stuff easier to bear?" Lily snapped open the lid on her salad. "Extra bacon. Now let me eat in peace."

Back at her station, Clarissa plopped into her chair and eyed her own salad with more resignation than anticipation. She should have gone for a burger instead. Then her cell rang, and anticipation took on a whole new meaning.

She pulled her phone from her purse and stared at it, set it on her desk and stared some more. *Noble.*

"What are you waiting for it to do?"

She jerked upright, hand on her heart, and frowned at Vaughn. "You can't just walk up on a girl like that."

Her cell stopped ringing. Her shoulders slumped.

"Aren't you going to call him back?"

"I'm not sure that's a good idea. I'm not looking for anything serious."

"Jesus," he muttered. "Must be something in the water."

"It's called self-preservation," she snapped.

Vaughn showed her his palms. "I just came out to see if you have any black pepper. I'm willing to trade for it."

She eyed him with suspicion. "Trade what?"

"How about I cover the dispatch station for as long as it takes you to return that phone call."

Fart. She knew it was the right thing to do. The man had bought her dinner and she was just going to blow him off? Then again, talking to Noble would make it harder to stand firm.

Stop going for easy peasy, chickie, and do the right thing.

"Deal," she said. She scooped up her phone, swiveled away from her desk and hustled toward the back door before Vaughn could change his mind.

"Wait," he called.

"Too late. Deal's a deal." She pushed through the door.

"Just tell me where the pep—"

The door swung shut. She wrenched it open again and poked her head back in. "Lower left drawer." She hurried as fast as her pencil skirt would allow to the stone bench behind the parking lot. Four crape myrtles sporting cone-shaped scarlet blooms provided shade, but still she cursed herself for forgetting her sunglasses. She dialed Noble's number.

"The least you could have done was tell me how you liked the rollatini," he said in his deep, rough-edged voice. The voice she had no trouble imagining coming at her out of the darkness as they lay side by side in her inexpensive but crisp percale sheets.

She straightened her spine and adjusted her glasses, channeling her inner primster. It was her best defense against the man. "I'm telling you now. I liked it very much."

"And the guy who bought it for you?"

"I like him, too."

"Be still, my heart."

She swallowed a laugh. "Noble. Thank you for dinner. I enjoyed myself, especially in the parking lot. I was expecting a noogie and got a crackerjack kiss instead. But I have a rule. You're a librarian, so you can appreciate rules."

"I've heard this part. You're not looking for anything serious. Which means you believe you're so irresistible that I won't be able to stop myself from falling for you."

It did sound fairly conceited when he put it like that.

"You don't have to worry," he said. "It's not like I care. I mean, I care, but I don't *care*." He mumbled something under his breath. "Don't forget I did save your life. You could have strangled at the book drop. Or starved to death."

"I will be forever grateful."

"But not grateful enough to go out with me again."

"If you don't care, then why are you trying so hard to talk me into a second date?"

"We were good together. Especially in the parking lot. I recognize a woman who wants more when I see one. Usually she's with another guy, but that's beside the point." He pitched his voice even lower. "You kissed me like you craved my taste. And you have a great ass."

"What an incredibly shallow thing to say."

"So we're on?"

It makes the sucky stuff so much easier to bear. Clarissa caught her lower lip between her teeth. Maybe she should consider taking her own advice.

She tugged off her glasses and slid the tip of the arm between her lips. "What did you have in mind?"

THEY GOT THE call a few minutes after two. Miranda was being released from the hospital, and CWS had identified a foster family to take her in. The social worker planned to drive Miranda there as soon as the girl was discharged.

Lily grabbed her keys, poked her head into Vaughn's office and explained. "We have to get there before she leaves."

He logged off his computer. "Let's go."

When Lily opened the driver's-side door and caught the subtle scent of vanilla, she offered Vaughn a nod across the roof of the car. "Thanks for cleaning out the cruiser. I don't think it's ever smelled this good."

"The wonders of baking soda." He regarded her steadily. "You going to be all right?"

"I'd be better if we didn't suspect Miranda's mother of abandoning her."

"We'll get to the bottom of it. Meanwhile, she'll be with a family who will take good care of her."

An hour later, Miranda, Vaughn and Lily were on their way to meet the family eager to foster the little girl. According to the social worker who'd been waiting for them at the hospital, the Panettis were a big, boisterous, loving family with two daughters near Miranda's age. That made Lily feel better about the situation, though she still planned to have JD check them out.

Feeling better about Miranda's new home didn't last, though. When it was time to leave the hospital, Miranda resisted the lure of a ride in a wheelchair because she didn't want to go. The little girl cried and begged to stay with Vaughn, who had to explain he wasn't qualified to care for her. He did promise he'd come see her often, for as long as he was in town.

After hearing that, Miranda cried some more. Her tears didn't slow when Lily said she'd visit her, too. At least they didn't speed up.

In the end, Vaughn worked a miracle by suggesting Miranda wear her new unicorn pajamas to meet the Panettis. That way, they'd know how special she was. Miranda countered with a suggestion of her own—that Vaughn and Lily drive her to the Panettis' house. The social worker was happier about the driving arrangements than the jammies—she wondered aloud to Lily whether they'd ever get the little girl out of them again.

Now, as Miranda sat with Vaughn in the backseat of the cruiser, he fielded questions about her mother, and assured her they were doing all they could to find her. That was Miranda's greatest concern. That her mother wouldn't know where to find her.

Lily intended to make certain that was exactly the case until they figured out what was going on with Heather Oakes.

She checked the rearview mirror again and caught Vaughn's eye.

"What is it?" he asked. The deliberate calm in his voice made it clear he'd sensed her tension.

"Tailgater. Guess he hasn't noticed that's not a ski rack on the roof of my car."

"Light 'em up. I guarantee that'll make him a changed man."

"Until I turn off, anyway." Lily glanced again in her mirror. The maroon Accord swerved to the right, then immediately corrected. The idiot had to be texting.

Or worse. A cold, buzzing sensation took residence in her chest.

Had he been drinking?

"Sorry, guys. We need to make an unscheduled stop." She switched on her take-down lights and thumbed her siren just long enough to let loose a high-pitched *whoop whoop*.

Miranda covered her ears.

Vaughn gave the little girl's shoulder a squeeze. "Hey, cupcake, you get to see the sheriff in action. She'll make us all safer by reminding this guy to keep his eyes on the road. That's a good thing, right?"

Reluctantly, Miranda nodded, but kept her hands over her ears.

The guy behind them had backed off. *Too little too late, jerk.* Lily had no intention of letting him back on the road. Not without a breath sample. She steered her cruiser in a gentle zigzag and continued to slow, sending the universal do-not-pass-me message. She nudged her turn signal on and moved her foot to the brake.

Behind her, Vaughn spoke softly to Miranda, who giggled.

An engine gunned. Lily's gaze jerked to her mirror and her fingers clamped around the steering wheel. The car was headed right for them.

"Hang on!" she yelled.

Bam! The cruiser jolted forward, then veered into a spin. The bounce against her seat belt slammed the air from Lily's chest. Miranda screamed. Vaughn swore. Glass shattered. Tires squealed and the trees at the side of the road swerved crazily past the windshield as Lily fought to control the slide. The acrid smell of burning rubber filled the car.

Another bone-jarring *whump* as they sideswiped the guardrail. Metal scraped and groaned.

Lily tasted blood. They bounced back onto pavement and she caught her breath.

No oncoming cars. Please, no oncoming cars.

They screeched to a stop in the middle of the road, blocking both lanes. The engine had stalled and ticked placidly as it cooled. The rushing thunder of blood in Lily's ears eased. Slowly, painfully, she relaxed her grip on the steering wheel.

She whipped around to peer into the backseat. Her neck protested and she grimaced at the hot stab of pain. "Okay back there? Vaughn, is Miranda okay?"

The little girl's restrained sobs finally registered and they slashed into Lily's chest like a blunt axe. Every muscle cramped with the need to see for herself that the child was okay. To hold her and tell her it would be all right.

Blindly, she groped for the door handle. She stilled when she heard the stuttering rumble of a truck downshifting.

Vaughn had already unbuckled Miranda and pulled her into his arms. "We're good," he said grimly, and banged open his door. "Get this crate off the road."

Brakes squealed. An upward glance revealed a tractor trailer bearing down on her. No point in looking in the other direction because if she didn't get out of the truck's way, it wouldn't matter what hit the passenger side. Lily turned the key. The engine coughed. She bit out a prayer, tried again and the engine caught.

"Go!" yelled Vaughn from outside the car, and she stepped on the accelerator. The cruiser fishtailed, but made enough progress to allow the truck to pass safely by.

Her entire body shook as she parked on the shoulder and pushed out of the car. Vaughn waited back by the trees, Miranda on his hip. The little girl had stopped crying, but she was wrapped around Vaughn like a clinging vine, her face buried between her arms, the legs of her pajamas hiked up to her knees.

Lily pushed a hand through her hair and walked over, her pace not quite steady, as if she were treading on uneven ground. Maybe she was. Her ears were still ringing from the impact.

Vaughn cupped her chin. "You okay?" His fingers were warm, but his voice cracked with frigid fury.

She nodded, and touched Miranda. The warmth of the little girl's skin beneath her top and the steady rise and fall of her back calmed Lily. She nodded again. "You?"

"We got jolted a bit, is all. We'll have the EMTs take a look, just in case." He hefted Miranda higher in his arms. "I called the accident in and asked Clarissa to put out an APB. I don't suppose he had a front plate." When Lily shook her head, he swore.

"Probably local, then. At least we have a make and model."

Lily rubbed her palm up and down Miranda's spine. The child made a snuffling sound and burrowed even deeper into Vaughn's neck. Anguish surged into Lily's throat. Elodie would have been this scared. Elodie would have needed someone to hold her.

There had been no one. Her little girl had strangled on her own blood before Lily could get to her.

She stumbled back, swallowing desperately. The sadness in Vaughn's face told her he understood the source of her struggle.

He made as if to dislodge his passenger. "Take her," he said gently. "One of us needs to work the scene."

Lily continued to back away, chest aching with the effort to rein in the emotion. "I can't," she whispered. Vaughn held Miranda to comfort her. Lily would hold her to comfort herself. The child deserved better.

Elodie had deserved better.

Lily swallowed again and jabbed a thumb over her shoulder. "I'm going to set out flares." She wheeled around and made her way back to her cruiser.

ONCE AGAIN, VAUGHN kept Miranda company while the EMTs did their thing. He also kept one eye on Lily, who held herself rigid as she placed flares on the road, took photos and measurements and swept the pavement of debris. A handful of lollipops had been enough to distract Miranda from what had happened. There wasn't a big enough lollipop in the world to distract Lily.

The cruiser was drivable. He intercepted Lily as she rounded the front bumper, Miranda half-asleep in his arms with a freshly unwrapped lollipop in her mouth. No doubt it would soon end up stuck to his shirt.

He couldn't miss the residual panic in Lily's eyes, or the tremor in her hands. The compulsion to snatch at her, to fold her against him, was strong.

"Hey," he murmured. "Why don't you let me take her to the Panettis? You need a break. Go home. Get something to eat. Watch something mindless on TV."

She looked at him like he'd suggested she should get fitted for a spacesuit. "What are you trying to do, punish me? Anyway, I promised I'd go."

When he opened his mouth to argue she gripped his forearm. "Vaughn. I need to see her there safely."

Her pleading tone confused him. She was the sheriff. She could do whatever she wanted. Then it clicked. She needed reassurance that she was making the right decision. That her presence wouldn't further upset Miranda.

That he didn't blame her for what happened.

Jesus. As if anyone would.

"This wasn't your fault," he said. "You did everything you could to avoid an accident. I don't think you should turn around and get right behind the wheel again, but only because you're shaking like a meth head after twelve hours in a holding cell."

"I need to stay busy. I need to not lose it."

"Going back to the station and writing up a report on that son of a—" he glanced down at Miranda's head "—you-know-what would keep you busy."

"But it wouldn't keep me from losing it." She inhaled and pushed back her shoulders. "And I'm okay to drive. I am. Miranda will need you in the back with her."

Still he hesitated, until Miranda raised her head and sleepily offered her lollipop to Lily.

Okay, then.

EVENING HAD LONG since fallen by the time Lily and Vaughn made it back to Castle Creek. They'd stayed for soup and grilled cheese sandwiches with all six Panettis, and afterward they'd admired Miranda's bedroom before saying goodnight. The exhausted little girl had barely put up a fuss as they backed out of her room.

But the wordless drive home had been thick with sadness, harrowing flashbacks and an uneasy intimacy. When Vaughn finally pulled into Lily's driveway, Lily barely had the energy to get out of the car, let alone walk to her front door.

She'd never admit it, though. Not to Vaughn. As ridiculous as it was, she couldn't bear to have him think she couldn't keep up.

She trotted up the porch steps and tried to remember which pocket held her house key.

Vaughn lingered at the bottom. "I'll check with Pete Lowry, see when he thinks he'll have my cruiser ready tomorrow. He said he'd drop it off here. I'll get you a rental, come by after and make the switch." He hesitated. "I'm glad the mayor ordered you to take a day off. You won't know what to do with yourself, so here's a suggestion. Get some sleep."

A night breeze fluttered by, smelling of fresh-mowed grass and honeysuckle, fanning her heated skin and tugging at Vaughn's hair. When she didn't move, he stepped up into the yellow glow of her porch light, his mouth unsmiling.

"You didn't eat much at the Panettis'. Sure you don't want to go grab something at the diner?" He took her hands and brushed her fingers open, lifted her palms to the light and showed them both the matching lines of purple gouges along the centers, where her fingernails had dug in. And that was on top of the scrapes she'd collected outside Snoozy's. "Or just hang out here for a while?"

She pulled back her hands. "So we can trade manicures, drink too much wine and talk about boys?"

"So we can delay the moment when you break out the guilt and start punishing yourself all over again for the day your daughter died."

Like a soda poured too quickly into a glass, the emotion she'd kept bottled up all day suddenly spilled over. Her eyes filled and her throat went thick. When a whimper escaped, she pressed one hand to her mouth and shoved the other in her pocket, digging for her house key. If the tears weren't already slopping out of her eyes, she'd grab the spare from its hiding place, but *damn* it, she couldn't see.

She slumped face-first against the door and jiggled the knob at her hip, but, of course, it didn't turn. Her breathing turned wet and ugly and her throat ached with the effort of holding back her sobs.

Vaughn stood silent at her side, probably trying to decide whether to curse a blue streak, pat her down for her key or run for his life.

His hand closed over hers and lifted it away from the knob. "Come here."

CHAPTER ELEVEN

LILY WENT TO HIM, her forehead bumping Vaughn's chin as he guided her against him. The fingers of her right hand glanced off his badge and curled into his shirt pocket while the fingers of her left dug too deep into the fabric, making him flinch. Her face found the side of his neck.

And the wailing commenced.

He held her loosely while she cried. The hard press of his cheek against her temple, though, was anything but offhand, and the warmth of his concern seeped through her skin. The cold grip of misery loosened.

"I let her down," she said in a strangled voice she barely recognized as her own. "I was so focused on making a good impression, so determined to be a good sheriff, that I didn't pay enough attention to my family. Then they died."

"I'm sorry," he said gruffly, and that was all. He didn't reiterate it wasn't her fault, didn't tell her time would help her deal, didn't suggest she discuss her feelings with someone. He simply held her.

Gradually, the pressure in her chest eased. Her

eyes drifted shut and she leaned into him, allowing herself to be soothed by his solidity.

Too bad she couldn't breathe. She had her mouth open against his neck, and cringed when she realized her nose was dripping. It was the first time since summer kicked in that she regretted not wearing a long-sleeved shirt.

She eased far enough away to keep the slobber to herself, but not so far that he could see her face. She huffed a self-conscious chuckle. "I don't suppose you have a tissue," she said thickly.

His barely-there beard grazed her cheek as he shook his head. "Let's get you inside."

She finally found her key—in her *back* pocket—then opened the door, flipped on the light and scurried to the kitchen. After mopping her face with a wet paper towel, she returned to the living room, heavy-eyed but back to breathing through her nose.

Vaughn stood facing the yellow-and-white-striped wall she'd crowded with family photos in frames of all shapes and sizes. He leaned in to get a better look at a photograph of Elodie on her fifth birthday. Even though it had been sixty degrees outside, she'd insisted on wearing the purple winter coat with the faux fur collar her grandmother—Lily's mother—had given her.

Vaughn straightened and faced her, but didn't say what she'd expected him to. "You smell like your house. Or vice versa."

She blinked. "I smell like dust?"

"Cinnamon."

"As usual, you smell like Good & Plenty." She willed him not to notice the wobble in her lips as she moved in close, so close she could see a smear of mascara on his throat. When he went rigid and inhaled, a tingle of satisfaction gave her the strength to lift her chin and skim her lips across his.

"Are you?" she murmured.

"Am I what?"

"Good? And plenty?"

He hiked an eyebrow. "Well, hell."

"What?"

"I never thought I'd see the day when Lily Tate flirted. With me, of all people."

She pressed her palms to his stomach and slid them up to his chest. His heart beat steadily beneath his shirt. Too steadily. Why hadn't she changed out of her uniform before starting this mess?

"Don't sound smug," she said. "Anyway, it's night. And I'm not flirting."

"What are you doing?"

She gave him a don't-even-try look.

He waited.

She sighed. "You're going to make me say it? Fine. I'm asking you to have sex with me."

He rubbed an eyebrow, and gave a sharp exhale that just missed being a laugh. "Want fries with that?"

"I'm sorry?"

"You just asked for sex like you're ordering a cheeseburger at the drive-thru."

Her eyes widened and she backed away until she came up against the recliner she spent the night in more often than not.

When she started working her way around the side of the chair, Vaughn frowned. "Where are you going?"

"I don't know." She had the recliner between them now, the bright blue-and-yellow-plaid slip-cover mocking her shame. "Trying to hide, I guess. I just begged one of my employees to have sex with me."

"That wasn't begging. That was an idle request. But you don't have to worry. My answer is no."

Her body went loose even as she nipped at her lower lip. Something she'd hoped *he'd* be doing by now. Still, she was relieved.

All right, fine. A little insulted, too. "You're saying no?"

He moved toward her, fingers dug into his hips, eyes gleaming with erotic intensity. When he stood right on the other side of the chair, he leaned in. He gripped the arms so hard the frame squeaked.

"When you want me so badly you're shaking with it," he began, the rasping timbre of his voice tripping her pulse. "When your mouth is soft and your nipples are hard and you can't sit still because you're vibrating with need…" He pushed upright, and offered the briefest dip of his chin. "Come find me then."

Her breathing was so out of control she was light-headed, and a heavy tension throbbed between her hips. "You do know you're a jerk, right?"

"Not in bed." He scratched his jaw, half hiding a smile. "In bed, I can be all kinds of thoughtful. When you want sex with me because you know we can be good together, and not because you want to screw away your sadness, give me a call."

FIVE DAYS. FIVE DAYS since they'd found Miranda, and they were no closer to locating her mother. Heather hadn't called again, and according to the service provider, her cell remained off.

Lily thanked the deputy on the other end of the phone and hung up. Miranda and her mother had moved to Buttonwood four months ago. The sheriff's department there had been checking in with Heather Oakes's apartment building, as well as the hospital and the morgue. No one had seen Heather since two days before her boyfriend had left Miranda on the side of the road.

And no one had any clue as to the true identity of "Lenny."

"Knock, knock." Ivy Walker poked her head

into Lily's office. "Remember that tour we talked about?"

Lily blinked. "Hi. Yes. When—"

"We're here," Ivy sang, and Lily's belly dove for the floor.

"I'll give you a minute," Ivy said with an encouraging smile, then disappeared.

Lily stared at the empty doorway, then reached out and locked her computer screen. She picked up the stack of folders in her inbox, shuffled them into alignment and replaced them. Straightened her tape dispenser and peered at the voice mail light on her phone to see if it was blinking. It wasn't. She stared at the phone and willed it to ring. It didn't.

Suck it up, Sheriff.

With a tug on her lower lip she got to her feet and carefully pushed her chair in close to her desk. She smoothed her hands down the front of her uniform pants and strode out into the common area.

Ivy's two stepchildren stood on either side of Clarissa, paying fascinated attention as the dispatcher demonstrated the call system and let them take turns wearing her headset. Nine-year-old Grace laughed when she got the mike stuck in her curly brown hair, and the sound both charmed Lily and scraped at her heart. Meanwhile Grace's brother, Travis, an earnest towhead a couple of years younger than his sister, spied Lily standing behind them. He turned and pressed back against Clarissa's desk, gaze riveted on Lily's sidearm.

Ivy tapped Grace's shoulder. "Travis and Grace, you remember Sheriff Tate, don't you?"

Grace turned, her smile fading but her eyes remaining lit with interest. Considering how Lily had reacted to Grace the last time she'd seen her, she was lucky the girl didn't kick her in the shins.

Lily pushed her lips into an upward curve and held out her hand, hating that she hadn't moved beyond this, praying she didn't give herself away again and hurt the child's feelings. It wasn't Grace's fault she could have been Elodie's twin.

"Hey, Travis. Hey, Grace," she said. "It's good to see you two again."

Travis squeezed her hand absently, his gaze focused on her equipment belt. His sister gripped Lily's fingers more forcefully.

"Your hand is shaking," Grace said.

Lily forced a laugh. "That's what happens when you drink too much coffee."

"You should see her in action, though. Cool as a cucumber." Vaughn strolled out of his office with a thick folder under his arm. Reports, no doubt, that he needed Lily to sign. She fought the urge to snatch them and make a break for her office.

Vaughn greeted Ivy and scratched his chin as he looked the kids over. "You two rookies?"

"Yes!" Travis shouted, while Grace rolled her eyes.

"We're too young," she said primly. "We're here for a tour."

Ivy gave her head an indulgent shake. "Grace, Travis, this is Deputy Fulton."

"I've been to your farm," Vaughn said. "I met Priscilla Mae. I meant to ask for her autograph, but I forgot."

"She can't write," Travis said gravely. "She's a cow."

"Kid's got a point," Clarissa said. She stood, picked up a pile of envelopes and waggled it at Lily. "Okay to make the post office run?"

Lily nodded. "I've got the phone while you're gone."

After Clarissa left, Grace turned to Vaughn. "When was the last time you arrested someone?" she asked, and Lily hid a smile. The girl's tone made it clear she doubted Vaughn was capable of working the cuffs.

"Just a couple of weeks ago, the sheriff and I arrested two men for disorderly conduct," Vaughn said. "They were fighting in public. And before you ask, no, they're not still here."

"But can we see the jail?" Travis bounced on one leg. When his sister poked him, he switched to the other.

"That's part of the plan." Vaughn shot Lily a questioning glance, then gestured at the back door. "But how about I take you outside and show you my cruiser first?"

"Your cop car? Cool!" Now Travis was bouncing on both legs. Even Grace looked impressed.

Lily couldn't help a surge of gratitude at the unexpected reprieve. Except she didn't want to need rescuing.

She didn't want Vaughn to pity her.

"When you're done checking out Deputy Fulton's patrol car," she said, "come back inside and I'll show you the holding cells. I'll even tell you about the only person in lockup who ever managed to escape."

"Tell us now," Travis begged.

"When you come back," she promised.

Vaughn had both eyebrows raised, and he bowed slightly in Lily's direction. Her cheeks warmed as she watched him steer the kids outside.

Ivy gave her a backhanded smack on the arm. "Look at you, acting all casual with my kids. I'm proud of you. And thank you for doing this. Travis brings it up every day. Every. Day. Since school starts in less than two weeks, I figured I'd better make good on my promise." She dropped into Clarissa's chair and gave it a lazy spin. "How's the new deputy working out?"

"He turned out not to be the jerk I thought he was."

"There you go." Ivy put down a boot and stopped the chair. "Hazel said he ordered five copies of our Pets Are People, Too calendar. She and June sing his praises every opportunity they get." She lifted an elegant hand and studied her fingernails, a little too intently. "Any chance he'll stick around?"

"Nice try, but no. He's returning to Erie once his uncle's house is on the market."

"You okay with that?"

"Why wouldn't I be? Anyway, the mayor made it clear from the beginning that he wouldn't be a permanent employee."

"You didn't answer my question."

Lily crossed her arms and perched on the corner of the dispatcher's desk. "Fine. Yes. You're right. I like him. A lot."

"Have you done anything about it?"

"I tried. After a really rough day I reached out. But he decided he'd rather not be used as a tranquilizer."

"Good for him."

"Whose side are you on?"

"Yours." Ivy leaned forward. "You need to let yourself feel, Lily. Life has been hard on you, but don't let it make *you* hard. You deserve better. Try again."

Lily blew out a breath. "I'm more than ten years older than he is."

"So? So what if you're twenty years older? Or thirty? Does he want you?"

Lily thought back to the way his body had crowded hers in his laundry room.

You want to touch me because you're curious, or needy? Go for it. I'm here for you.

"He wants me," she murmured.

"There you go. Try again. Let the rest take care of itself."

"The rest involves getting naked."

Ivy snorted and kicked the chair into another spin. "It usually does with sex."

"You don't understand. The whole cougar thing means he has expectations. That an older woman knows what she wants and isn't afraid to ask for it. That she's tried all sorts of toys and positions and knows the secrets to pleasing a man."

Ivy stood and leaned back against the desk at Lily's side. "I think you know as well as I do the secret to pleasing a man is taking off your clothes and having a good time."

"You think I'm being ridiculous."

"I think you're being a woman anxious to make a good impression." She poked Lily in the thigh. "We haven't talked since the day after you got rear-ended. The little girl doing okay?"

Lily nodded. "Nothing more serious than a few

bruises. It doesn't seem to be bothering her—her foster mother says she's adjusting well."

"I'm glad. And you and Vaughn?"

"Good as new."

"Excellent. So there's nothing to stop you two from playing a little good cop, bad cop." She nudged Lily with her elbow. "You give yourself permission to be bad and I have a feeling he'll be very good to you."

The back door opened and Travis, Grace and Vaughn filed in, faces red from the heat.

"Guess what?" Travis ran up to Ivy, who pressed a kiss to his forehead. "There's a computer in the car. It's, like, heavy duty, in case it gets shot. And bunches of switches for all kinds of sirens." He rattled on while Vaughn and Grace veered into the break room then emerged with bottles of water. Grace came up to the desk and pressed one at Travis before wandering over to the bulletin board, where wanted posters and county regulations and duty rosters were posted.

And photos of kittens needing a home. Two black ones and one gray one, to be precise. Grace stared at the photos, then glanced at Ivy, biting her lip.

While Travis continued to chatter about Vaughn's "cop car," Vaughn came around Lily's end of the desk, swigging his water. "Ready to take over?"

"I am. Thanks for stepping in like that."

"You would have been fine on your own. Though we do make a good team."

"So I've heard."

He watched as Grace leaned closer to the photo he'd tacked to the board. "Looks like my kittens have snagged someone's interest."

"Ivy may never talk to you again."

"They're good kids." He slowly twisted the cap back onto his bottle as his gaze moved from Grace to Travis and back again. "I wouldn't mind a couple just like 'em someday."

And there it was. The reminder that she needed to keep her emotional distance from Vaughn Fulton. Even if he weren't headed back to the city, they'd never have a chance. Because she was done having kids.

She squared her shoulders and pushed off the desk. Time to play tour guide.

"WHAT SMELLS SO WONDERFUL?" Hands pressed to her empty stomach, Clarissa eyed the array of foil containers that took up half her kitchen table. Noble pulled one last container from the cardboard box and waved it under her nose.

Warm cinnamon and honey.

"Oh, my gosh," she moaned. "Feed me now."

"That's why I'm here." Next he produced a bottle of red wine.

"Thank you, by the way." Clarissa retrieved two stemless glasses from the cupboard beside the fridge and set them on the table. "For not minding about having to push this back. I couldn't pass up the opportunity for an extra shift. I don't make a lot at Red Roof, but it's enough to make a difference."

"Are you joking?" His words practically fell over each other as he shot her a wide-eyed glance. "I'm just psyched you didn't cancel."

His fingers went still on the corkscrew, and he shrugged. "I mean, it's all good. I wasn't hungry earlier, anyway."

Clarissa moved to his side and crooked her finger. He leaned down, and she pressed a kiss to his cheek. "You're adorable."

He flushed, set aside the wine and turned to rummage in the box. He thrust a stack of books and a DVD into her hands. "Tonight's theme."

Plastic squeaked as she gripped the DVD and held it up. *"Exploring the Wonders of Greece?"*

"You mentioned that Greece was near the top of your wish list. I thought we could plan your trip together. Or at least, pick out the spots you don't want to miss." A muffled *pop* sounded as he worked the cork out of the wine bottle. He pointed at the containers. "Spanakopita, dolmades, chickpea soup, Greek salad, moussaka. I was thinking we could watch the DVD after dinner while enjoying our baklava."

He took the stack from her, set it on the seat of a chair and handed her a glass of wine. "To Greece."

"To Greece," she murmured, and sipped. Tart, but she could deal. She eyed Noble over her glass. "You're going to help me plan a trip you're not taking?"

He frowned. "I should have realized. You want to do this yourself."

"No, it's fine. Very thoughtful, in fact." Too thoughtful. Had she called him adorable? More like diabolical.

She plunked down her wine, grabbed the plates and silverware from the counter and arranged them on the table. "It'll be fun." She pointed at the basket of napkins on the shelf behind him. "So you've never been?"

"Nah. I've never had much of an urge to travel, but when I do, my first stop will be South America." He handed her the napkins and waggled his eyebrows. "I'm a big fan of the spicy."

He pulled out a chair for her, and her stomach jumped as he effortlessly lifted both her and the chair and moved her in closer to the table. He settled across from her and waited as she studied the wide stretch of his shoulders beneath a scarlet T-shirt that warned Don't Make Me Use My Librarian Voice.

He mimicked her scrutiny, lazily scanning the pale green, cropped cardigan she wore with black leggings. With a wink, he passed her the container of salad. "Nice berries."

She raised both hands to the needlework above her breasts. "I'm going to assume you're talking about my embroidered strawberries."

"Of course." He tried and failed to look offended.

They ate, leafed through the books Noble had brought and ate some more, made a list of the must-see sites and laughed at how long it was, refilled their wineglasses and discussed the timelessness of Mary Stewart's *The Moon-Spinners* and ate some more. By the time they'd finished their soup and salad and shared a square of spinach pie and several grape leaves stuffed with minced lamb, Clarissa couldn't face the moussaka, let alone the baklava.

"I'll never be hungry again," she groaned as she laid their dirty plates in the sink.

Noble stored the leftovers in the fridge and brandished the DVD. "This is an hour. Let's see how we feel after we've watched it."

When he loaded the disc in the player and grabbed the remote, Clarissa was forced to accept that "let's watch this DVD" was *not* a euphemism for "let's get busy on the couch."

With an inward sigh, she settled beside him on the secondhand sofa that was more comfortable than it looked. *She* wasn't comfortable, though. Not sitting beside this kind, quirky, muscle-bound man with his crushed-stone voice and dark chocolate scent.

Yes, he'd been crazy thoughtful, bringing her all this information about Greece, but she didn't want to spend the time they had left tonight staring at a screen. What she wanted to do was kiss him senseless.

She shifted around and faced him, leaned into the back of the sofa and tried to look kissable. "Say something in your librarian voice."

A flash of discomfort crossed his face. How was it possible to embarrass the man who joked about nipples and methane? Then the ends of his mouth tipped up and he pulled her onto his lap. She grabbed his shoulders and settled her knees on either side of him as he buried his face in the curve of her neck.

"I don't know what that is," he said. "If it's prim and proper, you sound more like a librarian than I do." He lifted his head. "You look more like a librarian than I do."

Another flicker of anxiety crossed his face.

"Are you okay?" she asked.

He nodded. "How about a quote instead?" He considered. "'There are darknesses in life and there are lights, and you are one of the lights, the light of all lights.'"

A delighted sigh shimmered through her. "What is that from?"

"Bram Stoker's *Dracula*."

With a laugh she collapsed against him, and he gave a pained grunt that thrilled her. She lowered herself onto his thighs and scooted in, brushing the rigidness behind his zipper. He hissed in a breath and she shuddered.

"God, that's good," she whispered into his hair.

He lifted his face and took her mouth in a frantic kiss. She moaned and lost her fingers in his hair. His hands clamped tighter on her hips, then moved upward, under her sweater, and the warm friction of his palms on her bare skin had her wanting more. Wanting to be closer.

Her hips tilted and swayed in a slow hula on his lap and a desperate moan tore from his throat. He pulled his mouth from hers and dropped his head to her shoulder, breath ripping in and out of his windpipe.

She started to pant, her hula jerking out of rhythm as she slid her hands from his shoulders to his lap. She fumbled for his zipper. She pressed and stroked his erection while she struggled to free him and he bucked against her hand, then let loose what sounded like a battle cry.

All at once she was weightless, and it took a moment to register the arm of the sofa digging into her back. Meanwhile, Noble had surged to his feet and rounded the couch and all she could think was that he'd come. He'd come in his jeans and was so embarrassed that he'd run for the bathroom.

She pushed a shaking hand through her hair and got to her feet. Scoured her brain for something supportive to say while her body quivered with need.

From behind the bathroom door came the unmistakable sound of retching. *Oh.* She pressed a hand to her mouth and swallowed a sympathy heave.

Oh, the poor man.

When he finally quieted, and the toilet flushed, she knocked on the door. "Noble? Are you all right?"

He grunted an affirmation.

"There's mouthwash and a spare toothbrush under the sink. Help yourself to whatever you need."

He mumbled his thanks. The water ran for a while then he moaned again, quieter this time.

Clarissa leaned her forehead against the door. "Is there anything I can do?"

The bathroom door opened. Pale-faced and sweaty, Noble leaned against the jamb. "Forget I was ever here tonight?"

She palmed his cheek. "What do you think happened?" She gave a tiny gasp. "Food poisoning?" Oh, no. *Please*, no. She couldn't afford to miss any work.

"It's too soon for that." He closed his eyes and inhaled. "I just… I ate too much, and I was nervous."

He opened his eyes again and she bit her lip at the misery swimming in the pretty blue depths.

"Stay here tonight," she said. "You can have the bed. I'll sleep on the couch. You need to lie down and you're in no shape to drive."

His mouth went flat. "We don't know each other well enough for you to see my insides."

"Then let me drive you home."

He pushed upright. "I'll be okay. I'm sorry to spoil the evening. What happened on the couch…" He stroked a finger down her cheek. "Hold that thought?"

She'd rather hold him. She'd rather he stay and let her take care of him. Let her bring him washcloths rinsed in cold water and stroke his hair and fetch him ginger ale and crackers. Let her love him.

Oh, chickie. You know better. You know better.

"Consider it held," she said, and led him to the door.

WHEN CLARISSA PUSHED into Lily's office without bothering to knock, Lily knew something was wrong. She was halfway out of her chair before the dispatcher got her first word out.

"Mr. Katz called. Spuds got out again. Mona's gone, too."

"Double fudge." Chasing that horse was not Lily's favorite pastime, especially in ninety-degree weather. Chase it she would, though. The longer the mare stayed away from home, the more worried Mr. Katz would be, and considering he was still recovering from a heart attack, worry was the last thing the old man needed.

Lily grabbed her water bottle and brushed past Clarissa. "Radio Vaughn." He was out serving a warrant not far from Katz's property. "Tell him to head over to the farm. I'll approach from the other direction."

"What if you don't find them?" Clarissa's skin had paled to translucent. When his heart had failed him on his daily trek to the mailbox, the old man had somehow managed to call 911. Clarissa had heard him gasp his one concern—that there wouldn't be anyone to look after his animals when he was gone. He didn't have any family. After that call, Clarissa had arranged a network of volunteers to make sure that at least once a week, Mr. Katz received a visit from somebody bringing either a meal or a willingness to gossip.

Or in the case of the Catlett sisters, both.

Lily considered Clarissa's question. If they didn't come across the animals on the road, it could mean a hike through the fields opposite Katz's place. She backtracked into her office, yanked open the bottom desk drawer and retrieved the bug spray. "Let's hope one of his neighbors spots the pair and calls it in. Oh, and check with Ivy, would you? See if her trailer's available for us to use as transport?"

Once Lily turned off Route 5 onto Katz's road, she kept her eyes peeled. If either of the animals went head-to-head with a moving vehicle, the worst would likely happen, and Katz would be inconsolable.

Her radio crackled to life. "Sheriff four-oh-one."

Vaughn. "Four-oh-one, Sheriff here."

"Fugitives sighted at bridge four miles west of home base. No sign of injury."

Lily's shoulders met the back of her seat with a muffled *whump*. "Copy four-oh-one," she said. "On my way. Dispatch?"

"Dispatch here. Ivy's not available, but Seth's on standby. I'll call him back and provide four-oh-one's location."

"Copy that." Lily exhaled. There shouldn't be much traffic where Vaughn had tracked down the runaways, and hopefully Seth and his trailer wouldn't be far behind her. She'd rather leave the horse-handling to the professionals.

Fifteen minutes later, she pulled off the road just past the tiny bridge Vaughn had mentioned. No sign of Vaughn, Spuds or Mona. Lily parked behind his patrol car, got out and listened.

Sixty seconds later, the back of her neck was already slick with sweat. Even the birds found it too oppressive to hold a conversation. She stood still, hesitant to use her radio in case the sound startled the horse. All she could hear was the gurgle of water in the leaf-clogged creek beneath the bridge, and the desultory buzz of insects. Sweat slid into her eyes and she blinked against the burn.

A horse neighed. *Finally.* She trekked up the road, grateful for the trees that blocked the worst of the sun. The muggy air lay heavy in her lungs. About a hundred yards beyond their cars, the trees opened into fields, some with crops, some without. In the distance, the flatlands gave way to a subdivision of scattered two-story homes. Spuds stood at the edge of a cornfield to Lily's left, helping herself to an exposed ear of corn, while Mona lay panting at Vaughn's feet.

The dog yipped a welcome and wriggled on the dry grass as Vaughn rubbed her belly. When Lily reached him, he stood and swiped an arm across his forehead.

"Damn, it's hot," he said, eyeing her water bottle.

With a smile, she held it out. "Seth's on his way."

He nodded his thanks and drank deeply. The sound of his swallows, the splotches of sweat on his uniform shirt and the scent of the honeysuckle in the brush behind them all lent the moment an odd intimacy. Lily averted her gaze.

"Any idea how they got out?" Vaughn asked.

"The paddock's not in the best shape. Every

now and then, a board drops out of place and if Spuds is feeling froggy…"

"She takes advantage."

Was it her imagination, or had he said that wistfully? Her wrists twitched, her brain scolding her body for wanting to touch. Still, she couldn't help staring at his mouth. His lips curved slowly upward. To cover her confusion, she dropped into a crouch. Her knees cracked and Vaughn chuckled. *Damn him.*

"You're looking a little overheated, Sheriff," he said lazily.

CHAPTER TWELVE

LILY'S GAZE SNAPPED to Vaughn's, and the gleam she saw there softened her knees. A bittersweet yearning rose in her throat as she straightened. She swallowed against it.

"We're in uniform," she said stiffly. "This conversation isn't appropriate." When he didn't respond, she parked her hands on her hips. "Deputy? Did you hear what I said?"

His gaze flicked up. "I got distracted by your mouth."

"It tends to move when I talk."

He looked again at her lips, and she could practically hear him imagining all the other reasons her mouth might be in motion.

"You're right," he said. "In uniform. Not appropriate. Got it." He adjusted his duty belt. "We'll just have to come back to it when we're out of uniform."

She drew in a breath. That gleam in his eyes again. Her belly dipped.

At the sound of a slow rumble, they both turned toward the road. Seth Walker's big green pickup—Lily had overheard him calling it Bertha—appeared around the bend, hauling Ivy's rear-loading trailer. Mona sat up. Tongue lolling, she watched Seth pull off the road and onto the grass. Spuds munched another mouthful of corn, no doubt realizing her adventure was about to come to an end.

When Seth emerged from the cab carrying a halter and lead rope, Vaughn strode forward and offered his hand. "Thanks for helping out."

"And for coming so quickly," Lily added.

"Not a problem." Seth pulled a pair of leather gloves from his back pocket and tugged them on. "How about we get these ladies loaded up and on their way?"

Mona trotted beside Seth as he walked right up to Spuds, slipped the halter over the mare's nose, attached the lead rope and led her easy-as-you-please to the trailer. The mare followed him inside without balking once—maybe because Seth had grabbed a few ears of corn for the road. Vaughn helped lift and latch the tailgate then gave Mona a boost into the cab.

"I don't know what we're going to find over there," Seth said as he yanked off his gloves and adjusted his ball cap, "but I brought some boards and tools so we can make repairs. That is, if you're up for it."

"You know it." Vaughn watched Seth shove his gloves into his back pocket. "Got an extra pair of those?"

"You know it." With the flash of a grin, Seth climbed into the cab.

After he started up Bertha and eased out onto the road, Vaughn swung around and started walking backward toward their cars. "Race you."

That edge to his voice. He expected her to flare up, maybe even launch into a lecture on safety. But she did have a sense of humor.

Didn't he think she had a sense of humor?

Hands clasped against the sweat-soaked small of her back, she tipped her head and pitched her own voice low. "You know, Deputy, you might just want to save your energy."

He stopped short. "Yeah?"

"You strike me as a thorough man."

"Oh, I am." The wicked promise of his smile tripped her pulse. "Very thorough."

"You don't know how glad I am to hear you say that." Despite the hammering in her chest, she managed a saunter. When she got close enough to see his jaw flex, she poked him in the chest. "Because *someone* has to stay late and write today's report."

"Well played, Sheriff." He shocked her with a grin. "Well played."

She rolled her eyes. The man was one big bundle of unpredictable.

Minutes later, Lily turned behind Vaughn into Katz's gravel driveway. She adjusted the visor against the sun and slowed so she could get a good look at the paddock on her right. The three-rail board fence was built for livestock, with the rails fitted against the inside of the posts rather than the outside. But several of the top rails were either missing or had broken loose, the boards slanting downward, gouging dirt. One section of the fence was lacking two rails altogether. That had to be where Spuds had escaped—it would have been a matter of simply stepping over the bottom rail.

She parked behind Vaughn. Before she could get out of the car, Mr. Katz was moving carefully down the porch steps toward her, one bony hand sliding along the railing. The stark relief on his face made Lily's eyes sting.

Mona had heard him coming. She came around from the back of the horse trailer to greet him, her tail wagging so hard, she waddled.

"That's my girl." He leaned down and stroked her head. "Kept an eye on Spuds, did you?"

"She really did." Lily smiled as Mona's rear left leg began to thump.

"That's why I brought these." Seth appeared, right hand leading Spuds. His left clutched a small resealable bag, which he handed to Mr. Katz.

The old man squinted down at the bag of dog treats. "Thanks," he said gruffly.

Seth nodded at Mona. "She earned it."

A bang and rattle from the back of the trailer

signaled that Vaughn had secured the rear door. He joined them at the foot of the steps and offered Mr. Katz his hand.

The old man gave him a once-over. "See you finally got yourself a shirt that fits."

"Yes, sir."

"And my Mona. Guess she surprised you today, didn't she?"

"She's a class act, Mr. Katz."

The old man nodded complacently.

Seth gestured at the fence. "Vaughn and I are going to replace those missing boards, Mr. Katz. Mind if we put your mare in the barn?"

"I'll do it," Lily volunteered, quickly, before Mr. Katz could protest the repairs. She understood his pride, but she was all for doing everything they could to avoid these catch-and-release episodes.

After settling Spuds in the barn, Lily encouraged Mr. Katz to bring Mona out of the heat. Inside, the older man suggested Seth and Vaughn could use a cold drink and handed Lily a discolored cookie sheet loaded with a pitcher of lemonade, three glasses with a nifty wave design, three spoons, a sugar bowl and three sugar cookies the size of toaster waffles. She made it to the top step before realizing she'd better put down the tray before she dropped it.

The front yard offered one heck of a view.

Seth and Vaughn had laid the paddock gate

flat on the ground. Vaughn was stretched across the red metal braces, mid-push-up, as he held the gate steady for Seth, who was manhandling the latch hardware with a wrench. Their backs were to Lily, their butts on glorious, stretched-denim display. Lily sent up a quick prayer of thanks that Vaughn's uniform pants hadn't come in yet.

She fumbled for the pitcher at her left and poured herself a glass of lemonade by touch only. Half of it was gone in one gulp. Seth's crazy biceps bulged as he worked the wrench, but it was Vaughn Lily couldn't drag her gaze from. His back and thigh muscles flexed enticingly as he moved. His sweat-soaked uniform shirt clung to his skin and Lily itched to touch both. How unfair was it that on him, the plastered look was supersexy?

Vaughn pushed up and away from the gate, then at a murmured request from Seth, lowered back down again, and Lily couldn't help but imagine her body under his as he moved up and down, just like that.

Minus his clothes, of course.

She shivered. Eighty-eight brain-frying degrees and she was shivering. Dear *God*, she was pathetic. She squeezed her eyes shut, pressed the icy glass to her cheek and started a mental list of county ordinances.

"You all right, Sheriff?"

Her eyes popped open. When she registered Seth standing in front of her, one eyebrow raised, and Vaughn strolling up behind him, slapping the dirt from a pair of gloves, heat barreled back into her cheeks.

"Fine," she managed. "Mr. Katz made lemonade."

Seth swiped his forearm across his face. "Mind pouring? I'm dripping sweat. I'll be lucky to hold onto the glass, let alone the pitcher."

"You don't have to worry about dropping these." Lily held up the tumbler and showed him the wavy pattern. "They're ribbed. You know, for a tight grip."

Seth's other eyebrow went up and Vaughn snickered. Oh, good God. Lily struggled to get past the moment by shoving the plate of sugar cookies in Seth's direction. One cookie sailed off the plate and landed on his boot. Wordlessly, Seth picked it up, dusted it off, accepted the glass of lemonade and sauntered away.

Vaughn leaned against the porch railing. "That blush about the tight-grip comment, or the fact that you were checking out our asses earlier?"

A quick glance showed Seth braced against the far side of the paddock, well out of earshot. "It's about the fantasy I was having while you were fixing the gate."

His smirk vanished. "What kind of fantasy?"

Lily hesitated. She was so not this person. So not the fun-and-flirty type like her dispatcher. Only... Vaughn's hot and heavy gaze watched her as if she *were* that type. His muscles were tense and his body canted toward her as he waited to hear what she had to say.

A thrill of empowerment shuddered through her.

She drew in a breath. Watched his chest expand beneath his shirt as he did the same. She blinked. His shirt. The one that matched hers because they were both *in uniform.*

Her spine snapped straight. Damn it, hadn't she *just* lectured herself on this?

"Easy, now," he murmured. "Don't go getting spooked."

She surged to her feet. "I'm not a horse."

The screen door squeaked open and banged shut. Mr. Katz looked at them suspiciously. "Everything all right out here?"

Vaughn's chin jerked in reassurance. "Yes, sir. We replaced the missing rails and reinforced where we needed to."

"I appreciate that." The older man peered closer at Vaughn and gestured toward the tray at his feet. "You should get something to drink. You're redder than roadkill."

"Nice," Vaughn muttered.

Lily would have tried a laugh if she weren't struggling for oxygen.

Seth walked up to Mr. Katz and, without looking at Lily, handed her his empty glass. "A mesh fence would be more effective at containing your mare, though it wouldn't be cost-effective for just one animal. Give me a call if you buy any more livestock. I can get you a deal. Meanwhile, let Vaughn or me know if you have any more troubles and we'll be right out to fix you up."

Mr. Katz shook their hands then stooped toward the tray.

Lily beat him to it. "I've got this, if you'll get the door for me."

While Mr. Katz opened the screen door, Lily turned to Seth. "Thank you for everything."

"Yeah, thanks, Walker." Vaughn offered a knuckle bump. "Good thinking, bringing those boards with you."

Seth nodded, looked from Vaughn to Lily and took off whistling.

An engine fired up and faded as Lily carried the tray into the kitchen. She waited for the sound of Vaughn's cruiser following Seth out of the driveway, then realized she'd blocked him in.

So much for hiding out in the kitchen until he'd gone.

Mr. Katz thanked her again and shooed her outside. She pushed slowly through the screen door, kneecaps loosening when she caught sight of Vaughn by her car. He stood with his hands low on his hips, face blank behind his shades.

"Try again," Ivy had told her. "You deserve it." But the words didn't matter. She'd already decided. If Mr. Katz weren't so protective of his animals, she'd suspect him of setting them free on purpose so he could score some company.

She was lonely, too. But she didn't have to be. Not tonight.

She walked up to Vaughn, limbs frail as froth, heart rising like a bubble. She mirrored his stance but couldn't formulate the first word. He removed his shades, revealing eyes so dark and savage with need that her brain spun and her stomach cramped.

"Are we done here?" he asked tersely. The fingers on his hips had gone bloodless from the pressure of his grip.

"We're done here." Any other time she would have despaired at the flimsiness of her voice. Now she just didn't care.

"I'll follow you home." He angled his head. "That okay with you?"

A swift inhale brought the dizziness back. "Will you be coming inside?"

His pupils went black. "That's the plan."

A sultry, syrupy anticipation rolled through her veins and slowed her breathing to languid. The promise of his hard muscles and hot skin surrounding her, stroking against her, stroking *into* her, nearly put her on the ground.

She leaned in and yanked once on his tie. "So what are we waiting for?"

VAUGHN LOCKED HIS car and walked faster than could possibly look cool as he made his way to Lily's front porch. He climbed the steps and didn't stop moving until she pushed away from the post she was leaning against and they were toe-to-toe. She gave a brief lift of her chin toward the dazzling orange of the sun.

"I didn't think this through," she said, focusing her gaze on Vaughn's tie. "It's light out. I always imagined this in the dark."

"How long have you been imagining this?"

A slow half smile. "Since you came out of JD's office wearing his shirt."

Damn, he loved her honesty. "This will be better than anything you've imagined," he said. When her pupils dilated, he let loose a ragged chuckle.

He bent and pressed his mouth to the pulse point below the left side of her jaw. A tremor skated through her and he inhaled. "You smell like warm cinnamon," he murmured. "All you need is icing. I'd warm it up and use a cold butter knife to smear it all over your skin. I'd lick you until you came, then I'd lick you some more."

When he lifted his head her eyes were round

and her mouth was quivering and he braced himself for the order to turn around and take his ass home. Instead she reached out and laced her fingers in his.

"Tell me more inside," she breathed. "We need to be naked if you're going to keep talking like that."

Hell, yeah.

She led him into the house and straight to her bedroom. As organized and thorough as she was at the station, and as tidy as she kept her desk and her cruiser, he'd expected her private space to be just as orderly. Not so much. But he didn't get more than a glimpse of light purple walls, clutter on the dresser and an unmade bed before her equipment belt hit the floor and she jumped him.

She threw her arms around his neck and fused her mouth to his. Her hands climbed his neck and she grabbed fistfuls of his hair as she pressed her chest against his. The lush weight of her breasts had him moaning around her tongue.

But when he slid his hands down to her ass and pulled her closer, aligning his painfully hard dick with the heat between her thighs, she caught her breath and went still. *Easy, jackass.* He swallowed a groan and lifted his head, lungs pulsing as he fought for air. He pressed a palm to her cheek.

"Lily." Her eyes were a mesmerizing hazel, with

streaks of rain forest green. He drew his thumb across her lower lip. "Tell me what you need."

"Sex." When Vaughn's eyes narrowed, she rushed to add, "With you."

Because of what he'd said. Because she didn't want him feeling like a cardboard cutout.

"It won't be just sex," he told her.

"What do you mean?"

He let her go and backed up a step, kept his gaze on her as he unfastened his rig. The flare of need in her eyes had his fingers fumbling, but he finally managed to shed his belt and laid it without looking on the dresser.

Items on the cluttered surface clanked and rattled. Vaughn's hands went to his shirt.

"I mean the way you and I set each other off. It won't be just sex. It'll be off-the-hook sex."

"Off-the-hook? Way to make me feel old." She followed his example and yanked her uniform shirt free from her pants. When she started on the buttons, Vaughn got a glimpse of soft, pale curves behind dark blue lace and his palms started to sweat.

"Would you feel better if I said 'epic'?"

"Is everything a joke to you?"

"Only when I'm trying to lighten the mood."

She threw her head back, her hair flopping over her forehead as she balanced on her right leg and attacked the laces of her left boot. "You don't think I can have fun."

"I know you can." They were about to put that to the test. "I think you choose not to." Today was the exception. *Please, Jesus, let today be the exception.*

She pulled off her boot and switched legs. "I don't know who told you that psychoanalysis is sexy, but they were wrong."

"Point taken." He dropped onto the bed and went at his own boots with a vengeance. "What can I do to make it up to you?"

When he looked up, both boots thudded to the floor.

She stood before him in a lacy bra and panties, the light seeping through the blinds painting her skin with shadowed stripes. A quick bolt of lust rolled through him and the room felt suddenly airless. Her body was toned but not hard, her lips swollen and damp, her eyes all invitation. He gritted his teeth, aching with the need to take her up on it.

"What?" She scowled and tried to find something to do with her arms. She crossed them under her breasts, dropped them back to her sides and finally moved her hands to the small of her back, where he could imagine her tucking her fingers in her panties. Then again, considering how little material there was in the front, there couldn't be a lot of room in the back for tucking.

He just about swallowed his tongue and somehow kept himself from asking her to turn around.

"You're disappointed," she said.

Aw, hell. "No. *No*, Lily. You…it's hard to breathe." His voice was as desperate as his dick as he moved toward her. She took a step back. Okay. Okay, he could fix this.

"You're beautiful," he said, and when her shoulders relaxed his erection gave a celebratory tap against his belly. "It's just that I thought I'd have to work harder to get your clothes off."

"I…" When she licked her lips, the waistband of his boxers threatened to cut off the blood supply to his hard-on. "I was determined to be confident for you," she said. "Sexy and intriguing. You know. All the reasons men appreciate older women."

"You don't think I'm nervous, too?"

She frowned. "Because of me?"

"No, because your mother might walk in at any moment. Of course because of you. You're a generous, badass, hotter-than-hell woman and I don't want to blow this. I get the feeling you haven't done much of this lately."

"That feeling would be right."

"So how about, instead of trying to impress each other, we try and have a good time?" He took a step forward.

This time she didn't retreat. "You make it sound like that might not be easy."

He kicked something aside—her shirt? her pants?—and took another step forward. "Nothing about you is easy, Lily Tate. But I'm willing to work hard to make this happen."

This time it was Lily who moved closer. "How hard?" she asked softly.

With one stride Vaughn closed the distance between them and pulled her in tight.

"Oh," Lily breathed. "*That* hard."

SHE LAY IN the dark on her back, her body boneless and satisfied but her mind refusing to shut down. After all this time, a man in her bed. And not just any man. A man who excited and challenged her. A man who understood her. A man she could imagine a life with.

A man who was leaving.

He slept on his side, facing away from her, his breaths deep and even. With every particle of her being she longed to turn and snuggle against him. Run her hand down his belly and bring him back to life so they wouldn't waste a moment of the time they had together.

But the poor man needed sleep. She'd sent JD off on his long overdue vacation, which meant she and Vaughn were both on duty the next day. The mayor had made noise about giving her the day off, but she'd rather be with Vaughn. Besides, she had the Spuds-and-Mona report to write.

When the AC kicked on, she took advantage of the noise to roll out of bed. She fumbled in the dark for her robe and tiptoed toward the door. Her toe snagged a piece of clothing on the floor and she stumbled, fell into the armchair and banged her knee.

She clenched her teeth and muttered a word that should have been *fudge* but wasn't.

Sheets rustled as Vaughn shifted in bed behind her. Lily held her breath, struggling not to picture all those hard, naked muscles sprawled across her percale. He gave a sleepy growl and her knees wobbled.

"Did we get a call?" The rough timbre of his voice kicked off a tingling sensation that traveled up and down her spine.

"No," she whispered. "I'm sorry I woke you."

The bedside lamp clicked on and Lily slapped a palm over her eyes. More rustling as Vaughn sat up, and a creak as he settled back against the headboard.

He yawned. "Can't sleep?"

She shook her head.

A thumping sound. He was patting the bed beside him. "I know a cure for that."

She dropped her hand and immediately wished she hadn't. He'd clasped his hands behind his head, showcasing his killer biceps. His hair was tousled, his cheeks were shadowed with stubble and his dark eyes brimmed with drowsy mischief.

She let her knees have their way and collapsed into the armchair. "Vaughn…"

"It's okay. I get it." He scrubbed both hands

over his face then let them fall back to the mattress. "When was the last time you had a man in your bed?"

"Not since my husband."

"I'm honored to be the first."

She tucked her knees against her chest. "You say that as if you know what I'm going to say next."

"That you don't intend to let it happen again?" He threw the covers aside and got to his feet. He was erect, and desire burst in her belly. Shamelessly she watched him walk to the foot of the bed, still craving the hot, hard weight of him.

"I knew you wouldn't make it through the night with me in your bed," he said. "I was this close to hauling out the handcuffs."

Her fingernails dug into her shins. "Morning-after remorse is such a cliché, but I can't help it. I'm your boss."

"Now say it like you mean it."

"I can't." She rested her chin on her knees and grinned. "You're much bossier than I am." Then it registered that he was scouting for more than his boxers. He wasn't headed to the bathroom. He was leaving.

Her feet found the floor. "You don't have to go. I'll just—"

"What? Drink coffee out on the deck while I get my snooze on?" He yanked up his boxers. When he let go of the waistband and it snapped, he flinched. "No way in hell I'm chasing you out of your own bed. You'd know that, if you'd been paying as much attention to me as I've been paying to you."

She stood. "You say you understand, yet you're angry."

"Not angry. Frustrated. And after I promised myself I'd be a man about this." He shook out his jeans and draped them on the bed, then frowned at the floor. "Have you seen my shirt?"

She stared at him, remembering abruptly how she'd promised herself that from now on, she'd ask for what she wanted. How he'd called her a badass.

Some badass.

She marched over to him and wrapped her arms around his waist. "I'm embarrassed about how messy my bedroom is."

His muscles bunched beneath her fingers. He kissed the top of her head then rested his cheek on her hair. "You don't straighten up because you can't wait to get out of the house in the morning. It's a sign of someone who enjoys her job." His hands roamed over her back. "And someone who's trying to dodge memories."

She leaned back and trailed a finger down the center of his chest. "Please stay. I like the kind of memories you're helping me make."

His eyes darkened. He captured her hand and pressed a kiss to her palm. "You sure?"

She nodded. "Remember when I said I didn't want to be a cliché? Forget about it. Let's break out those cuffs."

His laugh was brief and uneven as he reached for the tie on her robe. "Did you just say 'fuhged-daboudit?' I was right about that Jersey accent."

"Wudevah," she said. "Just kiss me."

VAUGHN'S MUSCLES BUZZED with an energy he couldn't remember ever feeling, not even when he and Faith had been tapped as backup for the takedown of a drug ring they'd been surveilling.

Pretending for his entire shift that he didn't want to pounce on Lily every time she'd come within reach had been some kind of hard. Hell, *he* had been some kind of hard, all damn day, remembering the night before and how she'd writhed in his arms. How she'd spent as much time bossing as she did begging.

He stifled a groan as he pulled into his driveway.

Unfortunately, he'd have to make do with memories until Lily finished up her meeting with the Pennsylvania Sheriffs' Association. The good news? The library had hooked her up with video teleconferencing so she wouldn't have to drive to Harrisburg. The bad news? She expected the meeting to last through dinner. He'd told her to pack a snack but save her appetite for him. He'd meant the steak he planned to grill, but the spark in her eyes and the fire in her cheeks had him preferring her interpretation.

He was lifting groceries from his trunk when the rumble of the lawn mower across the street cut off. He turned and waved at Jared Ensler, who ambled out of the neighbor's garage, slapping at the bits of grass clinging to his T-shirt. Jared's return wave was halfhearted at best.

Vaughn hesitated, then set the bags back down and jogged across the street. He greeted the kid with a knuckle bump. "What's up?"

Jared shrugged and picked up a broom. "Not much."

"Got time to cut my place after you're done here?"

"Yeah." Jared worked the broom with strong strokes, sweeping the driveway clear of grass. "I could use the cash."

Vaughn suppressed a grimace. The kid couldn't have sounded more discouraged if he were the only judge headed to a liver-and-onion cook-off.

"I'm sorry you didn't find Mrs. Yackley's coins," Vaughn said. "You put a lot of effort into it. I'm sure she appreciated that."

Another shrug.

"Those guys with the metal detector didn't find anything, either."

Jared stopped sweeping and leaned on the broom. "They weren't there for the coins. Nobody else knew she lost 'em."

"How did you find out?"

"She's my neighbor and I've been doing her yard work since I was like, eight. Mrs. Y told me about the coins after her husband died. She used to fix chicken sandwiches and lemonade and we'd sit outside and talk." He kicked at a piece of mulch on the driveway. It skittered across the pavement and into the grass. "I'm just sad I got her hopes up. You should have seen her face when I told her I didn't find anything. It just sort of… dimmed."

Aw, hell. Vaughn exhaled.

"Plus she was going to give me a prize. An eagle. I was gonna start my collection with it."

"Wait, she was going to give you one of her coins? An American gold eagle? How many did she have?"

"Lots." Jared propped the broom against the garage and gave his nose a good scratching. "When she told me about 'em, she said they were worth a couple hundred thousand. They gotta be worth more now, right?"

Vaughn's jaw dropped. A couple hundred *thousand*? Why hadn't the old lady filed a police report? Lily would have mentioned it if she had.

Jared had said nobody else knew about the coins. A secret like that was tough to keep. What were the chances Vaughn's intruder had been after them, too?

He rubbed his chin. "Feel like going for a ride?"

Jared's eyes lit up. "Where to?"

"Mrs. Yackley's. I'd like to talk to her, see if there's anything the sheriff's department can do to help." The conflict on the kid's face made him add, "Help *you* find her coins, I mean."

Jared gave a solemn nod. "I'm up for that."

Half an hour later, he and Jared were sitting with Verna Yackley at a four-seater picnic table tucked inside one of those roomy outdoor tents with the see-through mesh sides. He appreciated the shade, and the lack of bugs, but he appreciated even more the lemonade and sandwiches she'd served. Ham salad, this time. Jared had already eaten three.

Their hostess wasn't much bigger than the boy. She had smooth gray hair that hung to her chin and wide green eyes that beseeched with every blink. No wonder Jared didn't want to disappoint her.

Unfortunately, it seemed her husband had. Repeatedly.

"So, you see," she was saying, "despite Pug's intention to set money aside for a rainy day, I'm certain he sold the coins. His debts were substantial, but he still managed to pay them off. After he died I called Big Ed personally, and he said they were square."

"Big Ed was his bookie?"

She nodded. "Pug liked to bet on televised sports. Mostly women's volleyball."

That deserved a double take. "And why did you call him Pug?"

"Oh, everyone did." She took a dainty sip of lemonade. "You see, my husband was butt-ugly."

Jared coughed into his glass and Vaughn grinned.

"Young Jared here is right. We had amassed a decent-sized collection. I did look for it, but not hard. I know my husband. The coins aren't here."

Vaughn clasped his hands in front of him on the table. "Did he die suddenly, Mrs. Yackley?"

"You mean, did he die before he had a chance to tell me where he hid them? Yes, he went rather fast. That's what made me think Jared could be right, that maybe I gave the coins away with the items I donated to Emerson's cause. But I'm afraid that was wishful thinking."

Vaughn swallowed a grunt. "Emerson's cause." Also known as "help me screw with my negligent nephew."

Jared reached for the pitcher of lemonade and refilled Mrs. Yackley's glass before refilling his own. When Vaughn gave him a surreptitious thumbs-up, Jared's lips went into a spasm as he fought a self-satisfied smile. He gazed hopefully across the table. "Is there anywhere you haven't looked?"

Mrs. Yackley pursed her lips. "There is one place. The shed. I refuse to go in there because of the spiders. You're welcome to check it out."

Jared was halfway out of his seat before she'd finished that last sentence. Vaughn followed him across the yard to a small vinyl building that was immaculate on the outside but full of dirt and cobwebs and not much else on the inside. An old wooden workbench, a metal wheelbarrow missing its wheel, half a dozen paint cans stacked in the corner. Jared shook each one. Empty. The cement floor gave them no reason to bring in a metal detector.

"I'm sorry, boys," said Mrs. Yackley when they'd trudged back to the table.

"We're the ones who're sorry," Jared said.

Mrs. Yackley tipped her head. "You remind me of Pug, you know. He had a kind heart. He really did try hard to beat his gambling problem. Fishing, woodworking, chess. He tried them all. He even started going to the gun range again. He and Mayor Whitby used to go together."

Vaughn swallowed a mouthful of lemonade. "I didn't know the mayor was into shooting."

"He used to be. He hasn't had much time, since he's been in office. I suppose he won't have any time at all, now."

Vaughn frowned. "What do you mean?"

"Didn't you hear? He's engaged. Some girl he went to high school with, when he lived in Ohio. Isn't that wonderful?" She tittered. "Though I think it's supposed to be a secret."

Jared was shaking his head. "Woodworking? Mr. Y hated measuring anything."

The old woman gave him an indulgent smile. "Pug would try anything to shake the urge. He made those, all in one weekend." She pointed at the corner of the yard, where several metal poles each supported a sun-faded birdhouse. As they watched, a blue jay chased a sparrow from the largest of the houses.

"He hated measuring anything," Jared repeated.

Vaughn slapped his palms on his thighs and pushed off the picnic table bench. "Why don't we go take a look?"

Even from a distance, Vaughn could tell the birdhouses looked too perfect to be handmade by a beginner. Jared agreed.

"He wasn't making birdhouses out in the garage," the kid said disgustedly. "He was watching TV and placing bets."

They stood in the center of the birdhouse community, watching the birds dip and dive and the butterflies hover. The sun was strong on their backs, the smell of clover and straw enfolding them in a lazy, weekend-on-the-farm vibe.

"Wait a second." Jared walked around to the pole at the back of the cluster and stood on his toes. He pointed. "Look," he said excitedly.

Vaughn squinted up at the birdhouse. "What are you seeing?"

"The door," Jared squeaked, and started to bounce. "Check out the door."

Vaughn moved closer, and his heartbeat rocketed. "Son of a bitch," he breathed.

The entrance to the birdhouse had been plugged and painted black to give the illusion of a hole.

Vaughn lifted the house free of its hanger, and its weight told him what Jared had already figured out. Something was hidden inside. Something about ten pounds worth of heavy.

CLARISSA CARRIED THE thick brown paper bag with both hands underneath. Dusk meant relief from the heat, but she was already wearing enough sweat for three people. Who needed a hot gallon of soup on top of that? What she should have done was brought him some freaking ice cream. It would have melted on the way over and she could have dumped it on his head.

She marched up to Noble's door, admiring his welcoming front porch despite her inclination to kick the man's ass. His house was an older home in buff-colored brick, the entrance flanked by matching Adirondack chairs and circular stone planters mounded with purple pansies.

When he swung open the door, she took quick note of his sturdy stance and the healthy color in his cheeks. All right, yes, and the enticing fit of his faded jeans. *Damn it.*

"Why didn't you answer my calls?" she demanded, then said, "Nice plants."

He scratched his belly and anchored his hands on either side of the doorway. "Thank you. And it's called mortification."

"It's called don't be ridiculous. I was worried about you."

"I threw up all over your bathroom."

"An exaggeration. You did a good job containing the situation."

He grunted. "I did text."

"Once, and we all know once is not enough."

He went still then stepped out onto the porch in bare feet and held out his hands. "I see you brought me exactly what I've been craving."

"I figured I couldn't go wrong with Cal's chicken noodle soup."

"I wasn't talking about the soup," he said, and pulled her into the house.

A long while later, it was Clarissa's empty stomach that woke her. She lay unmoving, reveling in the sensation of Noble wrapped around her, basking in the soothing cocoon of heat. She didn't want to open her eyes. Didn't want to break the spell.

But she hadn't eaten since…she didn't remember. Noble had set the soup aside and feasted on her instead. Her skin tingled at the memory.

Her stomach growled. She kept her eyes closed and wondered, with a sudden, inexplicable feeling of unease, if she could ignore the hunger pangs and go back to sleep. But it wasn't meant to be. Nature wasn't just calling, it was screaming at the top of its lungs.

Cautiously, she scooted out of Noble's cuddle, rose to her knees and turned back to lean over him. She'd meant to wake him. He had to be hungry, too. But as she listened to the serene rhythm of his breathing, she realized she couldn't bring herself to do it.

First she'd heat up the soup and rolls, then wake him with a tray.

Maybe after they ate he'd be up for round three.

A delicious shiver gripped her as she scooped up his discarded bath towel and draped it around her body like a sarong. She made her careful way over to the door, switched on the hall light and padded downstairs.

Ten minutes later, she was back upstairs, cell phone in hand. Neither of them had noticed that when Noble had set aside the soup, the container had tipped. The soup had spilled, saturating the bottom of the bag, the rolls and the foyer's hardwood floor.

After she'd cleaned up the mess, she'd checked out his kitchen cabinets. They weren't empty, but Clarissa didn't have the energy to cook, and she didn't want Noble to do it, either.

Time to call for a pizza.

After flicking on the bedside light, Clarissa

bent over and licked Noble's ear. He didn't stir. When she replaced her tongue with her teeth, he grunted and rolled over. He blinked his baby blues open and exhaled a drowsy sigh, bent one arm behind his head and reached for her with the other.

"What're you doing out of bed?"

His slow smile did things to her stomach that put the hunger pangs to shame. She reminded herself of one sad but important fact. Another bout of sex without nourishment could very well kill her.

She waggled the phone. "What do you like on your pizza?"

"Come here." He tugged at her hand, pulled her down onto the bed and wrapped his arms around her. She stretched out on top of him and nipped his chin.

"I'm hungry."

He lifted his head, his mouth seeking hers. She sank into the heat of the kiss and groaned when she felt him hardening beneath her. She started to move her hips, then with a growl pulled back to straddle him.

"Oh, no you don't," she said sternly. "Pizza first."

He reared up, snagged her around the waist and rolled her beneath him. Somewhere along the way, she lost the phone.

She grinned up at him, but the solemn look in his

eyes robbed the moment of its humor. Her breath caught in her throat and her stomach knotted.

She knew that look.

Oh, God. Oh, Noble. *Don't say it.*

"We spilled the soup," she said quickly.

"What?"

"The soup. It ended up all over the floor." She clambered out from under him and stood. "Hence the dire need for pizza."

"Damn." He shoved the hair out of his eyes. "Sorry about that."

She readjusted the towel and tried to remember what had happened to her purse. "Sausage and mushroom?"

"Sounds good." He flung an arm toward his dresser. "Throw me my wallet, would you?" When she hesitated, he added, "You can get it next time."

Ten minutes ago, his words would have thrilled her. That he wanted there to be a next time. But with the specter of his unspoken declaration hanging between them, a cold, relentless panic was making her heart shiver.

You knew better, chickie. You knew *better.*

She should go. Staying would make things worse. Still she couldn't bring herself to leave—chances were she wouldn't be back again.

"Clarissa?"

She tossed his wallet and it landed with a *thwap* beside the bed.

"Sorry," she muttered, and dropped to her knees to collect the bits of paper that had fallen out.

Noble sat up and swung his legs to the floor. He reached down to help her at the same moment the numbers printed on the back of a grocery receipt caught her eye.

What the—? A scalding flash of anger swept through her, leaving nausea in its wake. She swallowed hard and jerked to her feet, eyes locked on the receipt. "What the hell is this?"

CHAPTER THIRTEEN

NOBLE STOOD, TOO, and peered down at the paper. His shoulders drooped. "It's a credit card number," he said.

"I know," she snapped. "It's *my* credit card number." With a slap of her palm, she pinned the paper to his chest. "What I want to know is, what are you doing with it?"

He swallowed and covered her hand with his. "I wanted to make a payment. I didn't mean for you to find out—"

"How would I *not* find out?"

"—so soon." He gave her a grin, though it wasn't up to his usual blinding standards. "Happy early birthday."

She stared, shock and anger and hurt backing up in her throat, making it hard to breathe. "Noble." Her voice sounded like she'd been gargling sand. "I don't know what to say."

"How about *Kaló taksídi*?" His grin went natural. "That's bon voyage in Greek. Now you can afford to go."

She saw spots. She could swear she was seeing freaking spots. "How big of a payment did you make?" she whispered.

After a pause he tugged her down onto the bed beside him and wrapped a beefy arm around her shoulders. He said a number, and she lunged up and away from him, leaving the towel behind in the process.

"You can't... I won't... That was *my* debt. Mine. Where the hell do you get off paying it for me?"

He blinked. "It was a gift. For your birthday."

"How could you think I'd be happy about this?" She yanked the towel off the bed and flapped it at him. "I'm embarrassed. More than that, I'm furious. You had no right to pry into my financial affairs."

"It's my business because I care about you. We're dating. I'm allowed to care."

With ragged motions, she wrapped the towel back around herself, hands shaking so hard she could barely manage the final tuck between her breasts.

"First off," she said hoarsely, "we're not dating anymore. And second, I will pay you back." She jammed a palm against her mouth in a vain attempt to hold back a sob, then started hunting for her clothes. "It'll take time, but you have my word. I will pay you back."

Her yellow pedal pushers appeared, draped

over a brawny arm. "I don't need your word and I don't want your money. Tell me how to fix this."

She stepped into her pants and accepted the sleeveless blouse he held out next. "This isn't your fault. I knew better. Being self-sufficient means everything to me. I won't have someone else make my decisions for me. Not again."

Noble appeared in front of her and lightly gripped her arms. She couldn't bring herself to meet his gaze, and instead focused on his stomach and the soft blond hairs above the waistband of his boxers as she shoved her feet into her shoes.

She wanted to touch his skin. Breathe him in. Fall forward into his arms and pretend.

But she'd already done enough pretending. She wrenched free and spun toward the door.

He got there first. "I'm sorry. I got carried away and I'm sorry. Pay me what you can, whenever you can, and I'll get you something else for your birthday."

She shook her head back and forth, because why should that be the only body part not shaking?

Both his hands were in his hair. "Don't do this, Clarissa. I screwed up, but it's not worth calling us quits. I'm nothing like that asshole who took you for everything you had. I'm interested in who you are, not what you can give me."

"We've had two dates. You don't know how I like my eggs or what side of the bed I sleep on, what my favorite color is or even if I'm allergic to peanut butter. Yet you sacrificed thousands of dollars to pay off a credit card. What'll you do for Christmas, buy me a car?"

She sidestepped him. He clasped her upper arms and shifted her around so he could shut them in. She ended up with her back to the door, Noble leaning over her. He reached past her and pressed a palm against the wood.

"Clarissa," he murmured, in that pitch he knew drove her bat-shit crazy. "Why won't you let me help?"

"I was straight with you from the beginning," she replied. "This? What's going on right now? This isn't casual."

"You weren't being straight with me because you weren't being straight with yourself. You're too scared to try for forever. I get it."

"Not anymore," she said. "Not from me."

Muscles rippled under his forearm as he pushed away from the door. She looked away from the starkness in his face.

"So that's it, then," he said, and it wasn't a question. "We're done."

She spotted her purse in the corner, scooped it up and fumbled for the doorknob. "I'll send you a check soon," she whispered. She started to add a goodbye but her throat muscles had seized, so she hurried down the stairs and out to her car.

The first thing she noticed when she got behind

the wheel was the pile of books and the DVD on the passenger seat. She'd meant to ask Noble to return them to the library. Now she'd have to take them to the drop box.

Where she and Noble had met.

She cried into her cucumber scarf all the way there.

LILY MADE A note on the clipboard, shut the drawer and moved on to the next item. Taking inventory was not her favorite chore, but Clarissa had requested a personal day and the mayor had already sent two emails asking for the numbers, so…here she was. Counting pens when she wasn't answering calls at the dispatch console.

Wishing she could be out on patrol with Vaughn. And though she knew that was wrong, she couldn't help it. The past few days—make that nights—had been incredible. Vaughn had made good on his promise. Being with him *had* been better than anything she could have imagined.

The way they made each other laugh, and throb, and cry out…

She fumbled the binder clips, sighed and started counting again.

"Problem, Sheriff?"

The sound of his voice sent a sizzle of need arcing through her. She turned as he came up beside her and slouched against the counter.

"No problem at all," she said. "Not if you agree to take inventory for me."

"What do I get in return?" he asked, voice nothing but gravel.

"I'll have to think about it. Maybe I could let you know tonight."

"Can't wait." His grin faded as he studied her face, and something fierce crept into his expression. "You are so pretty."

She flushed. "Thank you."

"So this is why I don't have my numbers yet."

They jerked apart. Whitby stood just inside the door, hands on hips, eyebrows halfway up his forehead. Vaughn swore under his breath and Lily's entire body flashed hot, as if she'd just stepped into her own private desert. *Busted.*

The mayor exaggerated a shrug. "When I heard the two of you had finally decided to play ball, I didn't realize that meant—"

"Watch it, Whitby," Vaughn said softly.

Lily eyed her office. Twenty feet and she could whimper in private.

The mayor cleared his throat, then snapped a nod. "My numbers?"

"I'm taking inventory now." Blindly, Lily patted the clipboard. "You'll have the results in less than an hour."

With a purse of his lips, the mayor disappeared. Lily sagged against the counter. Vaughn exhaled then pulled her close.

"I'm sorry," he murmured into her hair, squeezing tighter. "How much trouble did I just get you in?"

"If I'm in trouble, it's my own fault." Lily freed herself. What had she been thinking? Acting the vamp with Vaughn when anyone could have walked in? After all the times she'd scolded *him* for less than professional behavior?

She needed this job. Now more than ever. Without it, she'd never keep it together once Vaughn left.

She concentrated on straightening her tie. "I'm probably in for a lecture on fraternization, but it'll be a brief one. He'll want to spend most of his time gloating."

"About?"

The words tumbled out on their own. "How right he was when he said I'd end up appreciating you."

Vaughn tipped her head up, and swept the pad of his thumb across her lips. "I appreciate you, too." He dropped his hand. "But if I don't want to get you into any more trouble, I'd better do it from afar." He pushed away from the counter. "Where's Clarissa?"

Lily's lips tingled as she made a face and lined up the binder clips to count again. "She's not feeling well. She said she doesn't have a cold, but she does have serious congestion."

Beside her, Vaughn shifted uneasily. "Even I know what that means."

And Lily would be going through it, too, before she knew it.

She stared down at the highlighters in her hands and kicked the stool beneath the counter. Damn it, she'd lost count *again*. She dropped her pen and pressed her knuckles to her eyes. After her shift, she'd stop in on Clarissa. See if there was anything she could do.

"How can I help?"

Lighten up, Lily Anne. She raised her head and when she met his gaze, she didn't have to force her smile.

"We don't have enough inventory," she said. "And there's no money in the budget for more office supplies." She pushed the clipboard at him. "If you really want to help, I need you to figure out a way to fashion ink pens out of used toilet paper rolls."

"I'm good with my hands but not *that* good. You need to talk to June. She carried away an armful of pens and sticky notes the day I arrived."

A noise sent them spinning toward the door a second time. Paige hesitated at the end of the counter. She was holding a sheaf of papers and biting her lip.

Lily snapped upright. "I'm sorry, Paige, I didn't see you there. What can I do for you?"

"I hate to interrupt but I, um, I actually wanted to talk to Deputy Fulton."

Vaughn frowned at the papers in her hand. "Please tell me this doesn't have anything to do with the mayor's pet project."

"No, this was…" She gazed around the office, and pointed at the bulletin board. "I wanted to ask about the kittens. I promised a girlfriend I'd ask if they're still available."

"They are." Vaughn peeled a sticky note off the nearest stack, wrote his number on it and handed it across the counter. "Tell your friend to give me a call if she'd like to come by and see them."

"Thanks. I will."

As Paige pushed out the door, Lily turned and pointed at the stack of sticky notes Vaughn had raided. "I hope you know that's coming out of your paycheck."

"You awake?"

Lily nodded, her cheek sliding up and down Vaughn's sweat-dampened pillow as she pushed back against his hard warmth. Her skin tingled with sensations too fresh to call memories. Hair-roughened legs sliding between hers, an urgent mouth discovering her shape, lean hips alternately thrusting and stirring—

"Feel like talking?"

She rolled toward him and pressed her lips to his throat. His skin was warm and inviting, his pulse ragged. He ran a hand down her side and around to her butt and she wriggled closer. "After that," she said, "I don't feel like doing anything."

"Lily," he prodded. He flexed his fingers, and somehow through her haze of satisfaction, his tension registered.

She scooted upright on noodle-like arms, heels scrabbling over the sheets. Ignoring his murmured "Easy," she hauled a pillow into her arms and pressed her back against the headboard.

"What's wrong?"

He shifted around to face her, so he was sitting near the foot of the bed, his legs bracketing hers. He smoothed a hand up and down her calf and pressed a kiss to her knee. "Don't laugh, okay?"

She stared, then pressed her palms against her mouth, swallowing hard against the giggles that clamored into her throat as Vaughn's face darkened.

"I'm sorry," she choked out. She dropped her hands. "I thought you were going to suggest we call it quits."

His chest rose on a sharp inhale.

"I mean, I know it's coming, but…" She leaned forward and touched a finger to his chin. "When you asked me not to laugh, I knew that wasn't what you wanted to say. I got a little giddy."

"In the first place, I'd never do that while we were naked. I especially wouldn't do it ten minutes after I'd been inside you."

His words wrenched a shudder from her. "And in the second place?" She froze. "Wait, are you leaving?"

"Not yet. Here's the thing. We've been sneaking in and out of each other's houses for almost a week now." He grimaced. "I'm feeling like a booty call."

She wanted to pinch his head for scaring her like that. "I thought that was the point. I thought that was exactly what we agreed to do. Keep it casual."

"Yeah, like, maybe we could casually grab a burger together, or see a casual movie. This is all sex."

"You're complaining about the sex?"

"No. No, I'm not. I have absolutely no complaints about the sex. The sex is exceptional. Do not take the sex away."

Her chest felt suddenly vacant, as if her heart had dropped to her belly. "You feel like I'm using you."

"What? No."

She hugged the pillow harder. "You told me. You said that people were always looking for a way to take advantage."

His hand tightened on her knee. "That isn't the same thing. We're taking advantage of each other. I like it. I thought you liked it."

She nodded energetically, then wrinkled her brow. "But?"

"But I would like it better if I could take you out. Spoil you with a nice meal. See you in a dress."

"I'll wear whatever you want. Somewhere in my attic I even have a pirate costume I'd be happy to model for you." She scraped her teeth across her lower lip. "But you know dating was not part of our deal."

"I sound like a dick. Any man would give his left nut for what I have with you." He shifted around to sit beside her. His hand found hers and he threaded their fingers together. "I can't help it. I want more."

Shock punched at her lungs. This was one development she'd never expected. Pride, and an unhealthy dose of wistfulness, had her tipping up her lips to his. "I'm flattered, Vaughn Fulton. Truly."

"Flattered, but not interested."

She stared at the window, where a lime-green luna moth bumped rhythmically against the screen. Out in the hallway, a clock patiently ticked the seconds away. What he was asking...she couldn't quite wrap her mind around it. Which was just as well. They each had their own lives to lead.

Gently she shook their linked hands. "Even if I were, what good would it do? I don't want to leave Castle Creek any more than you want to leave the city. And you want a family. I've had mine."

"You've got to stop with the old lady talk."

"Watch it, whippersnapper. I may have a touch of the ol' rheumatism, but I can still work a paddle."

He rolled over to face her, the humor twisting his mouth absent from his eyes. "You're not going to let me in, are you?"

She touched a finger to his lower lip. "It's not fair to ask me to. Not when you're leaving."

"You're right." He exhaled and nipped her fingertip. "But you'll dig up that pirate costume?"

"There's not much to dig up."

"Even better."

"I'll wear it tomorrow night."

He hesitated. "Thing is, I have something going on tomorrow. I should probably—"

From somewhere under the clothes on Vaughn's side of the bed came the trill of a phone. He leaned over, grabbed his jeans and plucked his cell from a back pocket. One look at the screen and he groaned.

"Hazel Catlett." He sent Lily an apologetic glance. "If I don't answer she'll only come knocking on the door." When she nodded in understanding, he lifted the phone to his ear.

Lily could hear Hazel loud and clear. "We've been robbed."

An hour later, Lily and Vaughn sat with Hazel and June at their kitchen table, drinking iced tea and nibbling sugar cookies while the sisters did everything they could to drag out the interview.

Lily wanted to bang her forehead against the plastic, crumb-covered tablecloth. The Catletts' schnauzer seemed to sense this. He wandered over from the corner and sat beside her chair, no doubt counting on a few of those crumbs.

"Ladies." Vaughn tapped his pen against his notebook. "Can we get back to what happened here tonight?"

"Oh, well, I don't think that's anywhere near as exciting as what was happening over at your place." Hazel winked a lime-green eyelid, which reminded Lily of the luna moth. And bed. Vaughn's bed.

She bit back a sigh. "You don't think coming home and finding out that someone broke into your house is exciting? How often does this happen?"

"Not since we got Baby Blue," June said.

Hearing his name, the dog barked. Lily jerked and knocked the remains of her cookie to the floor. The dog was on it in an instant.

"Where was Baby Blue?" Lily asked. "We didn't hear him barking."

"I doubt you would have," Hazel said slyly.

June whacked her sister on the shoulder. "He was with us."

Vaughn rubbed his temple. "Can we get back to the burglary?"

"That's one thing I've never understood." June leaned forward. "The difference between a robbery and a burglary."

"Robbery is taking something from a person and using force, or threat of force, to do it," Lily said. "Burglary doesn't necessarily mean theft. It means entering a building with the intent to commit a crime."

"We've already established you two have been the victims of a burglary. Let's get back to theft." Vaughn put pen to paper. "Point of entry was the back door, which neither of you remembers locking. You said the only thing you found missing was your laptop, along with everything on top of your desk?" He checked his list. "Family photographs, digital clock, candy jar, the usual pens and notepads, and a solar calculator. Nothing else? No jewelry or other electronics missing?"

When Hazel and June shook their heads, Lily gave a thoughtful hum. "The thief must have started in the office and took off before having a chance to check out the rest of the house. Something must have scared him off." She gestured between the sisters. "Maybe you two pulling into the driveway."

Hazel pursed her lips. "Or you two going at it next door like a couple of feral cats trapped in a dryer."

Vaughn snapped his notebook closed. "I think we're done here."

VAUGHN BIT BACK a grimace as he opened the door to Mama Leoni's and waved his parents ahead of him. He was hungry, but not for Italian, and the heavy scents of tomato and garlic only smelled like lost opportunity. He should be sitting with Lily on his back porch, sharing an omelet before they went upstairs to bed or stayed and put the deck furniture through its paces.

What he shouldn't be doing was entertaining parents who'd only come to talk him into leading the kind of life they thought he should have.

Harsh? Yeah. But he was tired of playing this game. He knew they loved him. He loved them, too. That didn't mean he had to enjoy spending time with them.

Sadly, he couldn't remember the last time he had.

The hostess, a too-thin blonde in a wispy black dress, smiled excitedly when Vaughn gave her his name. "Oh, yes, Deputy Fulton, we've been expecting you. The mayor's running a little late. He asked us to seat you." After grabbing several menus off a shelf behind her, she gestured toward the dining room. "Please follow me."

She led them to a round table in the center of the glassed-in rear of the restaurant. Five places had been set—was the mayor bringing his fiancée? The windows reflected back the muted light cast by the chandelier suspended over the table, but still the undulating shadows of the lake could be seen in the distance. A trio of roses on the table, soft music in the background and the glimmering lake outside… Vaughn gave himself a mental kick in the ass. He should have brought Lily here. No matter what she said, women liked to be romanced. He'd complained about being a booty call, but what had he been treating her like?

A damn convenience.

"Your mayor sounded nice on the phone." His mother poked at the forks to the left of her plate. "You haven't been annoying him, have you?"

"I've only seen him a handful of times since I've arrived."

His father sat across from Vaughn. "Maybe that's the problem."

"There is no problem."

His mother clicked her tongue. "There must be, if he doesn't care enough to be on time."

"He's a busy man."

His father settled back in his chair and ran a palm over his thinning hair. "You would be, too, if you'd come work with me."

Vaughn couldn't believe his dad had said that with a straight face. Since their old neighborhood had become gentrified and his parents had made an obscene amount of money selling the restaurant, Thomas Fulton spent maybe two hours in the morning going over his holdings, then dedicated the rest of the day to the golf course.

"Being a cop keeps me plenty busy," Vaughn said.

His mother opened her napkin with a snap. "Apparently it keeps you waiting, too."

The hostess chose that moment to appear with the mayor in tow. Whitby approached the table with a lazy stride, all of his energy wrapped up in his cheesy-ass grin. No doubt he planned to reopen the subject of funding for his clubhouse.

Good luck with that.

"Mr. and Mrs. Fulton, Vaughn." The mayor shook hands with everyone, looking pale even in his light gray suit. "I apologize for keeping you waiting."

"Please," Vaughn's mother said. "We're Thomas and Amanda to you. And we were just saying how much we hoped you weren't fretting about not being here to greet us."

Vaughn's father patted his wife's hand to shut her up. "Being mayor must involve a lot of late nights at the office. One challenge after another, I bet."

"I am tardy because of a challenge, but it's the very best kind." He turned and reached for someone behind him. "Tom and Amanda, I'd like you to meet my guest for the evening."

Vaughn squinted as he got to his feet—the chandelier was bright enough that he was seeing spots. He got the impression of soft curves in a green, silky dress before the woman's face came into focus.

His knees threatened to buckle.

Oh, *shit*.

"Here she is." The mayor settled his smug gaze on Vaughn. "Castle Creek's very own sheriff. Lily Tate."

LILY ENJOYED EVERY second of Vaughn's shock as the mayor urged her forward. *Jerk*. He hadn't even mentioned his parents were in town, let alone that he planned to have dinner with them and the mayor. Instead he'd begged off tonight, saying he had some things to take care of. She'd been curious, but respectful of his right to privacy. The last thing she wanted to be was clingy.

Though at the moment, she was feeling all kinds of clingy. Especially seeing him for the first time in a suit. He wore a black one, over a crisp gray shirt. He'd left the collar unbuttoned and the tips of her fingertips tingled with the need to trace the skin he'd bared.

Why hadn't he told her about tonight? The question had been rattling around in her brain like a spent casing ever since Whitby had found her at her desk ninety minutes ago and wanted to know why she wasn't home primping for her meet-the-parents moment.

Once she'd swallowed enough hurt so she

could breathe again, she'd done exactly that. To some success, gauging by the stunned approval on Vaughn's face.

I owe you one, Clarissa.

The whirlwind inside her belly eased. Maybe she could pull this off after all.

Of course, the moment she got Vaughn alone, she'd indulge in a little assault and battery with the help of her borrowed stiletto.

"It's Thomas," said Vaughn's father, attempting to mask his irritation with a too-big smile. "Not Tom." He shifted his smile to Lily. "How nice that you could take time off from protecting your town. What if someone calls 911? Does it go to voice mail?"

"We have a dispatcher," Lily said smoothly. "And reserve deputies on call. They'll let us know if they need us."

"That's enough shop talk." Vaughn's mother, Amanda, offered a friendly smile. "What would you like us to call you, sweetie? Sheriff, or Lily?"

Not sweetie.

"Her name is Lily," Vaughn said curtly.

The mayor settled Lily to Vaughn's left. When Vaughn leaned over and whispered, "I can explain," Lily offered a neutral smile, careful not to meet his gaze.

"I wish you already had," she said.

When she faced forward again she saw that his mother, sitting at the mayor's left, had caught the exchange. Amanda gave the mayor's hand a pat. "So, Mayor Whitby. How long have you and Lily been dating?"

Whitby gave them his best crocodile smile. "Lily's not my date. I brought her to distract and disarm you while I put in a plug for the lakeside clubhouse I'm designing." He leaned over his plate and looked past Lily at Vaughn. "Your son knows all about it."

"That's not why I'm here," Lily said quickly.

The server chose that well-timed moment to appear and take their drink orders. While Whitby and Thomas talked wine, Lily grabbed hold of Vaughn's wrist. "We didn't conspire. I promise."

"I believe you." Vaughn didn't turn his head. "Still, you're letting him use you to use me." He inhaled. "Or did he threaten to fire you?"

"No threats. I let him talk me into dinner because I was hurt you didn't ask me yourself. Plus I owed him for never delivering that lecture on unprofessional behavior." She clenched her hands in her lap, the cool silk of her dress mocking the pleasure she'd taken in her appearance. "Would you like me to leave?"

The muscle jumping in his jaw paused. He seemed to be actually considering it.

"You're not going to leave us, are you, Lily?" When Lily turned to face Amanda across the table, she was surprised by the disappointment pulling at the other woman's mouth. "Vaughn hasn't told us anything about his time here. We were hoping you'd tell us a bit about what he's been doing. How many cows he's ticketed for jaywalking, that sort of thing."

Her laugh was teasing, and Thomas's snort was pure condescension, but Lily could see the concern in Amanda's eyes. Vaughn's parents might appear to be snobs, but that wasn't the only reason they wanted him off the job.

"He isn't planning to settle here, if that's what you're worried about. In fact, his talents are wasted in my department. Once he's back in Erie, I'm sure he'll make detective in no time. You should be proud."

"Stop." His jagged motions as he tugged at the cuffs of his shirt belied his mild tone. "I don't need you to defend me."

Lily swallowed against a hot rise of hurt and reached for her water. She cursed herself when her hand shook.

"Tell us about this clubhouse, Mayor." Thomas snapped his menu closed. "I assume it's an investment opportunity?"

Lily and Vaughn sat in awkward silence while Whitby described his plans for a facility that would allow public access to the water, provide an elegant venue for weddings and offer regular outdoor concerts. With enough land and capital, the next phase could involve building a world-class resort, albeit a small one. Thomas and Amanda listened politely, but didn't ask many questions. Lily could see signs of the mayor's frustration, but only because she knew how to spot them.

After the server returned and took their dinner orders, Vaughn's parents turned from the mayor to their son.

"Speaking of investments." His father fiddled with the knife and fork beside his plate. "What are you going to do with the proceeds from the sale of Emerson's house?"

Vaughn leaned back in his chair, but Lily could feel the tension rippling off him. "I haven't decided yet."

"We could set up a meeting with that broker I was telling you about." His mother poked at the nape of her neck, beneath a tidy chignon. "That would be a wonderful way to break the ice. I'll make lamb and we can talk long-term yields."

Thomas rapped his knuckles once on the table in front of Whitby's plate. "What do you think he can get for that property, Mayor? Three, four hundred thousand? That'd be a hell of a boost to your portfolio, son."

Amanda's eyes glowed as she wrapped both hands around her wineglass. "There's a house in our neighborhood for sale."

"That's a damn good idea. You get that job with the investment firm, you're going to need a place you can do some entertaining. And a woman to help you do it." Thomas avoided looking in Lily's direction.

Lily started as Whitby covered her left hand with his under the table and squeezed gently. She squeezed back, grateful for the sympathy.

When the server headed their way with two full trays, Lily released Whitby's hand and readjusted her napkin in her lap. Not that she would need it. She wanted food about as much as she wanted to listen to more of the Fultons' plans for their son.

"How about we change the subject?" Vaughn nodded at the server as she set an order of chicken Parmesan in front of him, and reminded him, sotto voce, to be cautious of the hot plate. "I can't afford a house, and I'm happy with where I live. What's Theresa been up to?"

"Your sister's fine." Amanda pointed her butter knife at Vaughn. "But she's not our concern at the moment."

Slowly, Lily turned her head and stared at Vaughn. A sister. He had a sister.

"You never mentioned a sister," she said, barely recognizing her own voice.

"You never had any complaints about our lack of conversation," he returned, his tone suggestive. But his eyes remained empty of passion.

"Oil and vinegar, those two." Amanda flapped a hand. "Don't be mad. Theresa doesn't talk about Vaughn, either."

Thomas huffed the first genuine laugh Lily had heard from him all evening. "You mean oil and water."

"Well," Amanda sniffed, "maybe I do."

"Maybe you can't afford a house right now," his dad said, twisting his fork in his fettuccine. "But that won't be an issue after you sell Emerson's property."

"Yes, it will. Half the proceeds go to charity."

Thomas stared, fork in midair. "What are you talking about?"

"Uncle Em earmarked half the profit for a handful of charities."

Amanda set down the slice of bread she'd been buttering. "There was nothing in his will about that."

"It was a decision he made right before he died."

Fettuccine unraveled as his father pointed his fork at him. "You weren't with him when he died."

Out of the corner of her eye, Lily watched Vaughn's fingers curl and whiten. "No," he agreed quietly. "But we talked about it the last time I saw him."

"He can't hold you to that," Amanda said. "It wasn't in his will."

"Speaking of wills." Whitby slapped the table and chuckled loudly. "Did you hear about the old lady who left her entire fortune to her cat? The day of the funeral, the hearse ran it over."

Lily didn't know whether to laugh or cry.

Actually, cry. It was cry all the way.

Amanda shook her head at her son as she sipped her wine. "He wouldn't expect you to honor something he said when he wasn't in his right mind."

"He also told me he loved me. Should I disregard that, too?"

"Of course not," everyone said at the same time.

Heat rushed into Lily's cheeks when four heads swiveled her way.

"I'm not asking your advice," Vaughn said. "I'm telling you I don't want a house, I can't afford a house, and I have no intention of changing jobs."

Blessed silence reigned for a full ten seconds, then Amanda leaned toward Lily. At the last moment she remembered her pearls, and barely avoided dragging them through her vodka sauce. "Maybe you could talk some sense into him, Lily. You wouldn't want to be responsible for holding him back, would you?"

Lily lifted her chin. "That's not possible. We don't have that kind of relationship."

Thomas scowled. "Rightfully so, since you're his employer."

"It's understandable, though." Amanda aimed

a fond smile at Vaughn. "My son is a handsome man. Though his sister insists on calling him something ridiculous, like…" Her fingers rediscovered her pearls. "What is it, Vaughn? Oh, of course. Booger brain."

"For God's sake, Amanda." Thomas winced at the Alfredo sauce clinging to his fork. He set down the implement and studied Lily. "How old are you, anyway, Sheriff? I'd say you have a good ten years on my boy. You should find someone your own age. Like the mayor here. Vaughn likes to snowboard, did you know that? Think you could keep up with him?"

When Vaughn remained quiet, slumped in his chair and rubbing his forehead with the heel of his hand, Lily felt the difference in their ages more than ever. She got to her feet, shook off Vaughn's fingers when he reached for her wrist and gathered up her purse.

"Excuse me, won't you? I've just remembered we had a DUI in the holding cell last night and I never cleaned up the vomit." She smiled at Vaughn's father. "He must have been eating Mexican food right before we arrested him, because there are big chunks of partially digested tomatoes and corn and pork all over the floor." Thomas paled and Lily pretended to shudder. "Lots of green goopy stuff, too, which I'm thinking was guacamole. Oh, and the entire station smells like boiled cabbage."

Thomas hiccupped and grabbed at his napkin.

Lily backed away from the table. "Good night, everyone."

She strutted out the door, already regretting leaving her lasagna behind.

VAUGHN PACED HIS living room, one hand in his hair, the other clutching his phone. Jesus, could he have been any more of a jackass tonight? Yeah, his parents made him crazy, but he shouldn't have taken it out on Lily.

Lily, in a dress. And *heels*. Looking fierce and confident and so damn sexy. Instead of appreciating her, he'd all but ignored her.

Her face when she'd walked out… He'd screwed up. Big-time.

He dialed her number again and swore when he got her voice mail. Again. He couldn't blame her for not taking his calls. What he should do was go by her house. Yeah. That. He'd go by her house. He'd beg.

And hope like hell she was still wearing that dress.

But first he wanted to know why she'd even been at the restaurant.

He dialed the mayor.

Whitby picked up before the second ring, and Vaughn didn't know whether to admire the man or pity him.

"What the hell were you thinking, Whitby? If I'd wanted Lily there, I would have asked her."

"I'm sorry, son." The mayor's voice was subdued. "I wanted it to be a surprise. I thought you two were involved."

"That was before she knew what my parents were like." Vaughn stomped into the kitchen, banged open a cupboard and grabbed a glass. "You may have sabotaged the best thing that ever happened to me." He slapped the faucet on, then slapped it off again. "No. No, this is on me. I should have told her what was going down."

"It's not too late, is it? I was hoping you two could make a go of it."

"Why does that matter to you?"

Whitby blew out a breath. "Truth is, I owe your uncle. I owe him big. I figured if I could get the two of you together, you'd stay, like he wanted."

Vaughn scowled at his reflection in the window over the sink. "Exactly what did he do for you?"

"That's between him and me, son. Anyway, I figured someone around here should get their happy-ever-after."

It took a moment for the words to register. "But I heard you were engaged."

The mayor's chuckle held no trace of humor. "Of course you did. Anyway, that's off."

"I'm sorry to hear that."

"Me, too. And you and Lily…it's a shame. The

kind of trauma she's been through... I don't know how you come back from something like that. Losing your family is one thing. Coming across them minutes after they died a violent death is a whole other level of tragedy."

"Wait." For a moment he didn't move, then a hot, greasy pain exploded in his gut and he jackknifed over the sink. Shit, he was going to puke. "Lily worked her daughter's accident scene?"

"No one knew who was involved. She was there before they could call her off."

Jesus. *Jesus.* He swallowed hard. Why hadn't she told him?

And she'd forced herself to work the scene of their hit and run.

An aching sorrow for what she'd seen, for what she'd had to do, spiraled through him. At the same time resentment heated into anger.

He'd deserved to know.

FIVE O'CLOCK SUNDAY MORNING, it was too early for even the sun to be up, but Lily knew her mother would be. Working on a crochet project, or rolling out a piecrust, maybe.

She curled into her armchair, allowed herself a small swell of pride because she didn't have to shove anything off it first and pressed her cell phone to her ear.

"Hey, Ma."

"Lily Anne. What a nice surprise."

Damp heat rushed to her eyes. She fumbled for the belt to her robe and pressed the cool material against her lids. "Can we talk?"

"As opposed to what we're doing now?"

"I'd like to reschedule that visit."

Her mother made a satisfied noise. "You have perfect timing because Rosemarie's son is visiting from Toledo. You'll like him. He can grill a bratwurst like nobody's business. When are you coming? How long can you stay?"

"In a couple of weeks. Once JD is back, I can take a long weekend."

"Are we going to chalk this up to guilt, or are you going to tell me why you're really coming to Florida?"

"Let's go with the guilt thing." Lily mopped her face with the hem of her robe and winced at her soggy inhale. "I'm not ready to talk about the rest."

"You don't have to, baby girl." Her mother hesitated. "But you will be ready eventually, right? Maybe after you've arrived and had a good night's sleep? You're not going to make me spend your entire visit guessing, are you?"

"No, Ma. I promise."

"You going to bring me some cinnamon rolls from that diner you like?"

"I'll bring you a whole box, Ma."

"Good, because the ones they make around here? About as tender as your father was, bless his hard-hearted soul. You know the secret to a flaky pastry? You have to…"

Lily dropped her head back and stared up into the graying shadows as her mother extolled the virtues of her own vinegar piecrust. Talking to her mother wasn't especially soothing, but it reminded her of what she could count on.

And Vaughn Fulton wasn't it.

LILY PARKED JD's cruiser and reached for her coffee cup, only to realize it was empty. She froze, fingers in midair. When had that happened? With unsteady hands, she unbuckled her seat belt. Just as well. Her stomach was already a riot of nerves, and the piece of toast she'd had for breakfast still hadn't decided to stay put.

She eyed the station door and seriously considered driving away again. But all that would do was delay the inevitable. It was bad enough she'd refused to talk to Vaughn last night. She should have given him closure. She owed him that much.

It was the sole reason she'd dragged her butt out of bed this morning.

As she pushed out of the car, the station door opened and Vaughn stepped out. *Here we go.* But this was better, wasn't it, than giving everyone inside an up close and personal view of their breakup?

Could you call it a breakup when there had never been any kind of commitment?

They faced each other in the middle of the lot, ten feet's worth of pavement between them. A giggle rose up in her throat. Vaughn was on the verge of leaving and he finally had his uniform pants. They must have arrived the day before.

Her chest rose and fell.

He set his jaw and jabbed a finger at her. "No," he said. "We are not over."

CHAPTER FOURTEEN

"Yes, I acted like an ass," Vaughn continued, "but you are not going to use that as an excuse."

"I don't need an excuse," Lily said, "and I'm sorry for not calling you back last night. You probably want to apologize, too, but you know what? You don't need to. I get it. Dinner with the mayor is not casual. Meeting the parents is not casual. I shouldn't have crashed your party."

"Screw casual," Vaughn said savagely. "We left casual behind a long time ago. Yeah, two nights ago in my bed we agreed we wouldn't try for more, but that was bullshit. You know it was."

Over Vaughn's shoulder, she could see the blinds in the station windows twitch and sway. She bit the inside of her lip. Things would never be the same after Vaughn left. Would JD and Clarissa be able to respect her now that she'd slept with a subordinate?

"This deserves better treatment than hashing it out in a parking lot." Vaughn gestured at her car. "What do you say we go someplace quiet and work this out?"

Her neck muscles ached as she shook her head. "There's nothing to work out. There never has been."

"Give it up, Sheriff," Vaughn growled, and started toward her. He backed up when a car approached and drove between them, scouting a space. After the car passed, Vaughn moved forward again, taking several steps to halve the distance between them.

"I'm on to you, Lily Tate," he said. "You think you're the only one scared shitless at the prospect of handing over their heart? The only one who struggles with second thoughts and insecurities and pure panic over the knowledge of how goddamn bad losing the one you love is going to hurt?"

Lily stared, ripples of shock, pleasure and alarm pumping through her blood.

"Yeah, that's right," he said. "I love you. You love me, too. Now what are we going to do about it?"

She shifted, and gravel scraped beneath her boots. "Maybe I am scared. But for good reason. Being on my own means never being used."

"Being on your own means being lonely."

"No. Not always, Vaughn, because you know what? I've never felt as lonely as I did last night."

Their gazes locked for several beats.

Vaughn skimmed a palm over the back of his neck. "I tried to tell you. The night someone broke into the Catletts' house. Anyway, there was a reason I didn't invite you to dinner."

"Was there a reason you didn't defend me?"

"I know. Lily, I know." Another car was heading toward them, but Vaughn didn't look away from her. "I made you feel like you didn't belong. Too many times in my life I've felt like an outsider and it's the worst goddamn feeling in the world. I can't believe I did that to you. You have to let me make it right."

The car got closer and Vaughn stepped out of its way, toward Lily.

A roar filled her ears. She jerked at the squeal of rubber as the vehicle accelerated, heading straight for them. Lily sucked in air, the heat searing her throat and burning all the way down to her lungs.

A maroon Accord. The same car that had cut them off on Route 5.

"Vaughn! Look out!"

Instinctively he lunged, but not fast enough. Lily watched in horror as the driver's door opened behind Vaughn. She drew her weapon, but it was too late.

A sickening thud and he was spun onto the pavement. The car raced away.

VAUGHN BLINKED, AND slowly a white tiled ceiling came into focus. *What the hell?* Distant voices. A wet, beeping sound nearby. Pain. *Shit.* His right hip throbbed like a son of a bitch. Carefully he raised his head, registered the IV in his arm and the thin ribbed blanket tucked over his ribs and finally put the pieces together.

Hospital. Right. Some jackass had tried to run him over.

He dropped his head back to the pillow and closed his eyes, but only for an instant. *Lily.*

He bolted upright, gritting his teeth as fire flashed through his lower body. Then she was there, with a firm but gentle hand on his shoulder, pushing him back to the pillow.

"What's the matter with you?" Her voice was crisp, but there was no mistaking the underlying anxiety.

"You're okay?" he asked, and winced. He didn't recognize his own voice.

She held a straw to his lips and he drank greedily. The ice water stung the roof of his mouth, but damn, it tasted good. When he signaled he was done, she set the cup aside. "I'm fine," she said. "You, not so much."

"No, I'm okay. If I sound like a crazy man, it's the morphine." He gestured at the IV stand beside the bed. "CT scan showed a hip contusion and a possible sprain."

"No broken bones?"

He shook his head. "Did you get the guy?"

"We're working on it. We'll get him, I promise." Her fingers were practically strangling the bed rail. "I'm sorry this happened to you. I... Is there anything I can do?"

"You can stop blaming yourself." When she sucked in a watery breath, he swore. "Son of a bitch. You are blaming yourself. Lily. This isn't your fault. This is on the guy who was driving that car."

Wordlessly she stared down at the wristband the hospital had given him. Desperation crawled into his chest.

"That car wasn't gunning just for me," he said harshly. "Either one of us could have gone down. The one thing that bastard did right was pick me."

"We've seen that car before."

He furrowed his brow. "Maroon Accord," he said slowly, then remembered. "The car that ran us off the road. This is about Miranda."

"You were right about Heather Oakes. Our guess is she wanted revenge because we put Miranda in the system. 'Lenny' is Leonard Briscoe, a known drug dealer with two child endangerment convictions. Heather had to realize once we identified him, she wouldn't get her daughter back. Though why she sent him after us when we had Miranda in the car... Anyway, we have an APB out on Briscoe."

"How'd you identify him? You got the plate?"

"Not me. Clarissa. She got it off our parking lot surveillance. Lenny is now wanted for attempted murder." She loosened her grip on the railing and backed away from the bed. "I need to get back to the station. That little time-out you took on the pavement will create a lot of paperwork."

"Before you go, tell me you know this wasn't on you."

"I can't," she whispered. "We were arguing. I wasn't paying attention. That's what I do. I let myself get distracted and someone else pays the price."

"Bullshit. I wasn't watching out for us, either. Anyway, you couldn't have known what that son of a bitch had in mind."

Her eyes were bleak as she shook her head. "I have to go. Someone will keep you posted."

Someone other than her, she meant. Damn it, she couldn't just shut him out. As soon as he was on his feet, he'd be back on the job and just let her try to ignore him then. Still, he couldn't help feeling he didn't have a lot of time to change her mind.

She was almost at the door when she turned back. He sagged against the pillow, his relief a better painkiller than the morphine they were pumping into his veins.

"I almost forgot," she said. "Your captain called. They want you back. Apparently they're rewarding your patience with a promotion. Congratulations."

The rush of jubilation wasn't a surprise, but it was damned inconvenient. "Can we talk about it?"

"What is there to say? That we can figure something out, that Erie isn't all that far away? It's far enough, and that isn't even the point. Whatever this is between you and me, I don't want it."

He clenched his hands to suppress the need to shout. "Don't you mean you don't deserve it?"

She stunned him with a half smile. "Nice try, Fulton. We both know this won't work. We want different things."

"I want you and you want me."

"You want a family and a fast life in the city. I want my life to stay the same."

His muscles tensed and pain ripped through his hip. "You're lying," he bit out. "I trust you. You should, too."

"I'm glad you're okay," she said softly. "But your parents are on their way and I have to get back to work. Take care of yourself, Officer."

Officer. Not *Deputy.*

If she thought he was going to accept that as goodbye, she had another think coming.

TWO DAYS LATER, Vaughn limped into the mayor's outer office. Paige looked up from her computer and gave him a friendly smile.

"Welcome back, Deputy. He's expecting you. Go right on in."

Whitby stood behind his desk, staring down

at the cluttered surface, face as rumpled as his expensive shirt.

Vaughn shut the door behind him. "You okay, Mayor?"

"What? Yes. Vaughn. You're out." The mayor rounded his desk and offered his hand. "How are you, son?"

"I'm good," Vaughn lied.

"Can I get you anything? Jelly bean? Tootsie Roll?"

Lily Tate, Vaughn wanted to say, but that wasn't something he'd discuss with anyone but Lily herself.

"You can get me the truth," he said instead. "Tell me why you owed my uncle a favor."

Whitby hesitated. "Lily told me you were heading back to Erie. Congratulations on your promotion." He gestured at a leather armchair and sank back against his desk. Scrubbed his fingers through his fading blond hair. "Maybe I do owe you an explanation, though it won't be an easy one."

Two taps on the door and the mayor lifted his head. Instead of being relieved at the interruption, he looked like he was going to hurl.

Paige poked her head in. "Sheriff Tate is here to see you."

"Ask her to wait, please," Whitby said stiffly, gaze trained on the window across the room.

Vaughn glanced from the mayor to Paige and

back again, then got to his feet. "I'd like her to join us, if you don't mind." Might as well get this all out in the open.

Whitby grimaced, then spread his hands. "Send her in."

Lily lost her smile the instant she saw Vaughn. That hurt. But the shadows under her eyes told him she was hurting, too. And they'd talk about that, as soon as he found out what his uncle and Rick Whitby had been up to.

"I can wait," Lily said.

Vaughn crossed to the door and shut it behind her. "I think you might need to hear this."

He gestured at the leather chair he'd vacated, but Lily elected to stand. Vaughn wandered over to the credenza and helped himself to a Tootsie Roll.

"Go ahead, Mayor."

Whitby was sweating like he'd spent an hour forging metal in the summer sun. "Emerson found out the title to my lake property is defective."

Vaughn froze, the candy halfway to his mouth. "Are you kidding me?"

Lily stiffened. "What does that mean? And how did he find out?"

Carefully, Vaughn rewrapped the piece of candy. "Uncle Em used to work in deeds processing. A defective title means the property transfer isn't official. Whoever sold the property to the mayor still owns it."

"That would be Helen Burkett." Whitby pulled a hankie from his back pocket and wiped his forehead. "She and her husband co-owned it, but she didn't sign the deed. It would have been a simple matter of getting a lawyer to rectify the oversight, except she never wanted to sell the property in the first place."

Vaughn gave a curt nod. "So if you told her, chances are she would have used it as an excuse to reverse the sale."

"I know I haven't been the most proactive mayor. The clubhouse was going to be my legacy."

"So Uncle Em agreed to keep this quiet? That's the favor you owe?"

Whitby sighed. "That, and he replaced the deed with a valid one."

Son of a bitch. Vaughn rubbed a hand over his mouth and started to pace. "I wasn't expecting that."

"Your uncle believed in the project. He believed in the future of Castle Creek."

Vaughn swore. "He also knew he was dying and that if he ever got caught, he wouldn't be held accountable."

Whitby's head bobbed up and down. "That, too."

Vaughn stopped pacing and his gaze drilled

the red-faced mayor into place. "Paige is shaking you down, isn't she?"

Lily gasped. *"What?"*

Vaughn never looked away from Whitby, who had started to squirm. "That's what the break-ins were about. She was desperate to get her office supplies back. My guess, Mayor, is that your devoted assistant listens in on your phone conversations. You must have discussed this title screwup over the phone with Uncle Em. Paige heard you, went to Records and did a little research, wrote down a tax map number or something on a sticky pad and accidentally threw that in with the junk she dropped off at my house. She had to get that piece of paper back because she didn't want anyone else to have the same leverage. She broke into my house but couldn't find it, came to the free-for-all and still couldn't find it because June Catlett had taken it the day I moved in."

"She's the one who broke into the Catletts' house?" Lily stacked her hands on top of her head and turned and stared at the door. She swung back to Vaughn. "That day she came into the station and asked about the kittens…"

"You could tell that was bogus, right? She probably came to ask about that box of supplies again."

Lily dropped her hands and strode over to the mayor. "What is she after?"

"She demanded I call off my engagement."

Whitby's shrug was pitiful. "'A woman scorned' and all that."

"Oh, my God." Lily rounded on Vaughn. "Can you prove any of this?"

"I don't know how. She's smart enough to have used gloves when she was doing her breaking and entering." He snapped his fingers. "Unless she kept some of the items she took from the Catletts. Talk to the judge, Whitby, and you can probably get a search warrant."

"You can't let her get away with this," Lily said to the mayor. "You have to come clean. Paige will go to jail and you may have to put the clubhouse on hold, but no one will be calling the shots for you anymore."

That's my girl, Vaughn thought, then gritted his teeth, because of course she wasn't.

"It's not so much the clubhouse anymore. What will I do when my fiancée finds out?" Whitby's face contorted. "My *ex*-fiancée."

Awkwardly, Lily patted his shoulder. "If she can't forgive you, you're better off without her."

Vaughn moved to stand beside her, and it was all he could do not to reach for her hand. "You're better off without Paige, too."

The mayor sighed and nodded. "As soon as I talk to the press, I'll tell Miss Southerly her services are no longer needed." He stood. "Thank you both."

Fortunately, Paige was away from her desk

when they left the mayor's office. Lily stood and stared at the woman's work space until Vaughn tugged her away.

"We don't want to engage her," he said. "Let the mayor work it out."

Once they were back in the sheriff's department, Vaughn exhaled. "I knew Whitby and Uncle Em must have been up to something, but I wasn't expecting that."

"It must have been quite a shock." Lily's tone was wooden.

"For you, too. I'm sorry about Paige. I know you were friends."

"I thought we were."

Vaughn touched her lightly on the small of her back. "Can we talk?"

Beneath his fingers, her spine went rigid. "Of course. My office."

Neither spoke as they walked through the reception area and into Lily's space. Vaughn's hip burned, but he fought to keep his stride even. No way he'd let this devolve into a discussion about his injury.

As soon as Lily's door closed behind them, she folded her arms across her chest. "You're here to say goodbye." The quiver of her lips belied the quiet calm of her voice.

"I couldn't go without asking one more time to be part of your life." He wrapped her in a hug and held her close, folded arms and all. "Lily," he murmured into her ear. "Let me love you."

She hitched in a breath and slowly unraveled her arms. But she didn't hug him back. "You're asking too much," she said thickly. "Anyway, you've seen for yourself that I'm a bad bet. That's not an excuse. That's my reality."

She eased out of his hold, and as she backed away it felt like she was ripping his heart out to take with her. Pain lashed at his chest and he clenched his jaw against the need to cry out.

Oh, hell, no. Not without a fight.

He snagged one of her hands before she could put any more distance between them. Her fingers were shaking. Or maybe those were his.

"When you and I were arguing in the parking lot," he said, "before that jackass tried to run me over, I told you there were times I felt I didn't belong. You know what my parents think of the career I chose. They bought the building next door to their pizza place, years later the neighborhood became trendy, and *boom*, they had money."

She listened silently, eyes damp, lips pressed tight.

He drew in a slow breath. "The restaurant had its perks. Truth is, I loved it. The heat, the smells, the customers and their stories. My sister hated it. My parents, too. They were always pushing me to be more, to want more. College, law school, medical school. They had big plans for me. When

I told them I wanted to go into law enforcement, you can imagine their reaction.

"I thought I'd found my home with the force. Then I find out my partner's on the take, and... you know the rest. The reason I'm telling you all this is because for the first time in my life, I know what it means to belong." He pressed her hand against his chest. "And it's with you."

When she tugged against his grip, he tightened it. "Let me finish. I had it out with my parents. They'll be contacting you to apologize but after that, they don't need to be a part of our lives. Not a big part, anyway. We can stay here or we can settle in the city. It doesn't matter because it's not the place we belong to, it's each other."

She reclaimed her hand and swiped it across her cheeks. Swallowed convulsively and shook her head. "It does matter," she said in a choked whisper. "You love the city. It's not going to work, Vaughn."

"Because you don't want it to. That bad-bet thing? That's bullshit." He fisted his hand so hard, his knuckles cracked. "You never told me you worked your family's accident. I can't even... You don't trust me, do you? Not enough to take a chance."

"I'm sorry."

His arms went stick-straight. After all they'd been through, all they'd meant to each other, "I'm sorry" was all she could manage?

He could see the look on his face scared her. She reached out, but didn't touch him. "I need you to understand."

"No, Lily. You don't need me at all." He groped for the door behind him. "I hope you can find a way to let yourself be happy."

Her lips trembled their way to a smile. "You will make an amazing detective."

He'd better, considering that was all he had left.

He shut the door quietly behind him.

CLARISSA TOOK A halfhearted bite of her sandwich, closed her eyes and lifted her face to the sun. They weren't far into September, but already the weather had cooled enough to make lunch out-doors more about relaxation and less about per-spiration. But even if the temperature had been one hundred degrees, she'd still have spent her half hour out here in her crape myrtle cave. It was painful, watching Lily pretend she didn't care that she and Vaughn were over.

Lily had accused Clarissa of doing the same when it came to Noble. But that was differ-ent. Noble was still in town. Clarissa just had to gather the courage to face him. And hope he could forgive her.

A shadow—a very large shadow—blocked the sun, and she knew without opening her eyes that she'd have to make do with the courage she had.

"I got your check in the mail," he said.

Her pulse started to buzz like the bees doing their thing with the scarlet blooms behind her. She opened her eyes and blinked up at the big man towering over her. He looked good—very good—in an untucked button-down shirt and jeans, his hair pulled back in a ponytail. He smiled and she could have kicked him in the balls for it. She hadn't felt like smiling in days.

He settled on the stone bench beside her and she resisted the urge to scoot to the end. The man smelled like chocolate, and damn, did she want to take a big-ass bite.

He exhaled. "Please tell me you didn't have to sell your car."

"I didn't." She concentrated on tucking her sandwich back into its plastic wrapping. "I took out a cash advance on a different card."

"Good. Listen, Clarissa—" he rubbed his palms up and down the thighs of his jeans "—I want you to know I understand the point you were trying to make, about needing to pay it off yourself."

She lifted an eyebrow and he lifted a hear-me-out hand.

"A couple of years ago, the library desperately needed new carpeting, but we had no funds. I got the idea for a book drive and spent days driving around, collecting used books. But when it came time for the book fair, they had to call someone in from another county to take over because I'd busted up my knee falling off a ladder. The drive made more money than we needed, but it wasn't the triumph it should have been because I didn't do the work. Not at the end, when it counted."

He tipped his head toward the library, on the far side of the courthouse. "That's not my carpet in there. It belongs to the librarian over in Meadville."

"You do get it," she breathed. She shifted sideways and lifted a knee onto the bench.

He mirrored her move. "I do. I'm sorry."

"You don't have to apologize again. Anyway, it's my turn. I know you meant well. I'm sorry I overreacted."

"I did what your ex did. Took control away from you."

"The motivations were very different. That's not why I overreacted." She toyed with the zipper on her lunch tote, peered up at him and shrugged. "Meeting someone like you…it wasn't part of my plan. I've been careful to keep my relationships casual because I had no intention of sharing that plan."

"Had?"

"I've told you some of the places I want to go. But now when I picture myself in Switzerland or Costa Rica or wherever, you're always there. Photobombing me."

"Am I naked?"

Despite the emotion clogging her throat, she chuckled. "You make me crazy, you know that?"

He straddled the bench and took her hand gently between his. "Were you ever going to come see me?"

"I haven't had the guts."

"Why would you be afraid of me?"

She gripped his fingers. "Not afraid of you, afraid you'd stopped wanting me. I was mean and ungracious."

"You had a right to be upset. And I'll always want you." He gripped her other hand and tugged her closer. Pressed his lips to her temple. "I love you."

Clarissa threw her arms around his neck and kissed his cheek, his ear, his jaw, his nose. "I love you, too."

His fingers flexed on her waist. "Yeah?"

"Oh, yeah."

"Enough to come home with me now?"

The need in his voice charged through her veins, boosting her own lust from a feel-good shimmer to a pounding blaze. She bounced to her feet and hauled him up beside her.

"Enough to go home with you *and* let you eat the other half of my sandwich," she said breathlessly. "Because, you know. Energy."

LILY SIDLED THROUGH an opening in the gate that blocked a little used dock and strode down the gravel incline toward the water. The early afternoon sun filtered through a mass of marshmallow clouds, leaving it weaker than usual for lunchtime in September. The lake was calm, rippling toward the rocky shore in a steady, murmuring rhythm. As Lily stepped onto the beach and the sun-bleached rocks clattered beneath her feet, a white crane lifted from the tip of the concrete dock and flapped silently away.

She breathed in and out, moved as always by the beauty that stretched before her. Five seconds later, she reminded herself she was on a mission. She made her way closer to the water, until she'd cleared the cliffs on either side of the access point. After peering left, then right, she exhaled two hours' worth of worry.

She'd found her.

Once she'd put in a quick radio call to Clarissa, who'd breathlessly requested the rest of the day off, Lily made her way down the beach. When she reached the rowboat with its bow just touching the water, she squatted down beside its sole occupant. Delia Frost.

Emerson Fulton's former girlfriend.

"Delia. We've been looking everywhere for you. Your daughter said you haven't been answering your phone."

Delia sat hunched over, waves of soft gray hair hiding her face. She wore denim capris, deck shoes and an oversized plaid shirt, and at her feet sat a small cooler, its open lid revealing an apple, cheese sticks and a roll of store-bought cookies, all packed around a partially frozen bottle of water.

A planned outing. Lily relaxed.

"Delia," she said again, softly. "Are you all right?"

"Just reminiscing." Delia slapped the side of the boat and Lily jumped. "I don't know if you remember, but this is the boat Emerson and I were making out in when you got the call about us that Sunday afternoon."

"I remember," Lily said. No doubt the family picnicking on the beach remembered, too.

"I thought about buying his house, you know. Just so I could sit inside it and feel like he was wrapped around me."

Lily swallowed.

The older woman raised her head and her sad gaze connected with Lily's. "I talked to his nephew about it. He was even going to cut me a deal. But that would be wallowing." She grabbed her apple out of the cooler. "Then again, I'm wallowing now."

"You're allowed to be sad."

"Everyone assumes that's how I feel, but it's not." The boat rocked as Delia shifted position on the bench. She polished the apple on her shirt. "What I feel is worse. I feel...relieved. I loved that old man so much it scared me. Being with him was exciting, but draining. Now he's gone, I can go back to my undemanding life. I can watch my shows and eat my grilled cheese and read until two in the morning if I want. I miss him, but he was so much *work*."

Lily couldn't help a smile. He *had* been a lot of work.

Delia grabbed Lily's arm. "You know I'm not talking about the kidney disease, right? I didn't mind looking after him when he was sick."

Lily nodded. "So you're out here sitting in this rowboat because…"

"I'm saying goodbye. Working my way through the guilt. Took me a while to understand I could have him and the heartache, or I could have memories and the heartache. Before I could tell him I'd chosen memories because they're less trouble, he got sick." She grunted. "Help me up, would you? My fanny fell asleep."

After advising Delia to call her daughter and reminding her to drink her water, Lily headed back to her car. The moment she'd spotted her on the beach where she and Emerson had spent so much time together, Lily had steeled herself to comfort a grieving woman. Delia's attitude had thrown her, but it had also helped her come to a realization.

She didn't want just the memories. She wanted the man.

FOR THE LONGEST time Lily sat outside Vaughn's apartment building, trying to muster the courage to get out of her car. The streetlight she'd parked under flickered on as dusk eased in and she tugged her keys from the ignition. If she didn't act now, she'd still be here when the dumb thing flickered off again. She wiped her damp palms on her jeans and grabbed her purse.

Minutes later, she stood in the hallway outside his apartment, staring at the slightly off-center wrought iron 6B on his door. It was going on nine. What if he'd gotten off shift at eight and went straight to sleep?

Nope. She'd have seen him. She'd been sitting outside his building that long.

She pressed a hand to a stomach that refused to stop churning. Would he be angry to see her, or glad? If he checked her out through the peephole, would he even open the door?

Before she could change her mind, she knocked.

No answer.

She tried again and slumped against the door. Then shot upright, in case it suddenly opened. It didn't. Either he wasn't home, or he wasn't answering. Because he wasn't alone? Chin to chest, she stared down at her sandals and the bare toes she'd painted a cheerful pink. In all the scenarios she'd invented when she'd imagined coming to see him, she'd never envisioned one where he hadn't been at home.

From around the corner came the elevator's *ping*. She blinked away the dampness in her eyes and slowly straightened. There were five apartments on each floor, so she had a twenty percent chance of seeing Vaughn come around the corner.

Her lips wouldn't cooperate, so she ditched her attempt at a smile. Her breath caught as a tall figure started down the corridor toward her.

Vaughn.

Her knees trembled as he approached. He hadn't seen her. He was staring at the carpet as he walked, jiggling his keys in his right hand.

He looked tired, but sexy as ever in his faded jeans and thin black pullover. He hadn't been at work, then. Or maybe he'd changed after shift? Left his uniform in his locker? His hair was disheveled, as if he'd been running his fingers through it. Or had someone else had the pleasure?

Pain stabbed and she welcomed it. She deserved it.

When he finally looked up, he jolted to a stop. His expression morphed from shock to caution.

Lily's smile felt as tentative as her breathing. "I hope you don't mind that I'm here."

His eyes grew Arctic-Ocean remote. He hesitated, then shrugged and moved toward the door. Her heart floundered as she backed away, giving him plenty of space. He seemed to need it.

He ushered her inside his apartment without a word.

She managed a quick scan of a small but tidy space with lots of brown and black before turning to face him. Her hands hung awkwardly at her sides.

After tossing his keys into a pink flamingo ashtray on the counter that divided the narrow kitchen from the rest of the apartment, he raised both eyebrows. "Why are you here?"

She wasn't ready to answer that. "Hello to you, too, Vaughn."

He sidestepped into the kitchen. "Hello, Lily. Why are you here?"

"I'd kind of like to work my way up to it."

"To what, an apology?" He shook his head. "Save it. We took a chance on something and it didn't work out." He strode over to his fridge and took out a beer. Tipped it in her direction.

"No, thank you."

She shouldn't have come. But she was here, with so much to say. The Lily she had been would skulk away. The Lily she'd become would apologize for all she'd done—and for all she hadn't. She'd ask for what she wanted.

No excuses, no hiding, no hesitation.

"I do want to apologize," she said.

"I figured."

"For everything."

"Consider it done."

She fingered her purse strap. "But I also wanted to ask—"

"I'm glad you're here," he said.

—*if we could try again*. She straightened. "What? Really?"

"Yeah. I could use an opinion."

Cautiously she approached the other side of the pass-through, maneuvered between two stools and set her purse on the counter. "On?"

"Ohio or North Carolina."

"Are we talking vacation?"

"We're talking job offers."

Her heart sank like the proverbial stone. "You're moving?"

"Thinking about it." He leaned against the sink. "IA cleared me, and the truth is out, but I'll be dealing with trust issues for a long time. I'm trying to decide if it's worth sticking with a unit that was so quick to turn on me."

"Sounds like you have trust issues of your own."

"It's hard not to."

And she had her answer. If he were prepared to leave his unit behind because they hadn't believed in him, no way he'd be willing to give another chance to the woman who'd let him down so thoroughly. She hadn't trusted him, she hadn't trusted herself and she'd let her fear ruin something precious.

How ridiculously ironic. They'd both finally realized the *where* didn't matter, but it was too late because the *who* had already called it a day.

He kept his gaze on her as he swigged his beer. "You wanted to ask me something?"

"Just…" She tucked her fingers in her back pockets. The back pockets of the jeans he'd once said he couldn't wait to see her in. Now he couldn't have cared less. How ridiculous, all that time she'd spent in the store trying on pair after pair, searching for just the right balance of offhand and come-hither.

"I was hoping you could forgive me," she finally said.

"That the only reason you came?"

"I guess I wanted to be able to picture you in your world. And see how you're feeling, after the accident."

He slapped his right hip. "Like it never happened."

"I'm glad. I feel bad about how we left things."

His expression hardened and he banged the bottle down onto the countertop. "You're not going to ask if we can be friends, are you?"

His hostility opened up a chasm in her chest, and the wound burned like nothing she'd ever known. "No," she whispered. "I don't see how we could. With the distance and…everything."

"Right." He moved toward the door. "Thanks for coming by. Call next time, okay?"

"I think we both know there won't be a next time." She tried, but couldn't maintain a smile. "Good luck, Vaughn."

"Goodbye, Lily."

She stared at the elevator doors and realized she couldn't remember the walk from Vaughn's apartment.

She'd tried. At least she'd tried.

You didn't tell him you love him.

She'd meant to. But it would have been too little, too late.

THREE MONTHS LATER, Lily jammed her hands into her gloves as she walked out of her favorite coffee shop. She winced as the bitter wind teased her for not buttoning her coat and hurried toward her car. The sidewalks had been cleared of ice, but with six inches of snow expected that evening, they wouldn't stay clear for long.

Ten steps from her Toyota, she heard the voice that had never failed to quicken her pulse.

"Lily?"

Heart slamming against her breastbone, she turned. She'd known this could happen, but still she wasn't prepared for the instant ache that gripped her bones.

"Vaughn," she said, and inwardly celebrated when his name came out as more of a statement than a plea.

He jerked forward as if to hug her, then stopped himself and jammed his gloved hands in the pockets of his hip-length coat.

"It's good to see you," he said.

Lily shivered, feeling the cold more than ever. "You, too."

He was wearing jeans and a gray turtleneck under his coat, with heavy black boots on his feet. His cheeks and the tips of his ears were red, his hair rumpled by the wind, and she wanted to just stand there and drink him in, like the cup of hot chocolate she'd just treated herself to.

He tugged on his ear. "Here doing your Christmas shopping?"

"I..." She licked her lips. "Actually, I live here now."

"You live here. In Erie." When she nodded, he glanced around, as if needing to get his bearings. He gave his head a shake. "Since when?"

Her gaze ran from his. "Since a couple of months ago."

"Did Whitby run you out of Castle Creek?"

She huffed a laugh, her breath a drift of white between them. "Believe it or not, he asked me to stay. When I turned him down, he polished off an entire bag of Snickers, appointed JD interim sheriff and informed me there'd be no going-away party." She began to button her coat. "I'm with the Gannon University campus police now."

She sensed his surprise as he hesitated. "Do you like it?"

"I do. Especially since they don't expect me to clean toilets."

That didn't earn even the glimmer of a smile. "Why Erie?"

Heat crawled across her cheeks. "I guess because I was too stubborn to picture myself here."

"I remember." Hands still in his pockets, he shrugged. "So what do you think?"

"Traffic sucks. I miss Cal's cinnamon rolls, not to mention everyone at the department. I find it energizing, though, being on campus. I still get to hang out at the lake, I've caught a few shows at the Erie Playhouse and the other day I signed up for a yoga class. You know." She dug her keys out of her coat pocket. "Baby steps."

"Hey, Lily." A man in a camel-colored coat with a tight grip on his briefcase waved from the door of the coffee shop. David Carroll, a guy who worked in campus accounting. Like Burke Yancey, he didn't know how to take no for an answer.

"See you at the Christmas party?" he asked.

"I'll be there."

"Looking forward to it."

When David disappeared into the shop, Lily turned back to face Vaughn.

"Right," he said. "Baby steps." His smile couldn't have been more remote if he'd flashed it from a mile away. He hunched deeper into his coat.

Lily took a step back. "You know what, I should go. It's cold out here and I have more errands to run and I'm sure you have things to do, too."

"Wait." Vaughn motioned toward her car. "Could we sit for a few minutes? Just to warm up?"

Not a good idea. He'd be close enough to touch. To breathe in. And it would be that much harder to watch him walk away.

"Sure," she said. "For a few minutes."

Once they'd settled inside and she'd turned on the heat, he removed his gloves. Ridiculous, how that made her heart beat faster.

"Ever miss your cruiser?" he asked.

"Sometimes." She pulled off her own gloves and flopped one toward the steady stream of cars passing them by. "Like I said, traffic sucks. By the way, did you hear about Miranda?"

"Yeah. Hazel told me a couple of weeks ago that her foster family had started adoption proceedings. Sounds like cupcake's going to be okay."

"She's pretty excited. But I wonder how Hazel knew."

Vaughn grunted. "What I want to know is why she didn't tell me about you."

Silence. Wind buffeted the car and Lily twisted her fingers in her lap. "Speaking of adoption, I heard Ivy ended up with Not Franklin and her brood."

"Licorice."

"I'm sorry?"

"I named her Licorice."

"That's a good name," Lily said huskily, and paused. "You must miss them."

"I do. But they're in good hands." He set his jaw. "Were you ever planning to look me up?"

Her breath stalled in her throat. She shifted in her seat and finally met his gaze. "You made it clear you didn't want to see me. After everything I put you through, the least I could do was respect that."

He ran a palm over his face. "You'd basically dug my guts out with an ice-cream scoop. I wasn't feeling kind. I didn't mean it, Lily."

"I'm sorry I hurt you." She stared blindly out her window. "Those job offers?"

"They were real. But I never seriously considered them. Both wanted someone right away and I still have a house on the market."

"I see," she said. "I have to go."

"Tell me one thing first. Are you happy?"

She sucked in a breath, and the tears erupted. He reached for her and she slapped at his hands. "I said I have to go."

"Not until you tell me what's wrong." He caught both hands in his and tugged her around to face him. He jerked his chin at the sidewalk beyond the car. "Is it the Christmas-party guy?"

"David? No. We're just friends."

When she struggled to pull away, Vaughn's grip tightened. "Someone else, then."

Lily gasped out a waterlogged laugh. "It doesn't work that way. You can't just—" She stopped and turned a shudder into a grab for her shoulder bag, which she'd plopped onto the console between them. She dug out a tissue and pressed it to her nose.

"Can't just what?" he persisted.

"That's the worst thing about being off duty," she said tightly. "Your stun gun's not handy."

"Lily." He grabbed her purse, dropped it on the floor and shifted closer, his knee sliding along hers. He reclaimed her hands, damp tissue and all. Her skin warmed from the heat of his, and when she caught the scent of Good & Plenty, she willed herself to breathe through her mouth.

He gave her hands a gentle shake. "Can't just *what*?"

She shook her head.

"*Jesus*, Lily, you're—"

"Stop loving someone, okay? You can't just… will yourself to stop loving someone to make room for someone else." She slapped both palms against his chest and gave him a push. "Yes. You were right. I love you. That's why I'm miserable. That's why I moved to Erie. Because even though we're not together, at least we're still in the same twenty-two square miles of city." She sniffled and leaned away to wipe her nose. "Besides, I had to prove to myself that I could step out from behind the grief. That I could stop making excuses and actually manage a life."

He closed his eyes briefly then leaned forward and gripped her leg. "Why didn't you come see me? *Tell* me?"

"Because. There was that whole ice-cream scoop thing, remember? And anyway, I didn't think you'd be able to trust me again."

"So you're not trusting me to trust you."

"Something like that." She threw a glove at him. "You told me not to come back."

"Because you were putting me through goddamn hell. Not that I didn't do the same to you." He pulled her across the console, ignoring her protests and settling her on his lap. He buried his face in her neck. "God," he breathed against her skin. "I thought I'd never hold you again." He clutched her tighter against him. "I'm so sorry."

She wound her arms around his neck and blinked back fresh tears. "I'm sorry, too."

"I love you, Lily."

She patted his hair, his ears, his cheeks. Her throat was scratchy and her eyes burned and her chest was one giant, chaotic mass of shimmering hope and she didn't think she could bear the big fat promise of having this man, here, now.

"I love you, too, Vaughn," she said. "Kiss me."

His fingers thrust into her hair and tipped her head as he reared up and claimed her mouth. He kissed her fiercely, jaw working, tongue stroking hers into a frenzy. His stubble scraped her chin and his hungry breaths heated her face and she couldn't stop shuddering.

She lifted up and straddled his lap and when she came back down again, they both moaned. His hips convulsed and she whimpered at the rigid press of his erection. She moved against him, lost in the need and the heat and the sparkling bliss of friction.

"Jesus," he gasped. "I've missed you so much."

Her fingers dug into his scalp and his, into her hips. Gradually, sanity filtered through the breathless greed, and she collapsed against him, forehead to his shoulder.

"We're going to get ourselves arrested," she said, panting.

"Don't worry. I know a guy."

With a strangled laugh she lifted her head. The fog coating the windows should have made her cringe, but instead she wanted to finger paint. Happy faces and hearts.

She let out a wondering sigh.

"Tell me something." Vaughn traced a finger along her jawline. "That day you came to my apartment."

"I was going to ask for another chance."

"Christ. And I pouted like a kid."

"Don't feel bad. I had some growing up to do,

too. It took me a while, but I realized I belong with you no matter where you are."

"I came to the same realization myself." He kissed her, lightly, sweetly, then scowled. "No more crap about our age difference?"

"That wouldn't make any sense, considering we just proved we're emotional equals."

"And you'll move in with me?"

Her insides began to vibrate as she scooted back, onto his thighs. "Vaughn." She palmed his cheek. "We have a bigger issue to settle than an eleven-year age difference."

"You don't like my flamingo ashtray."

Her lips gave an involuntary twitch. "I don't mind it. But you want children."

"I want *you*."

"Vaughn…"

Gently he pulled her hand from his face and kissed her fingers. "I can't deny I've imagined having children with you. But kids would be the icing on the cake. And it's the cake I can't live without."

Lily wilted against him, and pressed her lips to his throat. "That's sweet."

"Cake usually is." He tapped her on the shoulder. "Now let's talk about when you're moving in."

"Maybe you should see my place first. It definitely has the size advantage." She nipped his ear. "And it's only a few blocks away."

She shrieked as he practically launched her back into the driver's seat.

"Then what are we still doing here?" He fastened her seat belt for her, then pressed a lingering kiss on her mouth. "Let's go home."

* * * * *

LARGER-PRINT BOOKS!

GET 2 FREE LARGER-PRINT NOVELS PLUS
2 FREE GIFTS!

⬥HARLEQUIN®

Romance

From the Heart, For the Heart

YES! Please send me 2 FREE LARGER-PRINT Harlequin® Romance novels and my 2 FREE gifts (gifts are worth about $10). After receiving them, if I don't wish to receive any more books, I can return the shipping statement marked "cancel." If I don't cancel, I will receive 4 brand-new novels every month and be billed just $5.09 per book in the U.S. or $5.49 per book in Canada. That's a savings of at least 15% off the cover price! It's quite a bargain! Shipping and handling is just 50¢ per book in the U.S. and 75¢ per book in Canada.* I understand that accepting the 2 free books and gifts places me under no obligation to buy anything. I can always return a shipment and cancel at any time. Even if I never buy another book, the two free books and gifts are mine to keep forever.

119/319 HDN GHWC

Name _____ (PLEASE PRINT) _____

Address _____ Apt. # _____

City _____ State/Prov. _____ Zip/Postal Code _____

Signature (if under 18, a parent or guardian must sign) _____

Mail to the **Reader Service:**
IN U.S.A.: P.O. Box 1867, Buffalo, NY 14240-1867
IN CANADA: P.O. Box 609, Fort Erie, Ontario L2A 5X3
Want to try two free books from another line?
Call 1-800-873-8635 or visit www.ReaderService.com.

* Terms and prices subject to change without notice. Prices do not include applicable taxes. Sales tax applicable in N.Y. Canadian residents will be charged applicable taxes. Offer not valid in Quebec. This offer is limited to one order per household. Not valid for current subscribers to Harlequin Romance Larger-Print books. All orders subject to credit approval. Credit or debit balances in a customer's account(s) may be offset by any other outstanding balance owed by or to the customer. Please allow 4 to 6 weeks for delivery. Offer available while quantities last.

Your Privacy—The Reader Service is committed to protecting your privacy. Our Privacy Policy is available online at www.ReaderService.com or upon request from the Reader Service.

We make a portion of our mailing list available to reputable third parties that offer products we believe may interest you. If you prefer that we not exchange your name with third parties, or if you wish to clarify or modify your communication preferences, please visit us at www.ReaderService.com/consumerschoice or write to us at Reader Service Preference Service, P.O. Box 9062, Buffalo, NY 14240-9062. Include your complete name and address.

HRLP15

LARGER-PRINT BOOKS!

♦HARLEQUIN *Presents*

GET 2 FREE LARGER-PRINT NOVELS PLUS 2 FREE GIFTS!

PASSION
GUARANTEED
SEDUCTION

YES! Please send me 2 FREE LARGER-PRINT Harlequin Presents® novels and my 2 FREE gifts (gifts are worth about $10). After receiving them, if I don't wish to receive any more books, I can return the shipping statement marked "cancel." If I don't cancel, I will receive 6 brand-new novels every month and be billed just $5.30 per book in the U.S. or $5.74 per book in Canada. That's a saving of at least 12% off the cover price! It's quite a bargain! Shipping and handling is just 50¢ per book in the U.S. and 75¢ per book in Canada.* I understand that accepting the 2 free books and gifts places me under no obligation to buy anything. I can always return a shipment and cancel at any time. Even if I never buy another book, the two free books and gifts are mine to keep forever.

176/376 HDN GHVY

Name	(PLEASE PRINT)

Address		Apt. #

City	State/Prov.	Zip/Postal Code

Signature (if under 18, a parent or guardian must sign)

Mail to the **Reader Service:**
IN U.S.A.: P.O. Box 1867, Buffalo, NY 14240-1867
IN CANADA: P.O. Box 609, Fort Erie, Ontario L2A 5X3

**Are you a subscriber to Harlequin Presents® books
and want to receive the larger-print edition?
Call 1-800-873-8635 today or visit us at www.ReaderService.com.**

* Terms and prices subject to change without notice. Prices do not include applicable taxes. Sales tax applicable in N.Y. Canadian residents will be charged applicable taxes. Offer not valid in Quebec. This offer is limited to one order per household. Not valid for current subscribers to Harlequin Presents Larger-Print books. All orders subject to credit approval. Credit or debit balances in a customer's account(s) may be offset by any other outstanding balance owed by or to the customer. Please allow 4 to 6 weeks for delivery. Offer available while quantities last.

Your Privacy—The Reader Service is committed to protecting your privacy. Our Privacy Policy is available online at www.ReaderService.com or upon request from the Reader Service.

We make a portion of our mailing list available to reputable third parties that offer products we believe may interest you. If you prefer that we not exchange your name with third parties, or if you wish to clarify or modify your communication preferences, please visit us at www.ReaderService.com/consumerchoice or write to us at Reader Service Preference Service, P.O. Box 9062, Buffalo, NY 14240-9062. Include your complete name and address.

HPLP15

REQUEST YOUR FREE BOOKS!
2 FREE WHOLESOME ROMANCE NOVELS IN LARGER PRINT
PLUS 2 FREE MYSTERY GIFTS

✻✻✻✻✻✻✻✻✻✻✻✻✻✻✻✻✻✻✻✻✻✻✻✻✻✻✻

HEARTWARMING™

✻✻✻✻✻✻✻✻✻✻✻✻✻✻✻✻✻✻✻✻✻✻✻✻✻✻✻

Wholesome, tender romances

YES! Please send me 2 FREE Harlequin® Heartwarming Larger-Print novels and my 2 FREE mystery gifts (gifts worth about $10). After receiving them, if I don't wish to receive any more books, I can return the shipping statement marked "cancel." If I don't cancel, I will receive 4 brand-new larger-print novels every month and be billed just $5.24 per book in the U.S. or $5.99 per book in Canada. That's a savings of at least 19% off the cover price. It's quite a bargain! Shipping and handling is just 50¢ per book in the U.S. and 75¢ per book in Canada.* I understand that accepting the 2 free books and gifts places me under no obligation to buy anything. I can always return a shipment and cancel at any time. Even if I never buy another book, the two free books and gifts are mine to keep forever.

161/361 IDN GHX2

Name _____ (PLEASE PRINT)

Address _____ Apt. #

City _____ State/Prov. _____ Zip/Postal Code

Signature (if under 18, a parent or guardian must sign)

Mail to the **Reader Service:**
IN U.S.A.: P.O. Box 1867, Buffalo, NY 14240-1867
IN CANADA: P.O. Box 609, Fort Erie, Ontario L2A 5X3

* Terms and prices subject to change without notice. Prices do not include applicable taxes. Sales tax applicable in N.Y. Canadian residents will be charged applicable taxes. Offer not valid in Quebec. This offer is limited to one order per household. Not valid for current subscribers to Harlequin Heartwarming larger-print books. All orders subject to credit approval. Credit or debit balances in a customer's account(s) may be offset by any other outstanding balance owed by or to the customer. Please allow 4 to 6 weeks for delivery. Offer available while quantities last.

Your Privacy—The Reader Service is committed to protecting your privacy. Our Privacy Policy is available online at www.ReaderService.com or upon request from the Reader Service.

We make a portion of our mailing list available to reputable third parties that offer products we believe may interest you. If you prefer that we not exchange your name with third parties, or if you wish to clarify or modify your communication preferences, please visit us at www.ReaderService.com/consumerschoice or write to us at Reader Service Preference Service, P.O. Box 9062, Buffalo, NY 14240-9062. Include your complete name and address.

HW15

LARGER-PRINT BOOKS!
GET 2 FREE LARGER-PRINT NOVELS PLUS
2 FREE GIFTS!

⬥HARLEQUIN®

INTRIGUE
BREATHTAKING ROMANTIC SUSPENSE

YES! Please send me 2 FREE LARGER-PRINT Harlequin® Intrigue novels and my 2 FREE gifts (gifts are worth about $10). After receiving them, if I don't wish to receive any more books, I can return the shipping statement marked "cancel." If I don't cancel, I will receive 6 brand-new novels every month and be billed just $5.49 per book in the U.S. or $6.24 per book in Canada. That's a saving of at least 11% off the cover price! It's quite a bargain! Shipping and handling is just 50¢ per book in the U.S. and 75¢ per book in Canada.* I understand that accepting the 2 free books and gifts places me under no obligation to buy anything. I can always return a shipment and cancel at any time. Even if I never buy another book, the two free books and gifts are mine to keep forever.

199/399 HDN GHWN

Name	(PLEASE PRINT)	
Address		Apt. #
City	State/Prov.	Zip/Postal Code

Signature (if under 18, a parent or guardian must sign)

Mail to the **Reader Service:**
IN U.S.A.: P.O. Box 1867, Buffalo, NY 14240-1867
IN CANADA: P.O. Box 609, Fort Erie, Ontario L2A 5X3

**Are you a subscriber to Harlequin® Intrigue books
and want to receive the larger-print edition?
Call 1-800-873-8635 today or visit www.ReaderService.com.**

* Terms and prices subject to change without notice. Prices do not include applicable taxes. Sales tax applicable in N.Y. Canadian residents will be charged applicable taxes. Offer not valid in Quebec. This offer is limited to one order per household. Not valid for current subscribers to Harlequin Intrigue Larger-Print books. All orders subject to credit approval. Credit or debit balances in a customer's account(s) may be offset by any other outstanding balance owed by or to the customer. Please allow 4 to 6 weeks for delivery. Offer available while quantities last.

Your Privacy—The Reader Service is committed to protecting your privacy. Our Privacy Policy is available online at www.ReaderService.com or upon request from the Reader Service.

We make a portion of our mailing list available to reputable third parties that offer products we believe may interest you. If you prefer that we not exchange your name with third parties, or if you wish to clarify or modify your communication preferences, please visit us at www.ReaderService.com/consumerchoice or write to us at Reader Service Preference Service, P.O. Box 9062, Buffalo, NY 14240-9062. Include your complete name and address.

HILP15